William Robinson

THE BROKEN R

by
William Robinson

Eloquent Books
New York, New York

Copyright © 2008
All rights reserved — William Robinson

No part of this book may be reproduced or transmitted in any form or by any means, graphic, electronic, or mechanical, including photocopying, recording, taping, or by any information storage retrieval system, without the permission, in writing, from the publisher.

Eloquent Books
An imprint of AEG Publishing Group
845 Third Avenue, 6th Floor – 6016
New York, NY 10022
www.eloquentbooks.com

ISBN: 978-1-60693-527-9   1-60693-527-5

Printed in the United States of America

Book Design: Denise Johnson, Dedicated Business Solutions, Inc.

In loving memory of Novell Robinson

July 17, 1915–February 26, 1997

*May the sun always shine to your back
Providing warmth to your soul and
Light to your path.*

THE BROKEN R

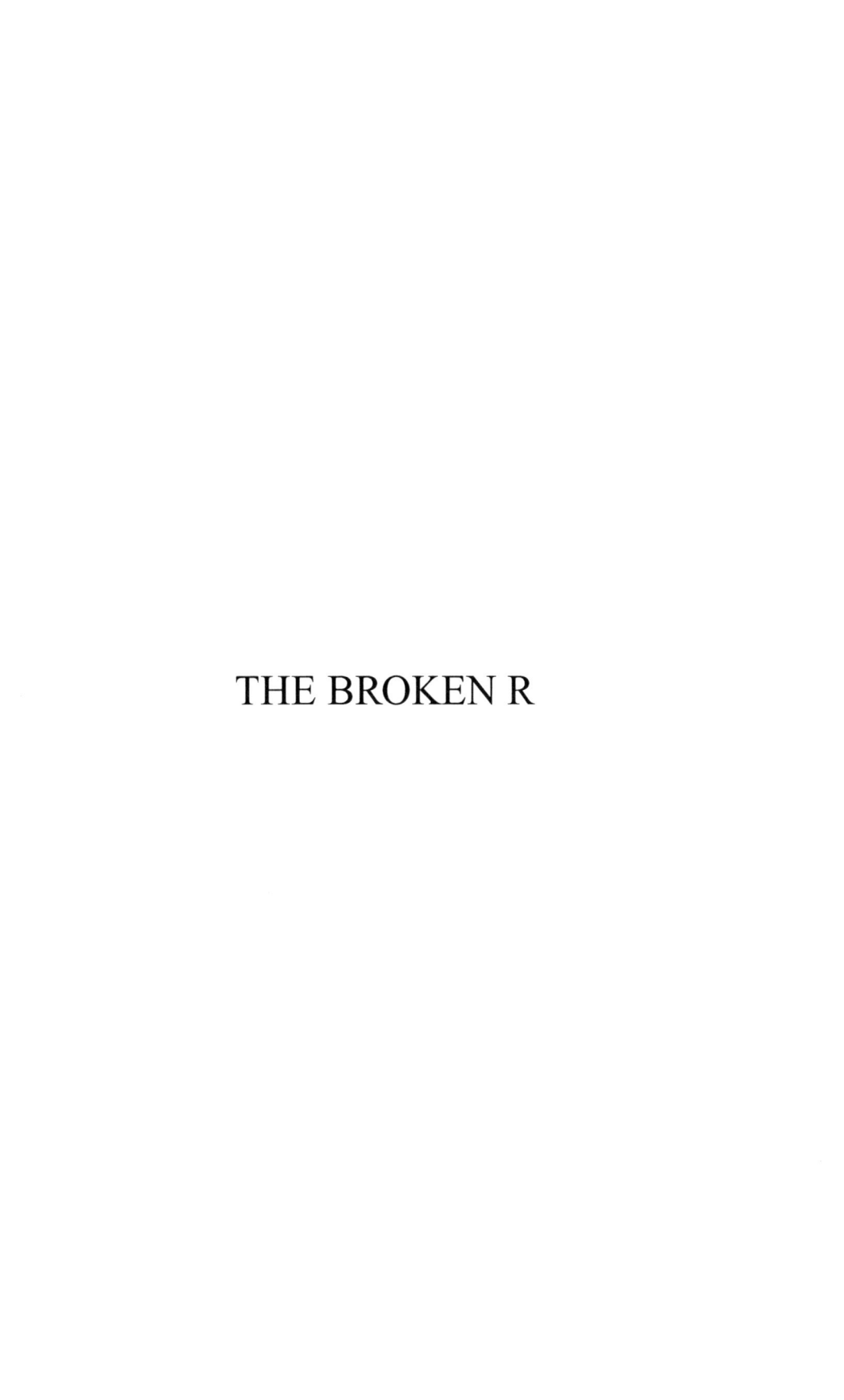

Chapter 1
The Homecoming

As Sam was driving up to the old house in Bryant, he questioned why he had allowed Mike and Cyndi to talk him into coming back home. The house looked the same as the house he had stored in his memory, and he could tell someone had spent a lot of time working to keep the old place up and running. Sam hadn't seen his father since his mother passed away, and now he was questioning whether or not he should have even bothered to make this trip back home. Some memories are too painful to rehash, and are probably best left buried in the past. Thinking of the past always seemed to put Sam on an emotional roller coaster that left him torn up inside, wishing for what he had missed with his family, and wanting to be able to change the past. It was all more than he cared to bear. He knew out of respect that he needed to be here, but it was a place he didn't want to be.

Sam was so deep in thought that he didn't realize another car had pulled in next to where he was parked. When a hand reached out and touched him, he almost jumped out of his skin. It was his youngest sister, Cyndi.

"Well, I see you haven't changed much, Samuel."

"Oh my, Sis, is that really you?"

"Yep, pure flesh and blood; a little older but a whole lot wiser . . . ."

"Man, you're really looking good! How is everything going?" Sam asked.

She could tell right off that Sam wasn't comfortable with the idea of being back home—let alone the prospect of being thrown into a family reunion. Unfortunately, this was how Dad had set up his will, and as he would have said, "Only by the hand of God would it have been handled any differently."

"Well, I'm doing fine," Cyndi said. "I've been keeping myself pretty busy. I talked with Mike last night and he should be back in town on Friday. He's at a convention in Texas and he was going to cancel the trip, but he promised Dad he would keep his appointments—although I know it's probably hard on him, working at a time like this. That should give you some time to kick back and rest up, after your long trip in from Montana."

"How is big brother doing?"

"You are not going to believe this. Our big brother, Mike, has become quite the executive! He has taken over the responsibility of running the Broken R Ranch and Simplicity, and believe me when I tell you this: neither one of those tasks are a small feat to keep up with these days. Hey, I'm sorry; we can go in and sit if you'd like. I don't suppose it's necessary that we stand out here in the heat all day. Mike said he sent a cleaning service over to clean the place up so it would be ready for you when you got here."

As they were entering the old house, Sam could almost feel a haunting presence, which increased as they walked through the house.

"You know Dad didn't stay here much after Mom passed on," Cyndi told him. "He spent most of his time out at the ranch. He never really changed a bit. He lived like a cowboy and died like a cowboy. Although Mom didn't care too much for the ranch, she knew it made Dad happy, and you know Mom's philosophy: if Dad was happy, she was happy. Anyway, tell me, what have you been up to?"

Sam stood there feeling like a duck out of water. "Not much, Sis. It's been such a long time. I had just about forgotten how hot it gets here in Arkansas."

"How long has it been, Sam?"

"Well, its 2025 and I will be forty-two this year, so it has been almost twenty years."

"Yeah, you're right. It has been awhile. I hope it's not too hard on you, coming back. Things have changed a lot, but I know even with your differences Dad would have wanted you to be here. Although you probably don't believe this, Dad really did miss having you here."

"Okay, let's find something else to talk about."

After visiting for a few hours, Cyndi had to leave for an appointment. She knew her brother did not want to stay by himself, but she also knew he had a lot of things he needed to work out on his own, and after his long trip, he was probably tired.

Sam was really starting to think it would have been better if he had just stayed away. Looking back into the past was still very painful, and he really didn't like being reminded of it. Just looking around the house brought back memories that made him feel like a scared little kid all over again. It seemed when he was young he was never able to do anything to please the old man.

In order to clear his mind, Sam called his wife Tara at home to make sure everybody was okay. After talking with her for a few minutes, he hung up the phone and found himself once again drifting back into the past. Lost in a dreamlike state, he wondered what good could come of all this, as he finally drifted off to sleep. After three days on the road, Sam was bone tired, and mentally weary. It seemed like time had stopped, and everything was in slow motion. He awoke to a loud noise in the back bedroom. As he eased his way down the hall, he wondered who was in the house with him, since he was supposed to be alone.

The memories were flooding through his mind so fast that it was hard to keep his mind focused on what he was doing. As he walked down the hall toward the bedroom, he scanned the pictures on the walls, almost getting lost in time. With the bedroom door shut, he could still hear somebody talking. Almost scared to open the door, Sam knocked lightly. No one answered. He listened more closely, and panic started to overcome him as his heart beat faster and he began to sweat.

"It can't be!" He was sure he had heard his Dad's voice coming from the other side of the door. The panic and fear had turned to anger. "That son of a bitch—he's not dead and they got me here on purpose," he said out loud. When the door opened, Sam jumped backwards, hollering out, "What the hell!"

Both men stood face to face: one in total shock, the other with a grin on his face. Sam couldn't even speak—his mouth was moving, but nothing was coming out. He turned to look at an old family portrait that hung on the wall in the hallway, and then looked back. Without a doubt, it was his Dad standing there, looking exactly like the photo.

"Well, what the hell are you doing here?" Sam blurted out after he managed to find his voice.

His father walked past him, saying, "I believe the last time I checked I still owned this old house, Bean Head."

Sam remembered hearing those words before. The memories were floating in his mind so rapidly that after all these years it was just too much to handle. "Sam, you have to get a grip. Oh, great. Now I'm talking to myself."

After a few seconds, he walked to the living room, hoping that this trip wasn't going to turn into the disaster of the century. That choked-up feeling was almost too hard to swallow, as he looked into the kitchen and saw his dad sitting there bigger than life, drinking a cup of coffee and smoking a cigarette. His father yelled out with a deep thunderous voice, sending shivers up the back of Sam's neck. "Get in here and fix you a cup of coffee, boy. We haven't talked in years. Surely you must have something on your mind. Last I heard about you was that you and Tara had moved off to Montana. I remember the trip we made up there, many years ago. You didn't seem to be too interested in staying there at that time, but you were just a kid. Things change when you age, and that is a fact. So how have you been doing up there?"

"We're doing good, making it the best we know how. The kids are doing well."

"Any of your kids make you a grandpa yet?"

"Yeah, we got three."

"That's a good thing, Son; I hope you're doing better at that than I did. I often wondered what I could have done differently; your momma sure missed not having you kids around. I just tried to keep busy doing something. It seemed as though I always had too much to take care of and never enough money to do it all with. All I knew to do was just keep going."

"What the hell are you talking about? You always had plenty of money, and did what you wanted. That's what I could never figure out about you. You were always so good at telling your bullshit stories—working all the time trying to convince us kids you didn't have . . ."

"Whoa, boy! You didn't come all this way just to try and pick a fight, did you?"

"No."

"Then let's talk and leave out some of that anger you always seem to carry around. My God, son, surely you have learned by now life is never what it's dreamed up to be. People do what they have to in order to get by. For some it is all materialistic; the more they have the better they count their life. For others it is a state of mind; happiness with whatever they have. Somewhere there has to be a line between the two. Just like love and hate. God knows I tried to figure that one out. Nevertheless, like many men before me, there will be many more behind me to make the same mistakes. By the time you figure out life, the best part of it has passed you by. Believe me—what I wouldn't give to be able to change it, but it is usually too late for most. I don't really care what you think of me now, because it is too late for me. The things

I tried to tell you when you were young and wouldn't listen."

At this point Sam wanted to get up and leave as he had done so many times before, but for some reason he just poured another cup of coffee.

"Look," he said, "if you think I feel sorry for you, I don't."

"Is that what you think, Son—that I want pity? Hell, that's the last damn thing I want, and that is what I have been trying to tell you. People always thought I was rich because I wouldn't accept pity. That's right, you remember 'Got More Money Than I'll Ever Spend.'"

"Yeah, I remember you got $17."

"See, you never could get past the bullshit."

"What's that suppose to mean?"

"I'll bet you one million dollars that I have seventeen dollars in my pocket right now. That's the way it went."

"Yeah—so what?"

"Did you ever take the bet?"

"No. Why would I?"

"Well, don't feel bad, Son. No one else ever did either. Nevertheless, there were as many times when I didn't have the $17 in my pocket. However, I never made a bet I couldn't cover. Anyway, like I said, that's why everyone thought the old man was loaded."

"Well, you were."

"Maybe to your way of thinking, but for me it wasn't even a good stake. Money couldn't be spent unless it was making more money—or eventually you went broke. I made that mistake enough times, and starting from scratch can make you see things a little differently. You see things differently now, don't you?"

"Well, sure I do, but I still don't understand you."

"That's because you never tried to understand me; you just couldn't figure out why I didn't think like you, and do things the way you wanted to. You see, Son, a lot of the hell you went through when you were young was because you chose to. The hell I went through was not of my own making—at least not most of it. By the time I was 14 years old, I had seen more evil than any one person should have had to see. It left me bitter at the world. Thinking back only made me angrier, and there were times when that anger consumed me. I wanted revenge, and was always trying to figure out how I could make someone pay for what they had done to me."

"Well, Dad, don't you still feel that way?"

"No. Don't you see it's a waste of time? Those people have been dead for many years, so even giving them any thought is a waste of my precious time. And for you to think ill of me, and that it's only my fault for your life turning out the way it did, is also a waste of your time. Besides, you got your revenge! You never wanted for me to see my grandchildren."

"The only reason you didn't get to see your grandchildren was because you wanted it that way."

"There you go again, Son, seeing only what you want to see. You have never been able to look beyond yourself for more than a second. But that's okay; I have rather accepted that somehow, some way, everything that has happened was my fault in some shape or form. At the young age of two, I went to live at an orphanage. Taken from my mother and siblings, I just knew it had to have been my fault; I had to have done something exceptionally bad in order for Mom to punish me in that manner. At the age of seven I had seen several foster care homes, and I'd already figured out that the reason people didn't want me around was because I was an awful kid. When it appeared that I was moving from the hellhole of a foster home I was currently living in, I realized I was just leaving one hellhole to move into the pit of hell—a hell far greater than any I had already been living in. This too, must have been my fault. Why else would this keep happening to me?

"For years, I suffered at the hands of those people. I suffered mental and physical torture to the point where

I didn't think there was any reason to go on. In addition, people who said they loved me did all this. They said they did these things to me for my own good. I am telling you all this so that you might understand how it was back then. I can't really explain it all, but I grew up with a twisted mind myself. I knew one thing for certain, even if I had a sick twisted mind: you don't treat people you love that way. Hell, you don't even treat animals that way. These were the kind of people who got a sick kick out of trying to bend a child's mind to their own will.

"I tried to let you live free and make your own decisions with your life so that you could experience a full, abundant, and happy life, but somehow between you and me there was always bad blood. No matter what I did or said, you always took it the wrong way. Maybe it's because we had the same blood and I passed all that anger over to you; whatever the reason, we never learned to deal with our problems. So we did what most people do when they can't get along: we just separated ourselves and went on with our lives.

"My time is short now, and I'll be moving on soon, so I wanted to share a few secrets with you. Maybe even explain some old ones."

"What do I need to know from you? Mom told me you cut me out of the will. Ten bucks and a handshake."

"Yeah, that's right, and that is why this meeting is for your best interests, and not mine. Years ago, when you just thought I was rich, really I was struggling along. When I was about your age, a package was delivered to me dating back to the early 1960s, containing information about me when I was just a kid. Now I am going to tell you: that is what turned everything around for me.

"From that day on, that package changed me forever. I have done all that I wanted and will leave enough for those grandchildren to do all that they can do or want to do. This also includes you, Son. Mike is well on his way and little Haley is tagging right behind him. Sissy isn't doing too badly either. However, you have always been the hard case. So you tell me: should I go on, or not?"

Sam realized that, for whatever reason, he was actually starting to relax, and this was somewhat neat, listening to his dad talking to him as if he were an adult. He nodded his head and said, "Continue on."

"The package was sent first to my adopted father. For a great deal of money, he only had to find and adopt me. There were only certain rules that had to be followed. I was supposed to have no contact with my natural family. I was to be kept as isolated as possible from the outside world. I was allowed very little contact with other people who might spoil the organization's plans. Why I was chosen is yet unknown. Maybe I was in the wrong place at the right time. Hell, who knows? Apparently, they needed a new name. After I was adopted, my records were sealed. This left my real name to be taken by someone else in a different state. They set in motion the biggest organization ever formed in the United States: judges, lawyers, who would in time, also go into Washington as senators, congressmen, and many very influential people.

"The plan at first was foolproof. If any one did get wise, they would wind up chasing after me. They refer to this as an 'endless run.' Because up until I received the package I had no idea what was going on. The buck stops there, so to speak. Therefore, they had a clean run for over 40 years. They were able to amass a great fortune; rumor has it that the last three presidents were placed into office by the backing of the organization. Their power and money were now so massive it protected them. I found out that I was just a pawn in a big game. Nevertheless, my adopted father said he only went along with the plan because he thought it would give me a good life, and he would have the son he always wanted to carry on his name. Alas, greed is a powerful thing when it gets a hold on some people, and my adopted mother couldn't have cared less if I lived or died. In fact, I was convinced she liked the idea of me being dead, because then she would have the money without the hassle of me being around. Therefore, when the organization approached her to do things that would make life hard on me, she found herself enjoying it way too much to stop.

"The plan worked for seven years. I lived under constant abuse from getting just enough to eat to survive, and sitting in a hard chair for eight to nine hours a day. I was told that if I said anything to Dad about it, things would just get worse. They got worse anyway. Mom started getting paranoid that someone was going to find out about the things she was doing. She started paying kids at school to spy on me. That way, if I talked to any of the teachers or anyone else, she would know about it.

"She would make me sit out in the cold for hours if she went out. Then, when she got home, she would make me clean the house until Dad would get home. Of course, once Dad arrived home I would be able to read or do schoolwork like a normal boy. I slept in the back utility room with the dog on an old army cot. Most of the time, I even ate back there by myself.

"She would make up stories that I did weird things like self-torture by sticking pins in my privates. She even took me to a psychiatrist once and told them that story. Good Lord, was I embarrassed! What I hadn't realized was that this was supposed to drive me crazy. Instead, it backfired on her. I really believe she lost her mind.

"I just got to the point where I didn't care anymore; living life this way just wasn't worth it. Death had to be better than this. I planned for months on ways that I could kill myself. I planned and thought about it so much, it became a comfort to me just thinking about it. Somehow, I just knew it would all be over soon. Then, one day, I grabbed a butcher knife and ran into the bathroom. I tried several times to shove that knife into my heart, but I couldn't do it! At first, I was angry with myself, and then

I realized there had to be a better way. The next day I ran away, and I never went back.

"This also worked out very well for the organization's plan, since I moved from place to place and made it almost impossible for anyone to keep up with my whereabouts. Many years later, my natural family and I were reunited. I was able to spend time with my true mother, brothers, and sisters. Well, you already know the rest of that story from here. I changed my name back, and that was the start of a new life. I tried to put everything behind me and really concentrate only on the future. I met your mother and we started our family."

"Come on, Dad, get to the package and what all this has to do with me!"

"Okay! My dad had kept a journal. Over the years he kept adding information to it, and because he knew they would have killed him for releasing this information, he made sure that the package would not be delivered until after his death. At first, I couldn't make much sense of the information. It contained a lot of names and dates, but then he explained that he had later joined the organization, and was able to learn just what the organization was really doing. He was devastated to discover that this wasn't all about just switching names and assuming new identities. He learned that they were actually conducting experiments in mind control. However, it wasn't until he had joined the organization that he found out Mom was in on it from the very beginning, and that's why they were selected as candidates eligible to adopt a child.

"He tried to say he was sorry, and hoped that this information would bring me some kind of peace. Now that I knew I wasn't the only one, and all those names in the journal were other kids that went through the same ordeal as I had, it made me want to do something about it. I took what money I had and went to work on trying to locate the others. There was one name that seemed to connect with all of them—and that's what changed everything.

It was my name. One day, as I was reading that journal, it dawned on me: I was the first candidate in the organization's game and somewhere there was another person using my identity. Because I broke the pattern when I ran away and entered back into what they referred to as 'the mainstream,' it had created a problem."

"I still don't get it."

"Hang in there, Son, I'm trying to give you almost 60 years of history in approximately two hours. Most of this may not mean much to you right now, but it will in the near future. I found myself learning more and more from the journal; things were starting to come together like a puzzle. I knew if I could find my double then the rest of the puzzle would come together. I hunted for over a year and didn't make any progress at all. Then one night, in a small town in West Virginia, I stopped at a little roadside bar. I got to talking with a fellow from that area, and he asked what I was doing in West Virginia, so I told him I was looking for an old friend. When he heard the name he almost stopped breathing. Then he wanted to know how I had come to know this friend. I explained to him that I had met him when I was with my adopted parents many years ago. He told me not to say anymore, and gave me a piece of paper with his name and phone number on it. When he finished his drink, he got up and left.

"Frank was the fellow's name, and I called him the next morning. He asked where I was from, and agreed to meet me here in Arkansas in two days. When he showed up, I was so excited. We had a long visit and Frank told of his years of abuse, and how it left him feeling cold and inhuman. He was 18 before he found a way to escape his adopted parents, but what was really interesting was that Frank had met the man I had asked about; he said he had visited his parents on many occasions over the years. He claimed he was an uncle, his mother's older brother. It was a lot like listening to my own story.

"Now when I told Frank my story, he was in shock and, like me, somewhat relieved at the same time. Things made a lot more sense to him; he could see what was going on. Then he commented, 'What I don't understand is, why are you looking for my uncle?' In order to try to make it easier for him to understand I just handed Frank my driver's license. When he read the name, he still didn't figure out the connection except that the names were the same. I took Frank at his word and made him swear that if I told him everything he couldn't tell anybody. He agreed, and even though we had just met I felt I could trust Frank—I felt we had a connection like brothers. I handed him the journal, told him to read it, and then we would talk more.

"The next day, Frank and I became partners. We tracked down my double in less than three days. Both of us were like ducks out of water, sitting in front of this mansion in upstate New York. We were about to leave when the gates parted open and the guard waved for us to pull in. When we got inside the gates, the guard asked if we were there about the job. We just played right along with the guard. When we got to the house, a maid came out and showed us in, took us to a big room and told us that the man of the house would be there in a few minutes."

"Come on, Dad, this is just a little too much," Sam said. "It sounds like you've been watching too much sci-fi. Next thing you're going to tell me is that it was you who came into the room."

"Well, maybe so, Son, but that's exactly what happened, except he was about ten years older than I was. I let Frank do most of the talking because I didn't want to slip and say anything to give myself away. Bill gave both Frank and me a job working as grounds keepers. We even had a little house on the back forty to stay in. To tell you the truth, it was a really nice set-up. When we were settled in and I had time to think, it dawned on me that Frank was supposed to have known this man as an uncle—so I confronted him. Frank swore he didn't know what was going on, but this guy wasn't the same man who claimed to be his uncle, and it made sense because the man acted as if he had never met or even seen Frank before. At that point, too much had happened to turn back without the truth, so I decided to trust that Frank was being honest, and we were on the brink of discovering the truth.

"A few days went by where we were working during the day and slipping around every night, trying to learn everything we could. There was a meeting coming up, and Bill was so busy making all the plans that I don't think he even remembered talking to us when he hired us. Everyone was busy cleaning; you could hardly get anyone to stop and talk to you, in order to try to get information or uncover anything.

"As luck would have it, though, Joe the cook was upset about something. Joe was about forty, and had been working on the estate for around fifteen years. When Joe yelled at me to give him a hand carrying in the groceries, I stepped in and followed, bags in hand. You want to know something? Get an angry man talking and he will fill your head with a lot of information. I found out that usually there is only one meeting a year, but for some reason they were having a special meeting as well this year. By what Joe was telling me, I couldn't help believing that it had something to do with me. It was just a feeling, but I had learned early in life to try and trust those feelings. That night I decided I was going to try to get into Bill's office. I knew the answers had to be in there.

"Frank said he was sick from working out in the heat all day. Therefore, I went snooping on my own. Determined to get to the truth, I had forgotten to keep my guard up about what was going on. They were all waiting for me. Yeah, you guessed it. Frank was in on it from the beginning.

"Now that they had me, Bill was just beside himself, as if his life's purpose had been fulfilled. I didn't figure there was any doubt as to what their plan was for me. However, to my surprise, they didn't just take me out and shoot me. Remember what I told you about someone with a sick twisted idea of trying to bend another person to their will? Well, Bill had it in his mind that he was going to finish the job that they had started on me when I was just a kid.

"I remember the crazed look he had in his eyes after the chains were on me and he sent everyone else out of the room. I had seen that look before from my adopted mother. 'I will break you like a toothpick!' he said, with so much hate that it sent that same scared panicked feeling through me I had when I was a kid."

"Dad, I think you've stretched this about as far as you can, and I still don't see what any of this has to do with me."

"See, Son, it's just as I said: you never understood me because you never wanted to."

"What's this got to do with me?"

"Well, I believe that whether or not you want to believe it, you inherited my bad side to life. I thought if I explained it to you that you might learn to control it, instead of it controlling you. Then maybe you would learn to appreciate life, share more with your family, show an interest in your children's lives and your grandchildren."

"Yeah, here we go again. Tell me how I screwed everything up; the things I did all wrong."

"I'm sorry, Son, but I don't have much time. What I'm talking about is learning to get past your mistakes; we can't change the past no matter what we do. So don't spend your time dwelling on it, because it will only make you angrier."

"Okay! Okay! Go on—maybe I'll figure it out."

"Where was I? Ah, yes. I had just been caught. There's no need to bore you with their torture tactics. Let us just say they were very effective. I would have confessed to shooting John F. Kennedy if it would have gotten me out of that place. Bill was starting to enjoy himself way too much. I think this comes from the idea of having total power over someone and making them say and do just what you want them to. It gives people a false sense of power, that they're in absolute control. I couldn't even tell you how many days had passed since I last ate or drank anything. Then Bill brought Frank in. I could hardly make out his face, as my eyes were so irritated by the light. Bill had Frank kneel in front of me. 'Now tell him you're sorry,' he said to Frank. 'You didn't last half the time before betraying your friend.' I then understood why Frank had done what he did.

"While Bill was removing the chains, he was steadily talking. 'Now, Bill,' he said to me, 'you must kill Frank for betraying you. He can never be trusted; you must shoot him for his betrayal so that you can be free from this problem and accept your place here working with me.' I never could stand people who bragged too much. I could tell my captor had never been beaten before. He was just downright proud of himself. He had broken Frank so bad that he was willing to kneel there and wait for me to shoot him, but I was so weak I could barely hold the gun up. Bill whispered in my ear, 'Go on, shoot him, and you will be rewarded with food and a good night's rest. Tomorrow will be the dawn of a new era for Bill and Bill. Just ease the gun up a little higher and shoot him!' He was looking over at Frank like he was no more than a sick animal that needed to be put down.

"I remember cocking the gun and looking Frank in the eyes. I thought I could still see a touch of my friend. 'That's it, now shoot him!' Bill said. With the last ounce of strength I had, I turned and fired twice, putting two rounds at point-blank range into Mr. Bill's chest. He dropped on the spot, never knowing what had hit him. Frank reached out and grabbed me to keep me from falling on top of him.

"Later I woke up in a makeshift hospital room. Frank was sleeping in a chair close to the door. A young woman walked in and, seeing me awake, she shook Frank and said, 'It looks like our fellow is going to make it.' I could hardly talk; they assured me I was safe for the time being. 'Just rest,' Frank said. 'Molly here knows her stuff; she will have you back on your feet in no time.' For the next few days, I just ate and slept. Frank spent hours telling me everything he knew. He started to tell me what he had done with his uncle, but I stopped him. Some things are better left unsaid. Frank had contacted his adopted parents; they flew in and I met them. They too had a great deal of information to share. George, his father, had been a judge, and had contact with almost every member of the organization.

"There wasn't but a few days left before the meeting was to take place. By the time I was back on my feet, I had worked out a plan with Frank, Joe the cook, and Molly. Now, Son, I know you're getting tired, so I'm going to have to cut you short on the rest of this. When you get back to Montana there will be a package delivered to you. Knowing now what I have told you, I trust you will make good choices and learn to enjoy life. There are people that would still kill for this information. You cannot trust anyone, and the less you tell your family, the better off they will be. As you go, try to remember: I always loved you, Son."

"That's it?"

"Yeah, pretty much."

"But, Dad, what happened?"

"You will know soon enough. May God bless you and give you the wisdom to carry on. Now I have to go lie down for awhile."

Sam stood up, and his dad gave him a hug. Almost choking, Sam heard himself saying, "I always loved you too, Dad."

"I know, Son. Now try to get some rest."

As Sam watched his dad walk down the hall, he wiped a tear from his eye.

When Bill got to the bedroom door, he called out, "Good night, Bean Head." Sam couldn't help but laugh, and hollered back, "Good night, Old Man!"

Chapter 2
A Rude Awakening

The next morning, Sam was cooking breakfast when Cyndi showed up.

"It looks like you're feeling pretty good this morning! Did you sleep well?" she asked.

"Sure did, Sis. Sit down; I was just about to wake Dad."

"What?!"

"That's right! You don't have to act surprised. We talked through the wee hours of the night. Well he did most of the talking. Actually, we got along quite well. At first, I was upset that you lied to me, but now I'm kind of glad."

"Sam, are you sure you're feeling alright?"

"Sure, I'm fine."

"Sam, Dad is gone—he's dead! The funeral is on Sunday."

"Sis, why are you doing this? Just a minute. I'll prove it to you."

Sam walked to the bedroom, knocked on the door and called, "Hey, Old Man! Come out and have yourself some breakfast!"

There was no answer, so he opened the door and found the bed still made, and no visible sign that his father had been there.

"Sis, I'm telling you he was here last night."

"Sam, please. This is not funny. Come back in here and eat your breakfast."

"Sis, I'm not trying to be funny! I've seen Dad. I talked with him just last night."

"Sam, that's impossible! You must have had a dream."

Sam sat down to eat, and when he looked at the spot he had made at the table for his dad he looked up to Cyndi and asked, "Are you hungry, Sis? Help yourself. I'm not feeling much like eating any more." Sitting there, he realized that he had actually been looking forward to seeing his dad this morning. Now he didn't know what to say; he was completely at a loss for words.

"Sam, would you like to go over to the funeral home and see Dad? Maybe it would help. You wouldn't believe how many people have come to say goodbye to him. Sam!"

"Yeah, Sis, I hear you. Maybe you're right—it would help."

Sam wasn't sure of anything at this point. It couldn't have been a dream; it had been too real. However, he didn't want to sound like a mental case, either. He went to take a shower and get ready for the trip to the funeral home. When he was finished he went back into the kitchen and saw that his older brother, Mike, had shown up.

"How has our big brother been doing?" Sam asked.

"I'm doing fine, keeping busy," Mike said. "How are you doing?"

"Well, right now seems a little questionable."

"I know what you mean. Sis was telling me about last night. Try not to let that stuff get to you, though. Just like you, there were times that I thought I could still hear Mom in the house every now and then, before I moved out to the ranch."

"So, are you guys ready?" Cyndi asked.

"Ready, Sis. Do you want to drive or would you like me to?" Mike asked.

"I'll drive. Come on."

They headed out, laughing and talking just like old times. Before Sam even realized it, they had arrived at the funeral home. He couldn't believe his eyes. There must have been close to 300 people there.

"My God, who are all those people?" he asked.

Mike looked back. "This is a small crowd compared to yesterday! Isn't that right, Sis?"

"Oh, yeah. They had to put out three registries to move everyone along more quickly."

"I can't believe this," Sam said. "I've never seen anything like it."

Sam was even more shocked when they got inside. Deep down, he still did not believe his father was dead, but his doubts were removed when he saw his dad lying there in the casket. A part of Sam wanted to run. Leave, and never come back to this place. Slowly, he made his way to the door. He was so busy shaking hands and thanking people that he lost track of Mike and Cyndi. When he finally got outside, he seemed able to blend in a little easier. He decided to go to the car and have a cigarette. He stood there watching in sheer amazement at the amount of people that had come to pay their respects to his father.

A man in a black Stetson hat walked out. It had to catch your eye if you knew Bill. Sam watched as if something magical was about to happen. He just couldn't shake the night before. As he got closer, Sam could see he was a younger man, maybe in his late twenties.

The young man walked up and said, "I don't want to be rude, but could I join you in smoking a cigarette?"

"Sure," Sam said, and handed him the pack. He lit the cigarette and thanked Sam. "No problem," replied Sam. "Did you know my dad very well?"

"Sure did. He and my father worked a lot together; I stayed out at the ranch more than at my own home for the last few years. Your dad gave me this hat on my 21st birthday.

"I can believe that. It's what caught my eye when you first walked out. So you know my brother, Mike?"

"Oh, yeah, the computer man, and your sister Cyndi. We met a few times over the years, mainly at parties at the ranch. I really hate to run, but I've got to go pick my dad up from the airport."

"Okay, but you never told me your name."

"My name is Frank," he said and shook hands with Sam.

"It's nice to meet you."

"Well, talk to you later."

As Frank walked to his truck, his name clicked in Sam's head. He wanted to call out and ask him what his dad's name was, but didn't want to make a fool of himself. Besides, Mike should know, so he would ask him later.

Haley walked up from behind him. "Hey Sam, what are you doing standing out here?" Sam turned to answer, but didn't recognize her. His silence gave him away. "Lord have mercy! Don't tell me you don't know me?"

Sam, trying to think on his feet, was stunned when Haley told him who she was.

"My God, girl, look at you! I would have never guessed. You have grown to be quite lovely."

"Well, thank you. I saw you talking with Frank."

"Do you know him?"

"Oh, yeah. I had a huge crush on him for a long time. Big Frank told him messing around with me would be sudden death if Papa was to find out. So we became more like brother and sister."

Sam was lost in his own little world; it was as though everybody was answering his questions faster than he could ask.

Haley had seen Cyndi. "I need to talk with Sis. I'll see you out at the ranch later, okay?"

"Sure thing."

As he watched the two talking, Sam could almost hear his dad saying, "You know they're cooking something up."

Mike came outside with a young woman who pushed a wheelchair with an older woman seated in it. He waved to Sam. "Could you help Miss Mary and her mother to their van?"

"Sure," Sam said, then asked Mary, "Where are you parked?"

She pointed. "Way out there. If you'll wait here, I'll go get the van."

"Okay, we can do that."

Mary headed across the parking lot. The older woman sitting in the wheelchair looked Sam up and down, and then said, "I guess I see a family connection."

Sam wasn't really sure what to say, but before he could try, she continued. "Your dad was a really special man; we're all going to miss him. You and your dad weren't very close, but he sure talked about you a lot. I'm sorry, Sam; you'll have to forgive an old woman for just rambling on. My name is Molly. Your father and I were good friends, and like I said, he talked about you a great deal, so when I heard Mike call out your name it was as if we had already met."

"I know what you mean. I felt it myself. Here's Miss Mary now. Let me help you."

"I hope we have a chance to talk again, Sam, before you leave to go back home." As the wheelchair lift was going up she pulled a card from her side pocket, and gave it to Sam,. "But if we don't, please keep in touch."

"I sure will. You ladies be careful driving home."

They waved as they were leaving. Sam waved back; his mind was racing as he tried to keep up with everything. For just a second, he thought things couldn't have gotten any stranger.

Then he noticed three black limos pulling up. Before they could stop, somebody grabbed Sam and pulled him back inside. He heard Mike yell out.

"Take him to the ranch; he will be safe there."

Without having time to think, Sam just followed the man as instructed. Once they were out the back door, a car pulled up.

"Quick, Dad, get in! Molly called and said there's more on the way."

"Okay. Go, Son, and get to the ranch. We don't want to turn this into a shoot-out here at the funeral home."

Sam hollered, "Wait! I don't know what's going on here, but my brother and sisters are back there."

"It's all right, Sam, they're protected. Besides, it's you they want!"

"Why do they want me? Who are they anyway?"

"Whoa, Sam, I think it might be best if we wait until everyone is together and then we can try to figure all this out."

"Okay, but who are you?"

"My name is Joe, and this is my youngest son, David."

Sam was glad to hear a name that he remembered, even if it was only a vague memory. He sat back, trying to relax and catch his breath. His mind told him there was no way this could really be happening. "My God," he wondered. "What did my dad do?"

About that time, three black SUVs pulled up beside them.

"What the hell now?" Sam yelled.

"It's all right," said David as he gave a honk and a wave. "See the Broken R brand? They're our escort home."

Joe leaned back and took in a deep breath. "Well, Sam, we are about two hours away, so you need to try and get some rest."

Sam shook his head and said, "Rest? Both of you act as though nothing has happened here. I want to know what the hell is going on. One of you, Joe, David, I beg you: please tell me the truth!"

"We really don't know much that we could tell you. We just showed up ourselves. We were talking with Mike when we found out you were there, and we wanted to meet you. That's the reason we were already at the door when everything started. Just how much do you know, Sam?"

"What do you mean? I don't know anything. Hell, I'm in the Twilight Zone."

"Your dad used to say that a lot," David laughed, and hummed the theme music. "Well, then, like I said, I think we had best wait until everyone is together and then we'll be able to get you caught up on things. Maybe you had better try calling home to see if everything is OK there."

Trying to keep his cool, Sam pulled out his cell phone, but Joe reached out and took it away.

"No! Here, use mine." Joe handed Sam's phone to David, who rolled down the window and passed the phone to one of the SUVs.

"No sense in taking chances now," said David.

The SUV turned off at the next road. Sam was now worried about his family. He made his call, but nobody answered. Joe could see the panic in his face.

"Hey, don't worry. It's all going to work out," Joe tried to reassure him. Reaching into his pocket, he pulled out a bottle of pills. "David, got anything to drink up there?"

"No, but I bet our friends have."

David made a sign to the men in the other car, as if he were drinking something. They understood what he wanted and, pulling up beside the car, passed him a small cooler. David tipped his hat as if to say thank you.

"Here you go, Dad."

Joe opened a Coke and gave Sam a couple of pills. "Take these. They will help you relax."

Sam knew he needed to relax, but he wasn't sure if he should take the pills.

"It's okay, Sam," Joe tried to reassure him. "Your dad used to take these when things got out of hand."

Giving in, Sam took the pills with a big swallow of Coke. He then pulled out and lit a cigarette. Taking big long puffs as if he were smoking his last one, he was deep in thought, replaying all he had been through over the last few days. The pills seemed to have kicked in rather fast, and his eyes were getting heavy. He looked over at Joe.

"Hey, you're the cook!" Joe didn't have time to answer him back. He just reached over took the cigarette out of Sam's hand as he slumped over into a deep, sound sleep.

"What was all that about, Dad?"

"I'm not real sure, Son, but Sam here knows more than he's telling. Maybe things will look better for him tomorrow. He has had too much excitement for one day. As his dad would have said, 'everything looks better after a good night's sleep.'"

David looked back. "I know, Dad, I miss him too."

They were pulling up to the gate. "Come on. Let's get Sam settled, and try to get us some rest as well."

Chapter 3
Welcome to the Broken R

Sam awoke late the next morning. Looking around the room told him right off he was in a strange place. His brain went right back into high gear. Remembering all that had taken place, Sam figured he must be at the ranch. Getting out of bed, he walked into the bathroom, having a hard time believing what he was seeing with his own eyes. This place was fit for a king. After climbing out of the shower, he found a note taped to the bedroom mirror:

> "Sam,
>
> You should be able to find anything you need in the closet.
> Just take your pick as to what you would like to wear.
>
> Love, Sis."

As Sam entered the huge walk-in closet, he was amazed at the amount of Western clothes and boots that were available for him. Selecting a nice brown suit and a matching pair of brown leather boots, he walked back out into the room. As he got dressed, he caught himself staring out of two large bay windows at an awesome landscape at the rear of the ranch. The picture he was seeing was like a photograph seen only on calendars and postcards.

"This place is huge," he said to himself.

He could see the riders moving a herd of cattle, at least 500-head or more.

"What an extraordinary place! Everything is picture-perfect."

The barns were red with white trim, and he counted 17 houses scattered across the way.

"That's dad's—number 17." He sat back on the bed, trying to clear his mind and talking to himself again. "I've got to try and call Tara again, and I need to check on Mike, Cyndi and Haley."

A knock on the door interrupted his train of thought. Sam started to yell "Come in," but cut himself short, walked to the door and opened it. It was his sister Cyndi. He grabbed her in a bear hug.

"Are you all right?" Sam said.

"Sure am. Good morning. Did you sleep well?"

"Sure, Sis, but of course I had a little help."

"Yeah, Joe told us he had given you something to help sleep. That is the only reason we haven't tried to wake you up until now. Molly is worried about you, though, so you need to come on down and get something to eat. Otherwise, Molly will have Mary up here sticking a needle in your arm to make you better."

"Okay. Give me a second."

As they were walking down the steps, Sam asked, "What can you tell me, Sis?"

"Sam, I really don't know; I've never seen such a fuss before. I can tell you this much: it sure has gotten everyone around here in an uproar, and it seems like you're the center of all the conversations. Dad never told me anything; he always said I was better off not knowing. It looks like you are going to have to figure this one out on your own. Come on, there's a surprise for you in the kitchen.

"What now? I don't think I need any more surprises."

"You don't, huh?"

As they both entered the kitchen, Sam stuttered, "Tarrrrrrra . . . Tara . . . Whaa . . . What are you doing here?"

"I don't know why I'm here, but aren't you glad to see me?" Tara asked as Sam reached out and hugged her tightly. He kissed her gently, and then continued to ask questions about his family, wanting to know everybody was safe.

She hugged his neck. "Boy, I just can't turn you loose for a minute without you getting into trouble," she said, laughing heartily.

"I tried calling you last night, but couldn't get anybody to answer."

"It was probably because we were on our way here."

"What happened? Where are the kids? Are they okay?"

"They're all fine and we're all here, lock, stock, and barrel." She pointed out the window. "They're checking the place out."

Sam took a deep breath. "Well, I wish I could tell you what's going on, but I'm just as lost for answers as you. I'm just glad to see you and the kids are okay!" He gave her another kiss to make sure she was real, then hollered, "Let's eat! I'm starving."

Joining the others in the dining room, Molly greeted them both. "I'm glad to see you back on your feet," she told Sam. "Are you both ready to eat?"

"Sure thing. Have you met my wife, Tara?"

"Yes, dear, we met early this morning. You have a very lovely family."

Mary came in. "Good morning, Mom. Are you going to stay here for a while? Haley wants me to ride with her up to Ronnie's, to let him know about the meeting tonight."

"Okay, that's fine," Molly replied.

"We should be back by three."

"Okay, but just be careful."

Sam was too busy eating at that moment, so he just waved as she was leaving.

"Who is Ronnie?" he asked, once he'd swallowed.

"He is the ranch foreman," Molly said. "Your dad took him in when he was just a kid. He lives in the first homesite built by your dad on the back forty. He is a quiet fellow, spends most of his time alone, but he is a good worker, he has taken your dad's passing hard. I think your dad was his best friend and mentor. I don't think he ever knew his father, and your dad filled that gap for him in a lot of ways."

"What meeting was Mary talking about?"

"Simplicity has a monthly meeting, and tonight is a special tribute to your dad. Everyone will be there. We are like a big family, Sam—what affects one, affects us all. They all want to meet you and your family. Now you two enjoy your meal. I am going to go lie down for a while. If you need anything else, just help yourselves."

After Sam and Tara finished eating, they went out for a walk to find the kids and check out the ranch.

"I just can't believe all this," Tara said.

"I know! This place alone is enough to blow your mind, let alone everything else that's going on."

"You didn't know anything about this?"

"Not really. Cyndi mentioned in one of her letters that Dad had bought himself a ranch, but I never dreamed it was anything like this."

"Hey, there are our kids."

"Who is that with them?"

"You don't recognize Mike?"

"You're kidding!"

"No, that's him."

"Hey, Sam, Tara," Mike said. "Well, little brother, are we feeling any better today?"

"Yeah, a lot better since I have my family close by. I see you've met everyone!"

"Yes, we've been having a good visit."

"Dad is this all for real?" asked Rick, Sam's oldest son. Pointing to the houses, he said, "Uncle Mike says this is our house, and over there is Brad and Donna's house."

"Grandpa, Grandpa," little Sara and Ben hollered. "Are we going to live here?"

Sam bent down and picked up his grandchildren. "We will just have to wait and see," he said, giving them both hugs and kisses.

Rick's wife, Patty, reached out and took Ben, while Rick grabbed hold of Sara. "Okay, now, let's give Grandpa a break," said Rick. "You two are getting way too big for him to have to carry around."

"But I'm only seven, Daddy," Sara protested.

"And I'm only five," said Ben, holding up his hand.

"That's right, and you're acting so grown-up today." Tara gave him a kiss on the cheek.

Mike looked over at Donna. "Who's this little fellow?"

"This here is Billy, and he is eight months old."

"Billy, that's a good name."

"Yeah, my dad's name was William too."

"Looks like little Billy is a namesake for both sides of the family."

Mike's cell phone rang. "Hello. Okay," he said to it, and then hung up.

Sam burst into laughter. "I guess some things never do change, huh, Bubba? Your answers are still short and to the point."

"Got to go, that was Eric at the communications center. We are having a problem with the security system. You two go ahead and take the cart. I will walk from here, since it's just around the corner. I'll see you later this afternoon."

They all watched him walk away. "Well I guess we should go back to the house," Sam said. "It's getting hot out here, and besides, we've got a lot to talk about." They all agreed and headed back toward the house.

"Mike!" Eric called out as soon as he walked in. "We've got problems! Someone has hacked into our system! What do we do?"

"Just relax," said Mike as he sat down at the computer and started typing. A few seconds later, he told Eric: "Call Tech Control and inform them our system will be offline for approximately two hours."

After the mainframe computer shut down, Mike went back to typing, and within a few seconds the system was back up and running.

Eric was just hanging up the phone from calling Tech Control. "What's the deal? You said two hours!"

"That's right; you have two hours to run a backup, just as a precaution. Whoever it is, they're after information, but I don't think they had time to infect anything."

"But if the system is running . . ."

"Well, it's not really. This is a program I designed many years ago."

Eric shook his head. "Okay, go ahead and tell me. I know I probably won't understand it, but I need to hear it anyway."

"It's really quite simple. I've just diverted the hackers from our mainframe to another mainframe. They want information, so we are giving them information. All they want plus more, and if they let their system run long enough our system will automatically run a trace. If they haven't covered their tracks well, we will know who the hackers are."

"Boy! I'm glad you're on our side," Eric said, patting Mike on the back. "Well, I guess I'll get busy running that backup."

"Good, I've got to run for now but I'll be back in time to show you how to switch everything back, so you can get back online," said Mike.

"Okay, thanks. I'll see you then."

While Mike walked back to the main house, he met up with Haley, Mary, and Ronnie coming out from the stables.

"Hi, Mike," said Haley as she reached up and gave him a big hug. "How's my big brother doing?"

"Good. Are you all heading over to the house?"

"Yep, Ronnie wants to meet Sam before everyone gets here tonight." Mike and Ronnie shook hands.

"It's been awhile," Ronnie said. "Are you doing all right, Mike?"

"Yeah, pretty good. How about you?"

Mary stamped her feet. "Hey, I'm here, too!" She had been sweet on Mike for a long time.

"I'm sorry, Mary," Mike said, reaching over to hug her and plant a soft kiss on her cheek. "Is that better?"

She stood on the tips of her toes, and kissed him back. "You bet."

They started walking toward the house, and Ronnie asked Mike how he felt about his brother coming back after all this time.

"Ronnie, I gave up a long time ago trying to figure Sam out. I hope this works out for Sam and his family, because that is what our dad wanted. No matter what he decides, it won't change much in the way things work around here."

"I hope you're right; it sure sounds like a lot of things are happening since he got here."

"I know, after what happened yesterday, and today we've got somebody trying to hack into the system."

"Have you found out who it was?"

"No, not yet, but we're working on it."

At the house, the driveway was already filling with cars. Mike asked Haley, "Would you please call the front gate and tell them to get somebody down here to show people where to park. It looks like we're going to have a big turnout tonight."

"Okay, Mike. Got it!"

"Come on, Ronnie," Mike said, "I will introduce you to Sam."

Mary started to walk away. Mike reached out to pull her back, kiss her, and ask, "Please stay with Haley."

"But why? What's wrong?"

"I'm not sure," Mike said. "I've just got a gut feeling, and I don't like it."

Mike and Ronnie headed into the house.

Haley asked, "Mary, what was all that about?"

"Girl, I don't know, but I liked it."

They waited for the security guards to show up before going inside. The place was packed. Mike was on the phone with Eric, telling him how to put everything back online.

"Okay, if you have any problems just give me a call back." He hung up. "Mary, Sis, you two stay close. I've got to find Frank in order to get this meeting started off."

"Okay, Mike. Try to calm down."

"I'm trying." He took off in search of Frank.

In the study, Sam was getting the rundown from Ronnie. "Listen, I'm not very good with words, so you may not like my rough-cut version of all this, but here it goes: your dad asked me to deliver this package to you. His instructions were clear. No matter what transpired after his death, I was to pass this package to you, and only you, if anything went wrong. I know things have been rough on you for the last few days. I don't have a clue about what is in this package, but I hope that maybe it will be something to help you understand what's going on here. Your dad was a great man; I highly respected and loved him. I always looked to him as the dad I never had. He controlled everything, and we just did our jobs. Now there seems to be a lot of confusion going on. I know it's because everyone is worried about what will happen now that he is gone. Sam, I owed your dad my life, and I'm happy where I'm at. I will do whatever I can to help; just let me know if you need me."

Sam stretched out his hand, thanking Ronnie. "I appreciate that, Ronnie," he said with sincerity.

Walking to the door, Ronnie said, "Well, then, I'll get on out of here, Bean Head. I need to give you some time to check this out."

"Wait! Where did that come from?"

"Your dad said you would understand."

After Ronnie left, Sam was still standing with the package when he remembered his dad telling him that he would receive one. "That is what he said, so I am not crazy, Bean Head or not."

He finally opened the package. It contained a videocassette tape. He walked to the TV, turned it on, and slid the tape into the VCR. Sitting back, he said, "Okay! Talk to me, Dad."

"Hi, Son!" his father said on the tape. "If you're watching this tape, it means something has gone wrong. I am sorry; I wanted everything to go smoothly, and that way you truly could make up your own mind as to what you wanted to do. I trust your family is with you, and safe. Well, you should have had enough time to look over the Broken R; she is worth her weight in gold.

"When I started Simplicity, I had no idea where it was going. The business grew so fast—Mike can tell you more than I can about the way it works now. As you must know by now, I have made many enemies. Enemies from the government on down; a line of people in high places. So trust no one unless they have proven their loyalties to you.

"If you want out right now, all you have to do is tell Ronnie, 'THE SNOW IS TOO DEEP.' He will take care of the rest. If you choose to leave, you must never come back. It would only put you and your family in danger's way. Now if you choose to stay, it works the same way; you can never leave. This is like taking new marriage vows—until death do you part. So if you have made up your mind to stay, go to the desk and pull out the bottom right-hand drawer. You will find a key taped on the backside. Get it and come back. The key opens the cabinet door under the TV."

Sam stopped the tape and went to get the key. When he came back and opened the cabinet door, he found a small box with a ring inside. He turned the tape back on.

"Okay, Son, take a good look at the ring. It bears the Broken R brand. It's like a wedding ring; when you put it on you become as one, bearing each other's burdens. Her secrets are now your secrets. Never lose this ring; it contains the answers you will be seeking. Now, if you have chosen to stay and you are wearing the ring; repeat after me: 'REAL POWER IS NEVER GIVEN, IT IS ALWAYS TAKEN.' Good luck, Sam, and welcome home to the Broken R."

Chapter 4
The Meeting

Sam studied the ring. He knew it was his dad's; he had been wearing it the night they had talked. A knock at the door brought Sam's attention back to the moment.

"Just a minute, I'm coming." He turned the TV off, and placed the videocassette tape back into the cabinet, making certain it was locked before he walked to the door. At the door, Sam stopped, rubbing his hands over his face and trying to regain his composure. The emotional stress of all that was happening was beginning to wear on him. He opened the door. "Sis! Good to see you. Come in."

"Well, just for a minute," Cyndi said. "What's going on? Come on, let's get you cleaned up. We can't let everyone see you this way." She went into the bathroom and got a wet rag.

"I don't really know, Sis; I guess it's all of it."

"Okay, here you go. Wash your face. Ronnie sent me to get you; he didn't want to leave Mike. It seems Mike is just a little worked up as well. Are you okay now?"

"Yeah, I'm good. Let's go and face the music."

Haley was waiting for them when they walked out the door. "Hey, you two ready to go?"

Sam and Cyndi both replied, "We are coming now."

"Well, come on, then. The meeting is about to get started and I don't want to be late."

"Are you just a little nervous yourself, girl?" Sam asked.

"Nah, this stuff doesn't bother me. I'm just a little scared for Mike, and I don't want him to feel all alone right now."

They all climbed into Haley's jeep and headed over to the meeting hall.

"The box back there in the seat is for you," Cyndi told Sam.

Sam opened the box and found a black Stetson cowboy hat. "Where did this come from?"

"It's a welcome-home gift from me."

Sam tried it on. It fit perfectly. "I have never worn a cowboy hat."

"Well, you do now. And it looks good on you, too," said Haley.

"What do you think, Sis?"

When Cyndi turned around to look, her eyes started to tear up.

"What's wrong?"

"I'm sorry, Sam, it looks really good on you. I was just thinking of how proud our dad would be if he could see you right now."

"You really think so?"

"No, I know so."

They pulled up out back. "Okay, now," Sam said as he handed Cyndi his handkerchief. "Dry it up, girl! We have work to do."

When they got inside, they spotted Mike, Mary, Ronnie, and Frank all standing by the stage. Haley gave Mike a hug, reassuring him everything was going to be okay.

"Come on, girls, let's go on ahead and make sure everything is ready."

As Cyndi and Mary walked onto the stage, Ronnie came over to Sam and reached out to shake his hand. "That sure is a mighty good-looking ring you got there," He said. Turning to Mike, Ronnie shook his hand too and said, "My job is done here for now."

"You're not leaving, are you?" Mike asked.

"No, I'll be right out front."

"Okay, then, we'll see you later," he said before turning to Frank. "Frank, how much time do we have before it starts?"

"Maybe twenty minutes," he responded.

"Are you guys all set over there?" Mike called to Eric.

"Yeah, everything looks good. We are just taking shots of the people now.

All four outside big screens are running, and the Internet is set on a two-minute delay."

"It sounds like you have everything under control. Good job, Eric, I will talk to you later."

They all headed up to the stage. Sam started getting butterflies in the pit of his stomach, but Mike was just plain nervous. Frank had been the M.C. since the beginning of Simplicity, and even he seemed a bit on edge. He asked everyone to take a seat so they could get started.

Frank, standing in front of the podium, turned to the gang and said, "Tonight's meeting will be changed in the manner from which we normally run our meetings. We are not going to run through the stats, for the sake of time. Molly will give a short rundown on the plans for the funeral tomorrow, and Mike will follow her. Are you all ready?"

They all nodded in agreement.

Frank moved over to Sam. "We have a memorial tape of your dad sat up; we would like you to say a few words, before they run the tape."

"I don't know if I can," Sam said reluctantly.

Molly and Cyndi both spoke at the same time: "Please, Sam."

"Okay. I'll do my best."

"Good," Frank said. "That leaves Cyndi to close the meeting."

Haley and Mary took their seats, one on each side of the podium. Frank stepped up between them. "All right, ladies, are we ready?" They gave him the okay signal.

He turned back to the podium. "I just want to tell you all, standing here tonight is a great honor for me. I know if my dear friend Bill is looking down here tonight, he is one happy soul. This was his dream, to see all his kids together again. I wish you all the best."

The lights came on, music played and the curtains started rolling back slowly. Frank waved to the crowd, and the music slowly faded out.

"I want to welcome everyone tonight, and we are honored so many of you have come out to show your respect and support. Since this is a special meeting, we will not be going through our regular program tonight. We have some information to share with you all."

Miss Molly rolled herself up to the microphone as Frank introduced her and stepped back. She began with a warm welcome, and Mary handed her a sheet of paper.

"My goodness, this is just amazing. Over 2,000 people and still counting. Some of you have already made plans to stay for the funeral. There are still 100 rooms available at the Broken R Inn, here on the ranch. Because we were sure there would be a large turnout, we contacted all the motels in Benton and Bryant, reserved all their rooms. If you do not already have arrangements made, just show any one of them your membership ID card. Rooms will only cost $10 for tonight. Tomorrow the services will begin at 9 a.m. The Broken R Family welcomes you to stay for open house afterwards. I personally want to thank each and every one of you present, and all that have sent their best wishes in cards and letters."

Frank stepped back up to the podium, "Thanks, Molly. Now let me introduce to you our new CEO at Simplicity. Please let us all extend a warm welcome to Bill's oldest son, Michael."

Mike stood and waved to the people. As he strode over to the podium, he glanced over at Mary, who winked as if to say "You'll do fine."

"I too would like to thank everyone for their support and best wishes as we go through this most difficult time," Mike began. "My dad started this company over twenty years ago. He committed his life to it, and to those who joined in. The greatest thing he did was to set everything in such an order that no one person could control the business or misuse her.

"Not one member here has more or less to say in any of the company's affairs. Once you are a vested member in the company, you are equal to every other member. It is my honor to step up tonight in my father's place, to reassure you that I will do everything within my power to see that Simplicity, and the memory of my father, lives on. I look forward to serving you for many years. Once again, I thank you." He waved as he backed away from the podium.

Frank patted him on the back, and whispered, "You did a fine job, Mike." Frank yelled out to the crowd, "Let's hear it for our new CEO one more time!" The crowd responded with the same enthusiasm. After motioning for everyone to settle down, Frank said, "We also have with us tonight Bill's youngest son. I know you're all eager to meet him." Sam was already standing next to Frank. "Okay, here he is! Take it away, Sam."

As he waved his hat, the crowd got deadly silent. Sam hadn't realized how much he favored his dad. He began, "There comes a time in every person's life when he must face himself and decide for himself, so that when he faces the world, he knows what they're looking at. Nobody knew this better than my dad." As Sam was speaking, Frank gave the signal for Mary to go ahead and start the tape.

Sam was so nervous he didn't even notice the lights had started to dim. When the projection screen came down and the tape rolled, showing scenes of his dad's life at the Broken R, he kept on talking.

"I remember my dad telling us when we were just kids, 'Above all things, learn to be honest with yourself.' To tell you the truth, I think tonight I finally understand just what that means. As we take time to honor my father, and your friend, I hope that I will be able to help in preserving his memory. While we continue his work, and make our own memories, I hope that one day we will meet again on the other side, with no more excuses and nothing to be ashamed of. As Dad told us many times, 'If you really did your best then no one has the right to ask any more from you—the secret is to figure out what you're best at and make it work for you.' Dad was a cowboy inside and out, as you see him here"—Sam motioned toward the scene on the screen — "riding with the herd. This is where he loved to be, and he was good at it—something we may never understand. In closing, I would like to use his words: 'Real power is never given, it is always taken.' May all of us tonight share in his thoughts: that nobody can run your life better than yourself." The film ended just as if they had rehearsed it a hundred times. "Thank you!" Sam said, and stepped back.

Frank was so choked up he could hardly make an introduction for Cyndi, so she went ahead without one. "I would just like to share with you, as a Daddy's girl who was spoiled, my memory of my dad, who I always thought was great. My heart is full, and can truly say he left this world a rich man, because he never measured his wealth in cash. He always said he would trade it all for his family and friends. He once told me if a man walked through life and could count five 'true friends' he had made in that lifetime, he would be a rich man indeed. Seeing all of you and his family all together tonight reminds me my father was indeed a rich man. I know his passing from here to heaven leaves us better people, just from knowing him. Thank you so much." She blew a kiss at the crowd, and stepped back from the podium.

Frank motioned for everyone to step up, and as they did he thanked the crowd one last time. The curtains closed as they all waved, and then the hugging and crying began. Frank ended the meeting with his final saying, "One, two, three, and cut."

The crowd started drifting out slowly. Ronnie came backstage. "Man, you guys did great. Dad would have been so proud of you all. Hey, are we all going to meet at the house?"

"Yeah, we will be there shortly," Mike responded.

"Okay. See you there."

Chapter 5
The Funeral

They all met back at the house, and for the next few hours no one had any problems. They laughed and talked, enjoying the time they had to share. Sam could not remember a time when he had had so much fun. After everyone finally gave up for the night, Sam lay in bed thinking of all that had happened to him in the last few days. As time crept by, it became easier for him to dismiss many of the unexplained things, and he finally drifted off to sleep.

The next morning came with a light rain. The cloud coverage was a welcome sight on a mid-July day. Everyone hurried around, trying to get ready. There seemed to be a peacefulness in the air that no one understood, but everyone seemed to recognize. When you have walked out into the country air, you just cannot help but lean back and suck your lungs full of it. That is what Sam was doing when Joe walked up.

"Hey, young man, how are you doing?" asked Joe.

"Just fine right now. How are you doing, Joe?"

"You remember me."

"Sure, why wouldn't I?" Sam said.

"Well, we only met the one time, and it wasn't under the best of circumstances."

"That's for sure. I feel as though I've lived a lifetime in the past few days."

"I bet you do," Joe said. "If you don't mind my asking, where did you come up with the idea I was the cook?"

"You wouldn't believe me if I told you."

"Why don't you let me be the judge of that?"

"Okay, but if I tell you, you have to answer one question for me. Do we have a deal?"

"Okay, deal."

"My dad told me."

"When was this?"

"Only one question. Now, it's your turn. Is it true?" Sam asked as he twisted the ring on his finger.

"Where did you get that ring?" Joe asked.

"Joe, stick with our deal and answer the question."

"Yes, I was a cook at one time." Seeing Mike and Mary coming their way, he added, "We'll talk about it some other time." Then he walked off.

"What was that all about, Sam?" Mike asked as he and Mary came up.

"I'm not really sure, Mike. When he noticed this ring, it seemed to set him off."

Mike looked at the ring. "That's Dad's old ring. Why would it bother Joe?"

"I don't know. Does it bother you?"

"What? That Dad left it to you? No, Sam—and I'm glad it means so much to you."

Haley had slipped into the kitchen without anyone noticing. "Everything okay in here? Or do I need to wait outside?"

Mike walked over and gave her a hug. "No, we're fine. Just talking. Well, I guess we should get going. By the time we get over there, it should be time to get started."

Sam went through the house, gathering everybody together. "Come on, it's time to go."

When they walked out, Ronnie was riding up, tipping his hat in greeting. "Is everybody ready?" he asked.

Sam replied, "Yes, we are."

"Good! Your rides are on their way."

Sam spotted the horse and buggy coming up the road. "Why am I surprised? Nothing should shock me anymore." Tara and the kids just laughed.

Mike slapped him on the back. "I believe there's going to be a few more surprises in store for you, my dear brother, you haven't even seen our little town yet." he chuckled.

Ronnie dismounted to help get everyone loaded up. "Sam, we weren't sure if you wanted to ride, but we saddled your dad's horse if you want to."

Sam started to say no, but before he could, Haley walked up and said, "Here's your ride, Sam." Sam took the reins, and the horse butted him with its head.

"Look at that! I believe old Samson likes you."

"Sure," Sam answered, rubbing his ears.

"Ronnie set the stirrups, so you may need to let them down a little more."

As the buggies were pulling out, Rick and Brad mounted up. "Come on, Dad, let's go."

Sam, still a little nervous, kissed Samson on the head. "Okay, boy, here we go," he said as he mounted the horse. As they started to ride off, he couldn't help thinking, "What a parade." As he became more comfortable in the saddle, he turned around to see a massive number of riders trailing behind the horse-drawn buggy for the trip into town. He looked over at Mike, "Yeah, you're right again."

Sam was not sure of the distance they had ridden, but it seemed as though they'd been riding for about half an hour when they came into town. It was just like watching an old Western movie, stepping back into the 1800s. About halfway into town, everyone came to a complete stop. Then, in front of the horse-drawn buggy, a wagon pulled out of the livery stable, with six more riders and a buggy following. They continued on, passing the saloon, hotel, and hardware store. Just outside of town, the buggy stopped at the cemetery. The preacher got out and directed the six riders, who removed the casket from the wagon and carried it to the gravesite. Everyone gathered as close as possible. Mike, Sam, Cyndi, Haley, and the rest of the family were escorted to the front.

Mike reached over and grabbed Ronnie by the arm. "Come on. You're as much family as the rest of us."

Ronnie might have objected, but was too emotional to speak. They all took their places around the casket. The crowd moved in as close as they could get.

The first sign of anything modern was when the preacher put on a headset. As he began to speak, it was almost like thunder at a slight distance.

"Family and friends, we come together today to pay our last respects to our departed brother. Brother Bill meant so much to so many different people. I myself owed him so much. We talked many times and shared each other's beliefs. That is why it is such an honor for me to stand here today. When I first met Brother Bill, I had already given up on God and myself. He found me in a bar, broke and bumming drinks. He bought me a drink and invited me to sit with him.

"I told him my story about never knowing my family, about how I was raised in a church orphanage and how it'd left me cold and indifferent to the world. He let me go on for about 30 minutes. Then he looked at me and said, 'I know exactly what you are saying, Brother Phil. I have been there myself, but tonight is the last time you'll have to tell that story to anyone ever again. God didn't leave you. Maybe everybody else in your life did, but God remains right where you left him, waiting for you to come back. And rest assured, my new friend, you will meet him again, either on your terms or his. I know that God would like it on your terms. Jesus did not give his life for nothing. He gave it for a price, and that price was to pay for your sins, as well for all humankind. You can't sit there and tell me you knew God and that you preached his words, and then claim he abandoned you. Now, you either know Him or you don't. Have you ever really confessed to God and accepted his gift of life through Jesus?' I bowed my head in shame. 'Do not be ashamed to admit your mistake. That is how we learn and grow,' he told me. 'Would you like to make that prayer now?'"

The preacher paused, then went on, "If anyone here today hearing the sound of my voice is where I was that night—alone and without God—Brother Bill and I invite you to join us in prayer." He bowed his head and prayed, "Our Father who art in heaven, please hear my prayer. I am but a sinner. Confessing before you, only you know my heart. I ask forgiveness and accept Jesus as my personal Savior, knowing that he gave his life for me, and I give thanks for this gift and I will always pray in his name. Amen!" The preacher raised his head before continuing. "That's the same prayer Brother Bill prayed with me, that night at the bar. After he finished, he got up to leave. I sat there feeling sober and clean, but didn't have anywhere to go. Brother Bill paid the bill and started for the door. Turning around, he asked, 'Well, Brother Phil, are you ready to go?' Needless to say, my friends, I have served here ever since. In closing, we now say goodbye to our dear brother, father, grandfather, great-grandfather, and friend. We will meet you once again, Brother Bill, one day in heaven." He paused again, and then said, "If you would please join us in singing 'Amazing Grace' as we all leave his resting place."

It was beautiful to hear so many voices singing Bill's favorite hymn. The family stood singing, and watched as the massive crowd dispersed. The riders gracefully circled around the family before they departed.

Chapter 6
Life Goes On

Sam stayed behind after everyone had left. In a quiet moment, he kneeled at the grave. "I wish I had said this sooner, Dad. I'm sorry. Please forgive me." When the tears had settled, Sam could hardly pull himself away. He still halfway expected his dad to say something back. The air buzzed with the sound of people talking. Everywhere he looked he saw people, but he didn't feel like being sociable.

He looked at Samson and knew what his dad would have done. It was getting hotter, and the clouds had broken away to reveal the noon sun. Sam said to Samson, "I know you understand, so let's find water." Samson threw back his head as Sam mounted and turned. "Let's go, boy," and off they went.

Sam didn't try to change his course. Sure enough, about half a mile away, they came to a stream. "Samson, you picked a beautiful spot. I bet you and Dad came here a lot." Samson walked right in and started drinking. Sam let him drink his fill before pulling up. "Okay, boy, guess we should be getting back before they send out a search party for us."

They made their way back toward town. Sam made use of the time by thinking about all that had taken place. What did he really know for sure? He still couldn't convince himself that his first night home had been a dream. If it had been just a dream, then why had so many things happened that his dad had predicted? Meeting Frank, Joe, Molly—and just this morning, what was eating at Joe about the ring? He and Samson were about to pass the cemetery again. It looked like a lonely spot now that everyone was gone. Sam rode closer to the fence. "You know, Dad, I hope I'm right, and you're out there someplace really enjoying yourself." He kept riding. Samson seemed content to mosey on along. When they came to town, Sam was still amazed at what his father had done here. He remembered his dad watching old *Bonanza* shows, and he could see where his father's inspiration had come from.

People were still walking through town, sightseeing. A few others were still riding. Sam just waved or nodded as he went by. He patted Samson on the neck and said, "You know, fellow, I think you and I are going to be good friends. You're a good listener. What do you think about all that?" Samson kept walking. "I can see why you got along with the old man so well. You never talked back."

At times like these, he could see why his dad loved it so much at the ranch. With so much excitement in today's fast-paced society, a person needs a quiet spot from time to time to think things out. Sam was still twisting things around in his head, trying to make sense of it all. "You know, Samson, I really don't know anything except what I've been told, and that isn't much. Like, who was at the funeral home, that they had to get me out of there so fast? Who made me so important? Why would anyone want me? I couldn't tell them anything! Mike runs the show around here. He knows the ins and outs. Pretty damn smart fellow, too—but keep that between you and me. Wouldn't want him to start getting a big head. One in the family is enough. You know something else? I think there's something going on between him and Mary, too."

Looking ahead, Sam saw they were almost back to the house. "Well, it's true, boy. Time flies when you're having fun. You and I will have to do this again real soon." As they made their way to the front of the house, Ronnie came running out.

"Sam, I'm glad you're back."

"What's wrong?"

"You need to get inside. Here, I'll take care of Samson. Now, go!"

Sam's heart was racing as he ran into the house. "What is it?" he said as Mike met him at the door.

"Try to calm down. Its little Billy. He's missing." As soon as he'd said it, Mike could see that all hell was fixing to break loose.

Sam's voice echoed throughout the entire house. "Somebody better tell me what happened, and tell me now."

Tara tried to hold Sam back. "The police are talking with Brad and Donna," she said.

Rick stepped in front of Sam. "Dad, please calm down. Brad is falling apart, and Donna is about to have a nervous breakdown."

"Got it, Son," he said as he pushed past Rick and went into the other room.

Brad stood up and said, "Don't be angry, Dad."

Sam grabbed him and hugged his neck. "I can't help myself, Son. You hang in there. We'll find little Billy."

The cop reached over and tapped Sam on the shoulder. "Who are you?"

"Didn't you just hear him call me 'Dad'?" Sam asked and walked over to Donna and sat beside her. "You, too, little lady. Don't fall apart on me."

"Sir, we're trying to conduct an interview here," the police officer said.

"I don't give a flying shit what you're trying to do here. This is my family you're talking to, and I'll tell you when you can interrupt me and do your job. Now sit down or get out."

The detective backed up. Ronnie walked in just in time. He and Detective James Ostrom were longtime friends. Ronnie had been the one to bring him into the Simplicity family.

"James, come on in here and let's give the family a few minutes," Ronnie suggested.

They went back into the kitchen, where Haley had made a fresh pot of coffee. "Help yourselves," she said.

Tara sat at the table with a cup of coffee, smoking a cigarette.

The detective poured a cup and sat down. "Were you here when they first discovered the baby missing?" he asked.

With tears still in her eyes, Tara replied, "Yes. When we got back, it was about 1:00. Billy was a little fussy, so we figured it was due to all of the excitement and not being used to the heat. Donna fed him some lunch, then they went into the study. I helped her push the loveseat up to the couch to make a place for them both to lie down. She lay down with Billy until he fell asleep. I guess she was in there about 30 minutes. When she came back, we fixed her a plate for lunch."

"Who are 'we'?" Detective Ostrom asked.

"Myself, Brad, Rick, and Patty were all still in here."

"Was there anyone else?"

"Just Ben and Sara. They were in the living room watching TV. Everyone else had left. Mary had left to take Molly home. Mike went to check on something. Haley and Ronnie went to the stables. Cyndi said she was going to town to pick up some groceries. After Donna ate, she said a nap sounded like a good idea, so she went back to lie down with Billy. That's when we found out he was gone. So just guessing it was probably about 3:00 by then."

"Thank you," Detective Ostrom said, and then turned to Ronnie. "I need to call the Feds in on this and set up phone taps, just in case this is a kidnapping."

Ronnie pointed to Mike and said, "He's the man you need to talk to."

Trying to keep his composure, Mike stepped up and answered, "The phone taps wouldn't be necessary. Every call on the place goes through the central computer system. All we have to do is set it for a trace."

"Okay, you let me know if you get a call for a ransom demand or if you get a good trace," the detective said, then added, "And you will share that information with us, right?"

"Sure we will."

"Here's my cell phone number in case you can't catch me at the precinct. All right, we're going to get out of here for now and start beating the streets."

Sam walked in just as they were leaving. "We need everyone back who was here this afternoon," he said. "Has anyone called Molly?"

"Yes," Tare said. "Mary and Molly are on their way."

Sam walked over to Tara. Rubbing her shoulders, he said, "It's going to be all right. We're going to get little Billy back."

"I called Donna's mom and dad. They said they'd call back as soon as they had a flight time."

Mary called out, and Mike opened the door for her and Molly. "Oh, Mike, this is terrible news."

"Sam, how are you holding up?" Molly asked.

"For now, Miss Molly, you need to check on the kids."

"Sure, dear," she said. Tara stood up and went with her.

Cyndi came in carrying some grocery sacks. "Reckon I could get some help with the rest?" she asked.

Ronnie headed for the door. "I got it. You guys fill her in."

She could tell by looking around that bad news was in the air. After Sam had told her what had happened, Cyndi got a notepad off the desk and started making a list of everyone she remembered being there.

Mike called Eric to fill him in on what was going on.

"Mike, have you contacted Frank?" asked Sam.

Glancing at the wall clock, he said, "Yeah, he should have been here by now. It's been over an hour." A car door slammed outside, "Maybe that's him now."

Haley finished putting up the groceries, and then gave Mike and Sam a hug. "I'm going to go lie down for a bit. If you need me, just holler."

"Okay. Try to rest."

Eric knocked at the door. "Sorry we have to meet like this," Sam said as he let him in.

"I know. Me too."

"Mike, I'm going to look around a bit. You guys have things to work out," Sam said as he headed off to the study. The truth of the matter was that Sam was about to break down himself. Maybe for the first time in his life, he felt truly guilty, as if this were his fault. He had been out just killing time, thinking of his problems, when he should have been thinking of his family and their safety.

He entered the study and looked closely at every detail of the room. As Tara had said, the loveseat had been pushed up to the couch. He walked slowly around the room. Surely there has to be a clue of some kind, he thought, but after circling the room, he found nothing.

Talking out loud, he said, "Dad, I sure could use some help from you on this one."

Thinking of his father, he reached into his pocket and pulled out the key to the cabinet. But when he opened it, the tape was gone. Almost in a panic, he felt around the inside of the cabinet. "It has to be here," he said to himself, but it was gone. He sat on the floor and wondered what in the hell was going on. Glancing up, he noticed a small shelf near the top of the cabinet. On it was a handwritten letter. When he opened it, he had no doubt it had been written by his father. In all his life, he'd never known anyone who could write like him.

> "Hi Son:
>
> If you are reading this letter, it must mean you're starting to trust your gut instincts, and you're still on the Broken R. Good. Nothing could make me happier. I trust that all is well. If not, I hope you will take my words to heart and not let your temper control you.

Everything you will need to know is written down, or I've already told you. Why didn't I just come out and tell you everything? First, I didn't know if you were going to stay, and second, I couldn't leave that much information lying around for just anybody to get hold of. If you haven't already, you'll soon find that there are a lot of people out there who would've loved to have seen me dead, and not of natural causes, either. You'll no longer be faced with any financial problems. All you need to worry about is taking care of your family and helping your brother take care of the business. The key you have in your hand opens many doorways. The first is right here in the study. If you are standing in front of the desk, turn to your left and walk straight forward, and locate Tom Sawyer. He will take you the rest of the way! Remember, Son, Simplicity is not always a sign of ignorance, but wisdom in its purest form.

Good luck,
Dad"

Sam stood in front of the desk, turned to his left, and walked to the bookshelf. Reading the titles, he found *Tom Sawyer* about midway down and on the end. He pulled it out, and there behind it was a key lock. He inserted the key and turned it, and the bookshelf clicked and opened into a hidden room. He couldn't believe his eyes. Although the room wasn't very big, it was well-organized. It held a high-tech computer setup with security monitors covering the entire north wall. Built into the south wall, just left of the secret door, was a large gun rack that stretched from one corner to the other, and contained a variety of 30-30 Winchester rifles.

Sitting on a hat rack in the corner was his Dad's old black Stetson hat and a double-holster gun belt holding two Colt 45 pistols. Sam placed the book back on the shelf and closed the door, leaving no sign that the wall hid any type of secret passage. It didn't take him long to figure out this was how his dad had been able to know about everything that had happened on the ranch. Now all he had to do was figure out how to operate the equipment.

Shuffling through drawers, he found all kinds of information, but nothing about the security equipment. He sat down and pulled out the sliding desktop, and there it sat—the complete diagram of everything he needed to know about operating the equipment. The screensaver was on, but when he clicked the mouse, the screen came alive. He found an option labeled "Security" and clicked it. There he saw everything he needed to do. He hit the "Monitors" option and the monitors came on. One showed the inside of the study. Another showed Molly and Mary in the living room. She must have given Brad and Donna something to help them relax; they were lying back on the couch and seemed to be resting easier. In the kitchen, he saw Mike sitting and talking with Eric. Ronnie stood by the coffeepot. Mary walked in and sat down by Mike. The other monitors showed what was going on outside the house and around the barns.

"Wow, what a system!" he said to himself. "All I need to do is figure out if this is recording, and how to retrieve it."

He checked the diagram again and found his answers. There were tapes, and they cleared every twenty-four hours. He realized he should be able to find out exactly who was in the study and who took Billy. After a few tries, he figured out how it all worked. Clicking on the option for the study, he rewound the tape, and after a couple of minutes, a recorded tape ejected under the monitors. While waiting for the tape to rewind, Sam had found a number of new tapes, so he inserted one into the tape drive to replace the recorded one.

He punched the old tape into a tape player and watched it play on another monitor. There he was, talking with

Ronnie. He fast-forwarded through the tape until he saw Donna and Billy, then hit play again. She was putting Billy on the couch, and then Tara walked over and helped her push the loveseat next to the couch so little Billy couldn't roll off.

Sam pushed fast-forward again, his adrenaline pumping. He realized he was about to figure this out. On the tape, when Donna got up to leave, he pushed 'play.' After a few minutes, Joe entered the room and checked to make sure no one else was around. Sam watched him walk to the window, pull back the curtains, and unlock the window, making sure the security alarm was disconnected, and then he left the room again.

Sam was trying to keep his cool. Damn, he'd been right again. He thought Joe had something to do with this. As he kept watching, he remembered what his dad had said: "Do not let your anger control you, but learn to control your anger."

On the tape, a young man was climbing through the window. He walked over and picked up Billy. As he turned to climb back through the window, the camera got a clear shot of the man and his face, but Sam didn't recognize him.

Mike must not even know about this room, or he would have already been in here when it happened, Sam thought. His dad's voice rang in his ears. "Her secrets are now your secrets." He knew he must get control of the situation. As the tape continued to play, he watched Joe enter the room again, walk straight to the window, lock it, reconnect the alarm, then straighten the curtain and leave. Sam tried to figure out why Joe would do this, but couldn't come up with a rational explanation. All he knew was that he had to come up with a plan. He looked at the time and realized he must act fast.

Chapter 7
The Truth Revealed

Sam pulled out the tape and was getting ready to leave, but he heard voices in the other room. Checking the monitors once more, he saw that Mary and Tara had just entered the study and were sitting on the sofa talking. "Great," he said to himself. "Now I have to figure out how to get out of here without giving myself away. Think, Sam." He looked around. Surely, there had to be another way out. He reached for his father's gun belt as if it were an everyday thing for him to do. He strapped it on his waist as if he had done it a thousand times before, then he picked up his dad's old hat and held it up. He could tell it was well-broken-in. It appeared identical to the one Cyndi got him.

As he started to hang the hat back on the rack, though, he saw another key lock. Hoping that it could be another hidden door, he inserted the key into the opening, and wasn't too surprised when a trap door popped up out of the floor. He grabbed the tape and lifted the door to find a set of stairs. Climbing down the first few steps, he found a light switch and turned it on, then closed the secret trapdoor above him.

At the bottom of the stairs, he came to another door. He slowly opened it, not knowing where the exit would take him. Looking around, he realized it led into a small tool shed with riding lawnmowers, rakes, shovels, and other tools. He flipped another switch to turn off the lights in the secret passage, and pushed the door closed. Once again, he couldn't even tell there had been a door there.

Walking out the shed door, he found himself behind the house. The bushes gave plenty of cover to look around and make sure the coast was clear. He walked toward the garage, trying not to attract any attention. He stopped and lit a cigarette, trying to make it appear that he had just stepped outside to have a smoke. Frank pulled up.

"Hey, Sam, what's going on?" he said. Then noticing the guns strapped to Sam's waist, he added, "Oh hell, we must have big trouble."

"That's right, Frank. Somebody has taken my grandson, Billy."

"Oh, God. What do you need me to do?"

"Find Joe and bring him here."

"You got it. I'm on it." Frank jumped back into his car and sped off.

Mike stepped out onto the porch and saw Sam. "Where have you been?" he asked. "We've been looking all over for you. Who was in the car?"

"That was Frank."

"Where is he going?"

"I sent him to find Joe." Sam walked back into the house with Mike. "Look, I don't have a lot of time for explanations right now, so just listen," he said. "I believe Billy is still here on the ranch somewhere. Call and have all the exits closed so no one leaves the ranch until we find him." Then Sam pulled out the tape and turned to Eric. "Can you pull pictures off of this?"

"Sure I can."

"I need a picture up on the screen as fast as possible—and whatever you do, don't lose that tape."

"Okay, give me fifteen minutes and you'll have your picture," Eric said as he took off.

Sam then hollered to Ronnie, "I need you to gather as many men as you can get together. I want every square inch of the town covered until we've found Joe." Ronnie left, no questions asked. Sam poured himself a cup of coffee, then turned and said, "This may take us awhile."

Mike asked, "Do you mind bringing 'us' up to speed on what the hell is going on, little brother?"

"If you'll get everyone together, Mike, then I'll fill you in on what I do know."

Within minutes Mike had gathered everyone into the kitchen. Sam felt confident for the time being. "Look, in a few minutes there should be a picture up on the big screens, of the man who took little Billy. We need to know as fast as possible who he is. I believe Billy is still here on the Broken R somewhere, and we also have to find Joe because he's involved in this up to his neck. Please don't ask me too many questions. Let's just concentrate on finding Billy, okay?"

Sam was walking to the door as the big screens were lighting up. He turned back and asked Mike, "Can we get this in here?" Mike picked up a remote control and turned on the TV. There on the screen was the man's picture.

"Does anybody know this person," Sam asked. "Or have you ever seen him before?"

Everyone shook their heads "no."

Ronnie came in and reported, "We have 50 men ready to ride and another 50 over in town."

Mike's phone rang. It was Eric. "There's nothing in our system on this guy, Mike," he said.

"We believe the man is still somewhere on the Broken R," Mike told him. "Put out a bulletin that if anyone recognizes this man, they should call in immediately. Keep searching, and let me know if anything changes." Mike hung up the phone and asked, "Where's Haley?"

"She's upstairs taking a nap," said Tara.

"I'm not anymore," she replied as she walked into the room. "Why? Do you need me for something?"

Mike wrapped his arms around Haley and gave her a big hug. "What's wrong, Mike?"

"Nothing. I just wanted to know where you were and that you were safe. That's all."

Sam could see the concern in Mike's eyes. Mike had helped raise Haley from a baby. She was like his child, so Sam understood the concern. Mike's phone rang again. This time it was Frank. "I found Joe over in town. What now?"

"Stay right there. We're on our way." Mike was ready to run, but Sam stopped him. "Please let me handle this one, Brother. You stay here and keep an eye on things." Before Mike had time to answer, Sam and Ronnie were already out the door and leading the way to town, with the other riders trailing behind.

When they arrived in town, Ronnie spotted Frank standing in front of the saloon. Sam told Ronnie to get the riders organized and close off all the exits. Then he walked up to Frank and said, "Where is that son of a bitch?" Frank turned and led the way into the saloon where Joe sat. Sam walked up and said, "Joe, you're only going to get one chance at this, so don't mess up."

Joe hung his head down. "I knew this would never work. You're just like your dad—always two steps ahead of everybody else."

"This isn't the time, Joe. Tell me where this man is with my grandson."

Joe shook his head. "I don't know. All I was supposed to do was help him get into the house."

Frank asked, "Why would you do this, Joe?"

"They have my son, David, and they said they'd kill him if I didn't help them. Sam, I'm sorry. I just didn't know what to do."

"Damn it, Joe, why didn't you come to us?" Sam answered. "Frank, take Joe back to the house and have Molly try to get some food and coffee in him. Maybe she can sober him up. We're going to make a clean sweep through town, and then we'll meet you all back at the house."

"Okay, come on, Joe," Frank said. "We'll work this out." He helped Joe to his feet. It was easy to see that Joe had had too much to drink.

As they got to the door, Sam was still barking out orders, and Ronnie was calling Mike to let him know Frank was bringing Joe to the house.

At the side of the building, Frank was trying to help Joe into the car. Sam had just mounted up on Samson when a figure ran out of the shadows toward the car screaming, "You stupid old man. They're going to kill us all!" He shot at Joe, but Frank gave him one last shove, finally knocking him into the car before Frank fell to the ground.

Sam charged the man and knocked him to the ground. Ronnie was right behind him and jumped on the man, trying to pin him down. As Sam and Ronnie were trying to subdue him, he continued to scream, "You son of a bitch! We're all going to die now."

Finally, Sam grabbed the man by the hair, placed the barrel of his gun against his ear, and said, "One more move, mister, and you'll be the first to die." Then turning to Ronnie, he said, "Get to Frank. I think he's been hit."

Ronnie called out to the riders for help and ran over to check on Frank. The riders formed a large circle to keep the crowd back. Joe was holding Frank and pleading, "Please don't die on me. I didn't mean for any of this to happen."

Ronnie called for someone to get a doctor, then got Joe back into the car. He could see Frank was still breathing, and that the bullet looked as if it had gone all the way through his shoulder.

Sam hollered, "Is Frank okay?"

"He's going to make it. The doctor's on his way," Ronnie answered.

Sam pushed the man out in the street and said to the riders, "If he tries to run, shoot his legs off." The riders pulled out their rifles, and the sound of them jacking a shell into the chamber was enough to humble any man. Then Sam hollered out, "If anybody here knows this man, or can identify any place this man has been, please come forward now. We may still be able to end this without anyone else getting hurt."

Quiet fell, except for the doctor, working on Frank, and Frank himself, who had regained consciousness and was demanding to be taken to Molly.

The doctor looked at Ronnie, who said, "Just do what he says. She's at the main house on the other side of the ranch." Then they headed out.

Ronnie joined Sam in the middle of the street. People looked as they walked by, but nobody seemed to know this fellow. Then a young man walked up, looking closely. "I'm not sure, but it could be," he said.

Sam's heart was racing. "Come on and tell us."

"Well, earlier this afternoon, we were at the boarding house up the street here, where a young lady watched our little one while we went to the funeral. I believe I might have seen him there."

"Watch him, Ronnie," Sam said, then turned back to the young man. "Take me there."

As they hurried up the street, Sam felt calmness come over him as he'd never felt before. They walked up to the door and Sam pounded on it, saying, "Wake up."

The lights came on, and a young woman answered the door. "Please hold it down. We have children sleeping." Sam walked in, and the woman recognized him. "What can I do for you? Surely, you're not looking for a place to sleep."

"You know me?"

"Well, yes."

"I hate to disturb you, but I have reason to believe my grandson may be here." He reached over, turned on her TV set switching the channels till he found the closed circuit where the mans picture appear.

"What are you trying to find?"

"There it is. Do you recognize this man?"

"Yes, he brought his son here this evening. He said he had decided to stay over for the night."

"You're sure?"

"Yes, he paid $200 in advance. That's why I remember him."

"Show me where the boy is."

She led them to the back of the house. "Why don't you two wait here? We don't want to wake everybody up." She opened the door and slipped inside. A small nightlight helped her find her way. She came back holding Billy.

Sam was almost ready to cry, and felt excited and relieved at the same time. "There's my boy!" he said. Billy's eyes opened, and he reached out. Sam took him and said, "Thank you." Billy hugged his neck and said mama. "You bet we're going to go see Mama. She sure is missing you," Sam said.

Sam thanked the woman again and told her if she watched the TV, everything would be explained. Then he turned to the young man and thanked him for coming forward.

"I'm just glad I could help, but I've got to get back to my family now, if that's okay," he said.

"Sure, but before you leave, please bring your family by the house."

"I will."

As Sam came back into sight, Ronnie saw he had little Billy. Sam said to the man under guard, "Tonight must be your lucky night. You might get to live after all," then he turned and asked Ronnie, "Do we have a jail in this town?"

"Sure do."

"See that he's locked in it, and let's all go home."

A couple of riders carried the man down the road to the jail, and Sam handed little Billy to Ronnie so he could mount up again. Once in the saddle, he took Billy back and said, "Come on, big boy. Let's ride."

Ronnie felt good as he leaped back onto his own saddle. "Yeah, let's ride," he hollered, then added, "Thanks, men. You can all go home now." The men who had ridden with them from the house took off on a run, whooping and hollering.

Sure enough, everyone knew good news was on its way. Sam never felt so proud. His heart felt as if it would explode in his chest as he held little Billy. "One day you'll run the Broken R," he whispered.

They rode through the night with Ronnie at their side. "Hey, by the way, thanks for all your help tonight," Sam said.

"No problem, but you know I need to get to the house and take care of the stock up there. You have to come up after you get everything straightened out. Besides, I've got a surprise for you," Ronnie said, mysteriously.

"All right, we'll sure do it."

"I'll see you in the morning, then." Ronnie cut off and headed across the field.

When Sam arrived at the house, everyone was standing on the porch, and Brad and Donna ran out. "Look, Billy," Sam said. "There's your mama and daddy." Handing the baby to Donna, he added, "There we go, little man. There's your mama."

Brad hugged both of them and said, "Thanks."

"You bet, son," Sam replied. "Now y'all go on in. I'll be inside in a few minutes." Then he said, "Come on, Samson. Let's get you bedded down for the night." The horse turned and headed straight for the barn.

Chapter 8
Time to Regroup

Sam made sure Samson got an extra ration of oats, and then bedded him down. He was more than just a horse now. He had become Sam's best friend. As Sam headed toward the house, he realized everybody would want answers to their many questions. He decided to try slipping back into the house the same way he got out. He slipped back around the house to the shed door, and made sure no one was around before going inside.

Once inside he used his lighter to find the light switch, then looked around the secret door for a key lock. He couldn't find one, and started talking to himself again. "Come on, Sam, think. There has to be a way, a simple way." From watching too much television, he started pushing on things and looking for anything that might twist or turn, but found nothing. "Maybe it would be better if I came back when I have more time to look around," he said. Reaching for the light switch, he saw a dead-bolt lock in the shed door. He tried his key, and it fit. When he turned it, the dead bolt clicked over and he heard a buzzing sound as the hidden door opened. "Well, now, isn't that something," he said, shaking his head in near-disbelief. "This is just too neat."

He climbed back up the stairs and entered the security room, then took off the gun belt and hung it on the rack. He took one last look at the monitors to make sure nobody was in the study, then he slipped into it through the secret door. He sat at the desk and tried to appear as though he had been sitting there for a while, reminding himself he needed to get his adrenaline under check. "Just relax and breathe." Taking a moment to gather his thoughts, he tried to figure out what all of this was about. Who was behind it? Why kidnap David, then Billy? It must all somehow tie back to him, especially in light of the incident at the funeral home. What did he have that they wanted?

Too many questions and not enough answers.

The sound of voices brought him back to reality. Heading to the door to check on everyone else, he noticed his legs were sore and he was walking a little funny, but he didn't have time to worry about that right now. When he entered, everyone was so busy they didn't even notice him come in. Molly and the doctor had bandaged up Frank, who was flying high on painkillers. Joe was in the bed next to Frank's, trying to sleep off his binge at the saloon.

When Molly saw Sam at the door, she got so excited that she stood up in front of her wheelchair and took three steps before she knew what she had done.

Sam ran to catch her. Frank started laughing and said, "I knew you had it in you. I knew you'd walk again one day."

The doctor was just as excited. Molly was so beside herself, she was crying. The doctor hollered out, "Mary, come here."

Mary came running as if the house were on fire. "What, what is it now?" She stopped dead in her tracks when she saw her mother standing. Molly regained her balance by holding onto Sam. Then she walked over and grabbed Mary. They were hugging, laughing, and crying all at the same time.

Mike and Haley came down the hallway, almost afraid to find out what was going on. When they realized what it was, they too were excited. Cyndi stood at the end of the hallway, crying, because she thought something bad had happened to Frank.

Molly looked at her and took a couple more steps. "Come on, girl," Cyndi said. "At least meet me halfway." Cyndi, like Sam, ran to meet Molly.

Sam went back to Frank and the doctor. "Doc, you make sure you get this old man better. We have a lot of business to attend to." Sam gave Frank a pat on his good shoulder.

"Don't you worry about this 'old man,'" Frank said. "You better go get some rest yourself."

"That, I believe, is an order. I'll see you tomorrow, then," Sam said.

Sam went back to the living room, where he found everyone still laughing and crying. Molly had walked all the way across the room, a few steps at a time. Tara was in the kitchen cooking, so Sam eased his way in there.

"It sure does smell good in here," he said.

"You don't even know what it is."

"It could be a pair of old boots boiling, and it wouldn't matter to me. Just add a little salt and pepper, and I think I could eat them. I'm starving."

"It's beef stew," Tara said, fixing him a bowl. "Cyndi and Haley cooked this up, and I must say it is delicious."

Sam didn't care who cooked the food. He was just thankful someone had cooked. It didn't take long until the table was full, and everyone was eating. They talked and carried on for hours. Sam started to nod off at the table, so he excused himself, and Tara helped him off to bed.

Mike was left to regroup everyone. He sent Rick and Patty, with their children, to their new house, then sent Brad, Donna, Billy and Donna's parents to theirs. Frank's and Joe's wives both came in, so they moved Joe and his wife into another room where they could be together, while Frank and his wife remained. Molly and Mary took Mike's room, and Cyndi bunked with Haley.

Mike sat in the kitchen after the house was finally quiet, and thought, "Thank God everything worked out." So much had happened that it was hard for him to believe they'd just had their dad's funeral that morning. Tired and worn out, he turned out the lights and made his way to the big sofa in the living room. Whispering so that only his dad could hear, he said, "Good night, Dad. Rest easy."

The next morning brought with it a beautiful sunrise. Sam was the only one to witness it. He had been up for an hour or so, and already taken a hot shower and shaved. He sat, fully dressed, on the front porch with his morning coffee, knowing everyone still had a big problem to face. He saw a rider coming across the open field and could tell right off it was Ronnie. What a beautiful picture he made in the early morning light! Sam could tell he was going through some kind of change; he looked at the world as though for the first time. Everything had new meaning and a fulfilling purpose.

Cyndi came out with a sleepy "Good morning" and a big yawn, and added, "What, no breakfast cooked?"

Sam pointed to the coffeepot. "There you go."

Ronnie was almost to the house. Cyndi waved at him, then turned back to the house. "I'll go see what we have."

"No, Sis. You don't have to do that. I've already ordered breakfast, and it should be here any minute."

"Okay, then I think I'll get me a cup of that coffee. Ronnie, you need a cup?" she asked.

"Sure. Sounds good."

They chatted a few moments while having coffee. Cyndi was telling Ronnie about Molly's walking when Sam interrupted them.

"By the way, what happened to Miss Molly to put her in that wheelchair?"

"That's right; you didn't know her back then. She was in a really bad accident almost two years ago. She broke both legs and her hip. The doc told her there was no reason for her not to walk again, but because she had been down for so long, it was going to take a lot of therapy. Being stubborn, Molly wouldn't go to therapy. She said if it could be done, she'd do it on her own."

Sam laughed. "She sounds like someone else we know," he said, then added, "Hey, look. We have three big covered wagons coming up the road. What do you think they're doing?"

Now it was Cyndi's turn to laugh. "Sam, you said you ordered breakfast. Well, here it comes. Come on, let's wake everybody up. I wouldn't want them to think you called them out for just a couple of people."

Sam was feeling a little confused. "What did I do?"

"It's okay, Sam. Matter of fact, I would've called myself if I'd thought of it," Cyndi said, then started for the door. "Why don't you help get them set up, Ronnie?"

Sam just shrugged his shoulders and followed her into the house. People were already moving about. Molly had Frank at the kitchen table, and was changing his bandages.

Tara called out to Sam, "I'll be down in a minute."

He walked to the steps and hollered back, "Okay."

He noticed the study door was open, and wondered why anyone would be in there so early in the morning. Looking back toward the living room, he saw Mike getting up from the couch. Sam walked to the study and looked inside, but didn't see anyone. That strange feeling was coming back over him. He slipped inside and closed the door, slowly, so as not to draw any attention to himself. He went straight to the cabinet and opened it with great anticipation. Inside he found another letter, which set his heart racing. Without any hesitation, he opened it and started reading.

"Dear Sam,

Enclosed is a plane ticket to New York, a credit card, and $500 in small bills. Here is all you need to find Joe's son, David. When you arrive in New York,

> expect a man by the name of John to pick you up. You will know him by these words: "When pigeons fly south." He will help you find David, but it will be up to you to get David out of there. Be sure to take the pager. If you should run into any trouble, just turn it on. It has a built-in tracking device. You will have to do this on your own. You cannot take any more chances of anything else going wrong. Take care!
>
> Dad"

Sam folded the letter and placed it in his pocket. After taking the pager and locking the cabinet again, he hurried back to join everyone in the other room. He found them all gathering outside around the wagons. With the tables set up, people were coming from almost every direction. He found Tara and the kids already at a table, and joined them for some breakfast. He tried not to show what he knew was in front of him. For the next few hours, he just wanted to enjoy being with his family. They laughed and talked and had a good time. Sam couldn't believe how good things could be, yet how wrong at the same time. The sight of everyone gathered around for a meal was a memorable one for him, but he knew it would soon be interrupted with more unfinished business.

Three men pulled up in one of the Broken R's black SUVs. As he watched them get out, Sam knew they had to be lawyers. All three of the men were dressed in black Western-cut suits.

Ronnie walked out and met them, shaking hands and inviting them to eat.

One man spoke for the other two, saying, "No, thanks. We've already eaten." Then, checking his watch and noticing it was 8:30, he added, "Tell us where you'd like us to set up. We'd like to get started by nine because we all need to be back in Little Rock by noon."

Ronnie motioned for Mike to come over, and they all walked to the house, where Mike told them to set up in the study. Then he went back to get Sam, Cyndi, and Haley, saying, "The lawyers are here to read Dad's will."

They quickly finished eating and headed into the house. Once all were present in the study, the oldest of the three attorneys began to speak while the other two passed out copies.

"What you are about to receive is a copy of your father's last will and testament," he said. "It is very simple to read, but in order to make it legal, I must read it for you." He read the will, and then asked if there were any questions.

Sam stood up. "That's it? We all get a handshake and ten dollars?"

"You must be Sam," the lawyer said, walking to him and shaking his hand. "Gosh, it's good to meet you. My name is John, and before you ask too many more questions, I want you to know we're not exactly through yet. Before we can go on, though, I need you to bring in the rest of your family."

Sam left to get Tara and the kids, and John sent Ronnie to get Mary, Molly, Frank, and Joe. By the time everyone was present, John had placed a stack of folders on the desk. He held one up and said, "When I call out your name please raise your hand, and one of these two gentlemen will bring you one of these files. Mike. Sam. Cyndi. Haley. Ronnie." He called everyone's name on the list until he'd passed out all but three files. "These last three files are for Ben, Sarah, and Billy. Will their parents please stand up and receive their files."

After all of the files were handed out, he continued, "Some of you already know what is in these folders. Mike here will be able to answer most of your questions in more detail than I could, so let me explain what little I do know about these files. You are vested members in Simplicity, which means you are worth at least one million dollars each, depending on the length of time that you've been 'vested.' Time determines exactly how much each one is worth. For example, the children are vested now, so by the time they have reached the age of eighteen, their money will have rolled over several times, making them multi-millionaires.

"I was instructed by your father as his friend to tell each of you a special message. I will close this meeting with his words to you. And I quote, 'You cannot inherit what is already yours, and remember to whom much is given, much will be required.' May God bless you and good luck to you all.' Thank you. I look forward to many more years together in the Simplicity family."

Turning to Sam and Ronnie, he said, "Would you two please stay for a minute after everyone else leaves?" They both nodded, and waited as the others left the room. When everyone was gone, John also sent away the two men who had come with him. Then he said, "I have one more message for the two of you: 'When pigeons fly south.'"

Ronnie looked a little baffled, but Sam nodded his head. "Ronnie, I'm going to be gone for awhile, and I need you to stay here and help take care of things," Sam said. "Mike has too much on his plate to worry about any more."

"Consider it done, Sam, and good luck," Ronnie said, then left to join the others.

Sam said, "John, give me about an hour to pack and say goodbye to my family."

Chapter 9
In New York

Sam tried explaining to Tara and the kids why he had to leave so suddenly. After packing a small bag and saying his goodbyes to his family, Sam walked out to the SUV. Running into Molly and Frank, Sam said, "Molly, I'm going to be gone for a few days." Giving her a hug, he whispered in her ear, "You take care of yourself and keep an eye on Frank."

Turning to Frank, he said, "You keep Joe busy, and out of trouble for the next few days." Sam reached out, shook Frank's hand and then slapped him on his good shoulder.

"You bet I will, Sam. Be careful."

"I will." Sam walked the final steps to the SUV and climbed inside. He waved goodbye to everyone. As Mike walked out on the porch, looking confused and half-waving back, Sam and John drove away toward Little Rock.

Once they arrived at the airport, John climbed out with Sam. "Okay, remember: when you get there, don't speak a word until you hear the code. Good luck. You have approximately forty minutes before your flight. You might want to get a drink, and relax a minute before take-off. Look for me here when you get back." John said his goodbyes and left.

Sam pulled out his ticket and headed for the check-in counter. He thought to himself that, for as long as he had lived in Arkansas, growing up just twenty miles from here, this was his first time inside the Little Rock Airport and his first time to fly in an airplane. Butterflies were in full bloom in his gut. After checking in, the young lady at the ticket counter pointed the way to the boarding area. "Gate four, sir. Have a good trip."

As Sam headed toward the gate, he saw a bar. "Maybe just one drink," He thought. He walked into the bar and ordered a shot of Crown Royal. The bartender smiled very big while he poured Sam's drink.

"First time to fly, huh?" the bartender asked.

"Yeah. Hopefully this will take the edge off."

"You bet it will, sir. It will be alright.

Sam swallowed the shot of whiskey, and the warm, peaceful feeling that came over him chased the butterflies from the pit of his stomach. After paying for his drink, he continued down toward the boarding area for Gate 4; mere minutes after checking in, he boarded the plane.

When they were in the air and leveled out, Sam leaned back and closed his eyes. He prayed that everything would go well, and already missed the Broken R and his family. He drifted off to sleep, thinking of taking an early morning ride with Samson while the sun rose over the horizon for the beginning of a brand-new day.

Sam awoke to hear the pilot announce they would be landing in New York in approximately twenty minutes. Sam wished the pilot had waited until there were only five minutes left before making that announcement. He was glad he had been able to rest during the flight, but would be much happier once his feet were back on the ground. The landing went smoothly, and once the plane came to a complete stop his heart went back to a normal beat. Everybody exited the plane, and Sam followed the crowd as though he knew where he was going. As they approached the front of the airport, he saw arrows pointing the way to the baggage claim section. Sam slowed his pace to give the crowd time to clear out; he hoped he would stand out, but nobody approached him.

He slowly made his way to the front doors. Stepping outside and a bit away from the doors, he stopped and lit a cigarette. Leaning against the building, he watched for a sign. After about ten minutes, he started to worry that something had gone wrong. Then he spotted a black SUV coming around the corner.

Sam thought to himself, "Maybe this is the person with whom I'm supposed to meet."

The SUV pulled up and stopped. A big man stepped out, and walked around to open the door. Sam was almost in a panic. John was supposed to speak first. Was this him? "Say it, come on, say it," Sam thought.

The man finally looked straight at Sam and said, "When pigeons fly south." Wiping the sweat from his forehead, Sam climbed into the SUV. The man returned to the driver's side, and as they drove away from the airport, he turned and introduced himself. "Hi, Sam. My name is John. Welcome to New York. I can tell this is your first time here."

"How's that?" asked Sam.

"Oh, you can tell a lot about a man by the way he dresses. We are heading to my place and we will take care of that problem." John was full of questions about the Broken R and Arkansas. "My wife and I have been talking about coming down there on vacation, but we haven't made it yet. I'm sorry, Sam; I'm just one of those men that love to talk. I really don't mean to be insensitive."

"Continue on. You're not bothering me at all."

"Well, we're really sorry about your dad and all; he was a fine man and will be greatly missed."

"Thank you."

"I can tell you there's one good thing about having someone that likes to talk with you on a trip; it makes the trip go a lot faster. We are only a couple of blocks away, so I guess we need to get serious about the tasks we have at hand. When we get to the house, you will have about two hours to prepare yourself. You are welcome to take a shower before changing clothes, if you would like. We want you to look like a tourist while you're in New York, instead of a cowboy on a mission."

John turned the car into the driveway and parked the car in the garage. Both men climbed out and headed straight into the house. John showed Sam to a bedroom, and pointed out the bathroom. He reached under the bed and pulled out a suitcase, telling Sam, "Here are your new clothes." He handed him a box. "You can put the clothes you have on in here, and we will send them back home for you. When you are done, just meet me in the kitchen."

Sam was now programmed to accept unexplained or questionable dealings without asking too many questions. After all, look at all he had been through in the last few days since he had been home! However, he could still hear *Twilight Zone* theme music in the back of his mind. He took a hot shower and dressed for the task at hand. As he looked in the mirror, he thought that just a short time ago, his new outfit—khaki pants and polo shirt—probably would have been more his style of clothing. Now, the modern flash just didn't seem to fit him anymore. Sam boxed up his things, and then headed for the kitchen.

John was talking on the phone and pointed to the coffeepot; he had already set a cup out for Sam. Helping himself to a cup, Sam heard John say, "All right, then, pigeon is in the coop.' Okay. Bye." John hung up the phone and asked, "Do you got that, Sam? 'Pigeon is in the coop.' All right. Here are some photos of the place where you're going, and here is a map showing you the route out." As Sam looked them over, John added, "I suggest you try and memorize it. I have a gut feeling you are going to be in a big hurry on your way out. Go ahead, take a few minutes. I'll be right back."

Sam sat studying the photos and the road map and thinking of home, but was soon interrupted by John, carrying his box and suitcase. John handed Sam a billfold. "This is who you will be while you're here in New York. Give me your wallet and ID." John took out the cash and handed it back to Sam. "There is a credit card in there matching the name. If you have to use it, the firm will add it to your bill later. You are about set to go, 'Tim Bryant.' One more thing: there is a card in there with our numbers on it. If by any chance you have any trouble with the local police, say as little as possible and call the firm. Ask for John. We will handle it."

Another car pulled into the driveway. "Okay, here's your ride. Good luck. I hope we get to meet again under better circumstances. Oh, here, take your map; it's a good scenic route so no one should question that."

Sam picked up the suitcase and headed for the door. John walked out to the car with Sam, and told the driver to pop the trunk. Sam placed his suitcase in the trunk and closed it back. John introduced him to the lady who stepped out of the car. "Tim, this is Martha."

She politely stuck her hand out. "Glad to meet you, Tim."

"Likewise, Martha."

As they climbed into the car, Sam figured it was just like acting in a movie or a play. Martha waved to John as they drove off. After several minutes of silence, Martha asked, "So, Tim, what are you in such deep thought about?"

"Just trying to keep my head glued on straight. I have never been here before, and I want to see as much as possible, and get everything done on time."

"I understand. It can be frustrating to try and do too much all at once. Do you have your whole trip planned out?"

"Just about. I'm looking for an old friend of mine that's supposed to be living in these parts. That would top the trip off, if I were able to find him after all this time."

Martha pulled into a gas station. "Come on," she said, "let's get us a Coke."

When they were far enough away from the car, she said, "Man, you're really good at this. I hope you're around if I'm ever in trouble."

They walked in and got Cokes to drink. Martha said, "There are a couple of booths over there; do you mind if we sit for a few minutes and have a cigarette?"

"Mind?" Sam asked. "I was just about to demand that we take five for one."

As they sat and talked, Martha told the man she knew as Tim, "We should be at our destination in approximately one hour. I will show you where the truck will be parked, and then I will drop you off at your pick-up point. You know the code, right?"

"Yes."

"A delivery truck will pull in between seven and eight. If he says the magic words, you climb aboard. He will deliver you to where your friend is. Is there anything you would like to ask me before we get back into the car?"

"No! I think we've pretty much covered it."

They finished their cigarettes before returning to the car. The remainder of the trip was filled with idle chit-chat.

Sam was really getting into his part. Tim, now a businessperson, was sightseeing in New York, and hardly knew what was really taking place, or what was really at stake. He had come back home to be caught up into a whirlwind of deception, lies, and danger. Where it was going to lead him? He didn't have a clue. For now, he was just trying to stay focused on the task of getting David back from the kidnappers without harm.

Martha pointed to a large mansion. "This is the place where you are going."

When Sam saw it, he was amazed. From his conversation with his dad back at the old house in Bryant, Sam had already had a mental picture of what to expect, but upon seeing the place for the first time, the fact that it looked just as he had pictured struck him as a little strange, if not miraculous.

Sam questioned himself again: How had he talked with his dad that night, if he were dead? Did he really have a dream? He was having a hard time believing his dad could still be alive; after all, he'd seen him lying in the casket.

Sam looked things over as best he could as Martha drove. They continued to drive for another two miles to get to the backside of the mansion.

Martha said, "This is where your truck will be parked, and the keys will be left in the ashtray." Martha continued talking all the way to their next stop, giving "Tim" all the details she could without giving anything away.

About fifteen miles up the road, there was a motel with a gas station beside it. Martha pulled in; when she climbed out of the car, she got his suitcase from the trunk and said, "If you would follow me, please, Tim."

They walked to room number ten, on the end. Martha pulled a key out of her pocket and opened the door. Once they were inside, she asked, "Well, do you have any questions?"

"No."

"Okay, looks like you're ready. You will have a few hours before you have to go. I would suggest that you study the map so you'll be more prepared." She reached up, gave him a hug, and wished him lots of luck.

Martha left Sam standing in the room of a small motel. The only thing he knew was that he was here to rescue David. He felt lonely and isolated from everyone he knew, the two feelings Sam hated the most. He tried sitting down for a few minutes but he found he was too restless and agitated, so he decided to go for a walk to work off some of the nervous energy that seemed to be distressing him.

He had seen a pavilion just over the hill from the motel. He thought that might be a good spot for thinking. There was something eating at him, so he pulled out the letters from his dad and read each one as if for the first time. He remembered what Dad said to him the first night he was back home: "Trust no one! Simplicity is not always a sign of ignorance, but wisdom in its purest form! Real power is never given; it is always taken!" One he hadn't heard in a while flashed in his head. "Above all things, learn to be honest with yourself!" With that running through his mind, Sam had to ask himself, "What the hell am I doing here?"

He read the last note again. "When you arrive in New York." A light in Sam's head came on. "Wait a minute—no one was supposed to know anything until I got here. Oh, shit. What the hell have you done, Sam? You played right along with them. Here you are, where nobody knows you, carrying a fake ID. That has trouble written all over it." The revelation of this sent Sam into a silent rage. Nobody likes to be played for a fool, but Sam had let his guard down, and so they had gotten to him.

Reverting back almost twenty years, he thought, "Those sons of bitches want to play head games, huh? Well, bring it on, 'cause I'm the best there ever was and the best there ever will be."

Chapter 10
The Chase Is On

After stewing for a spell, Sam knew that everything was working against him, even time. He started back to his room to make sure he had what he needed. Looking down from the hill, he saw it was too late. Somebody was already in his room. Sam hid in the shadows, trying to make out who it was. After a few minutes, Martha and a cowboy walked out. Sam could tell the cowboy was upset. Raising his voice at Martha, he asked, "Why didn't you stay here with him? We have got to have that ring."

Martha tried to calm the man down. "Would you shut up? You're going to wake the whole damn place up." Sam strained to get a good look at the man, but he wasn't close enough. Martha and the cowboy climbed into the truck, backed down the road for a short distance, and parked again.

"It looks like they're going to wait for me to come back, huh?" Sam turned and headed into the woods. "I hope they enjoy their wait." After putting the letters back into his pocket, he started a slow jog, hoping to put as much distance as possible between himself and the pair in the truck. He wondered why he just didn't tell everyone "The snow is too deep" when he had the chance. He knew now that time was his enemy.

By morning, Sam had made his way into a small town. He needed to make some phone calls and let everybody know he was all right. When he spotted a truck stop in the distance, he knew he would be able to take care of all his needs quickly. He ate a small breakfast between phone calls, and drank plenty of coffee. He felt a little better, knowing that Martha and the cowboy were some distance behind him. He still did not know what their plan was, but he knew that the quicker he got out of New

York, the better his chances of survival. After eating, he went shopping and bought some work clothes. By the time he'd changed into them, it was almost six in the morning. He wondered just how long Martha and the cowboy would wait before they finally gave up on Sam's returning to the motel.

A middle-aged truck driver came through the front door. Sam had no time to beat around the bush. He followed the man back into the dining area. When the truck driver sat down, Sam introduced himself and offered to buy the man breakfast. Jimmy Martin, the truck driver, was kind of a loner, and didn't quite know what to say, but went ahead and accepted the offer.

"Where you headed?" asked Sam.

"I'm on my way out to Washington."

"Are you going to go through Montana?"

"Yeah, I have to make a drop in Bozeman."

"Do you think you could drop me off there?"

"Sure. Are you from there?"

"Live just outside of Bozeman. My truck broke down, and it appears that it is going to take some time to get it fixed. The company I work for wants me to come in and pick up another truck. That way, they don't have to pay me to just sit around here."

By the time Jimmy was ready to leave, Sam was getting a little nervous. It was almost eight in the morning, and he knew Martha and the cowboy would not be too far behind. When the big rig pulled out onto the main road and started picking up speed, Sam set his heartbeat to the sound of the engine. Jimmy seemed more at ease as well; when he got started, he talked over the sound of the engine. They were off!

After thinking things over, Sam realized he had not really put anything together, so he decided that at the next truck stop, he would buy a notebook and start his own journal. His dad told him that is what had protected him over the years. "Bingo," Sam thought to himself. "That's it! They're after the journal, and this ring. They don't give two hoots about me. Just like Dad said, I'm just a pawn in a big game. Well, well. For the time being I guess it's safe, because even I don't know where the journal is."

At the next truck stop, Sam bought a notebook and started a journal of his own. Things somehow made more sense when they were put in writing. It definitely added a new meaning to each word. After the first night in the rig, Sam started driving some to help Jimmy, which he knew would get him to Montana more quickly. After two days on the road, they finally arrived in Bozeman. After calling his friend Kelsey Lancaster for a ride, Sam helped Jimmy make his drop. Then they parted company with mutual thanks.

Sam told him, "If you ever find yourself in the state of Arkansas, then look me up."

"I will, Sam! You take care now. So long."

Kelsey pulled up in a truck and honked its horn. Sam waved to Jimmy as he climbed into the truck.

"Hey!" Kelsey said. "How are you doing?"

Sam, not wanting to answer the question directly, replied, "Kelsey, we've been friends for a long time."

"We sure have. What's the problem?"

"Well, that's just it. I've got a mess to clean up, and I need to know that I can count on you when and if I need you."

"Hey, you know me. If I can, I'll be there."

When they arrived at Sam's house, Kelsey asked, "Do you want me to hang around for awhile—or will you just call me when you need me?"

Sam thought for a second. "Kelsey what do you have planned for tomorrow?"

"Nothing. Sue and the kids are planning to spend the day at her parent's house."

"Okay, call me in the morning. Maybe I'll have some kind of plan worked out. And by the way, let's keep my being back in town just between you and me."

Kelsey nodded. "Okay, then I'll see you in the morning.

Sam walked around to the back of his house, getting the hidden key taped to the bottom of a small flowerpot. Once inside, he looked around the house and saw that everything appeared to be in order. Now that he was in his own home, he began to feel more secure and at ease. He made a pot of coffee and sat down with his journal. He had already written as far back as July 14, 2025, and documented everything that had taken place since the day he arrived in Arkansas. After reviewing all the entries, he called Mike and told him to tell Frank and Joe that he was in trouble and needed their help. Then he told him to lock both of the men out of the computer system, and make sure they did not handle any business transactions until he got back home. In addition, he asked Mike to find out about Frank and Joe's kids; how many they had and where they were located.

He talked to Tara, and told her to keep a log of everyone coming and going in the next few days.

He talked to Cyndi, telling her to find out everything she could about Molly. He wanted to know if she was involved in anything besides Simplicity, but he did not want her to say anything to Mary about it. "In addition," he said, "the next time you see Ronnie ask him if he can remember when Dad started wearing his ring, and if he knew which jeweler made it."

After talking with everyone, Sam closed his journal and poured himself another cup of coffee, looking forward to some quiet time, and rest. "For the next few hours, I am going to try and pretend none of this has ever happened," he said to himself.

Unbeknownst to Sam, there was trouble in paradise back in New York. Sam's disappearance had everyone in an uproar. John was beside himself, because he never wanted to let Sam leave once he had made the identification swap. They had him right where they needed him, and there had been no need for the rest of the charades. Now, it appeared, they had bigger problems. While Martha and the cowboy were waiting for Sam, somebody must have seen the open door, and entered the hotel room. The cowboy jumped the man, thinking it was Sam. As the two men struggled, the cowboy's gun went off, killing the man instantly. The cowboy, seeing that it was not Sam, fled the scene, knowing that he and his friends now had bigger troubles at their heels.

Witnesses told police the man was approximately six feet tall, wearing a pair of faded blue jeans and a black shirt. The man was dressed like a cowboy, and wore a black cowboy hat. With this description from witnesses, the police issued a statewide manhunt for their "pigeon named Tim," while Martha and the cowboy continued to search for Sam, knowing they were running out of time.

Sam, knowing none of this, had thought about what he needed to do the following morning. When Kelsey showed up, they went to get Sam a new driver's license. Then they went by the bank, where Sam closed all of his accounts. Having a little over $10,000 to his name, Sam called the airport and booked a flight back to New York. He and Kelsey stopped to eat at one of Sam's favorite steakhouses.

Sam said, "Order what you want, Kelsey. I'm going to fill up. I don't know how long it will be before I get another good meal."

For a short while Sam enjoyed his meal and the visit with his friend. When it came time to leave, Sam told his friend, "Kelsey, you go on home. I'll catch a cab to the airport." Sam went shopping, to kill a little time, and bought himself a new wallet.

While standing outside the store waiting for a cab, Sam remembered the journal he'd left at the house. "Damn it!" When the cab pulled up, Sam had already made up his mind to go back and retrieve his journal. After giving the cab driver directions to his house, he knew he would still have plenty of time to make it to the airport. As the cab pulled up to the house, Sam spotted a red Ford Blazer sitting across the street. As he hurried into the house to get his journal, a man stepped out of the Blazer and met Sam as he was coming out of the house.

"Excuse me. I hate to bother you, but it looks like you are in a hurry. Are you, Sam?"

Almost scared to answer, Sam said, "Yes."

"Do you have a minute?"

"Well, I'm on my way to the airport."

"Sir, I have a package for you, but I can't release it unless you answer some questions properly."

Sam moved back a step, thinking how funny it was that one word could jog his memory banks. "Wait here. I'll get rid of the cab driver." Sam paid the cab driver double the fare and got his cell phone number in case he needed him to come back.

The man walked over to the Blazer and came back carrying a briefcase. "Shall we go inside?" Once inside, he asked to see Sam's ID and checked it off his list. "I've already verified the address given. Next question: what was your father's middle name?"

"O'Dell."

"What was the name of the family dog when you were a child?"

"We had a lot of dogs, but 'Tazzman' is the one that my father was the fondest of, as well as everybody else."

"Last question: what was your pet name that your father always called you?"

"It had to be 'Bean Head.'"

The man checked everything off the list. Opening the briefcase, he pulled out a package wrapped in plain brown paper. "All right. If you will just sign here, I will give you your package, and get out of your hair."

Sam signed the receipt, and the man ripped off a copy and handed it back to him. Releasing the package to Sam, the courier apologized for the horrible timing and wished Sam a good day.

As the man was leaving, Sam asked him, "How did you know I would be here?"

"My orders read that this package was to be delivered on July 20, 2025. If undeliverable, I was to deliver the package to Arkansas. I suppose whoever sent the package figured you would be in one of the two locations. I sure am glad I caught you before flying out today. I would have hated to have to drive all the way to Arkansas. Well, anyway, I am glad it worked out for the both of us." The man stepped outside onto the porch, telling Sam, "Hope you have a safe trip."

Sam was totally beside himself at this point. He called the airport and canceled his flight, and informed the ticket office that he would call back when he was ready to reschedule it.

CHAPTER 11
THE JOURNAL

Sam sat down with the package. "Was this fate or what? How would Dad have known I would be in Montana on that one particular date?"

With so many questions running through his mind, one right after the other, he was almost afraid to look. "Lord, I need help to understand all of this." He opened the package rather slowly, as if he had just received the greatest Christmas gift in the world. The package contained a large, hardbound leather book with "The Broken R, By: Bill" engraved on the cover.

Sam thought, "Dad's journal. Hell, this looks like a book that belongs on the bestseller list." It read like one, too. Flipping the book open, Sam started reading: "I am sitting here wishing I had started this journal about ten years back. Maybe it would have saved me a lot of time and grief. Therefore, if you have not started a journal of your own, I highly recommend you start one today, Son; there is no better time than now to start. The truth to life is only what you leave behind.

"In death, I have not wasted one minute thinking about what I had gained in life. Nevertheless, all my thoughts are with you, Mike, Cyndi, and Haley, that you will be able to have a better life than I had. Most of the people that I knew, just like myself, never learned to live life to its fullest potential; we only reacted to it, the cause-and-effect law. Because I work, I do not have time to fish anymore! Because I am poor, I do not visit with friends and family! There are a million examples of them, but they all say the same thing. Excuses. I can tell you: if you are looking for an excuse, believe me you will be able to find one. Today is all you have; make no more excuses for yourself. Learn to enjoy every minute of your life, no matter where you are or what you are doing.

"Some of the things that you will learn about me in this journal are not good. I spent a lifetime searching for what I could call a normal life. It began with this one simple little truth: 'ABOVE ALL THINGS, LEARN TO BE HONEST WITH YOURSELF!' For if you can be honest with yourself your conscience isn't always following you around, leaving your mind free to explore new ideas, new possibilities and the ability to enjoy the memories you're making without the burden of a troubled soul.

"So, Sam, if you still smoke, burn one and have that cup of coffee. Relax and kick back. Blame nobody else for your mistakes, but do not take credit for anyone else's mistakes either. After you finish reading this journal, you and I will always have a special bond between us. I do not know where you are at right now, but if you choose to stay in Montana, that is fine! With everything that has happened the way it has, nobody could fault you for your decision, nor would I hold it against you. However, the latter details of this journal need to pass to Mike and Ronnie if you decide to leave.

"If you have chosen to stay on at the Broken R, you should have received another package and you should be wearing my ring. If this is so, it means you have learned the second truth I discovered in life. 'REAL POWER IS NEVER GIVEN, IT IS ALWAYS TAKEN.' You should not have to think too hard on where the idea of the ring of power came from. Nevertheless, guard it with your life; the ring is the tool that reveals the great wealth of the Broken R, and her secrets. It protects the journal that my dad had left to me. This place is where our journals shall rest in time with your sons, and then their sons. Maybe by then our families will have bonded and healed."

Sam decided to stop reading for a minute, and have that cigarette and cup of coffee. The sun was setting so he took a break out on the back deck, watching as the sun went down for another day. Sam remembered watching the sunrise in Arkansas the morning before, and thought to himself, "I know now what Dad is saying. I am knee-deep in all of this, and it is my fault. Nevertheless, the sunset of another day is still a beautiful thing, especially in big-sky country."

When the sun had set, Sam returned to the journal, and curled up on the couch like a young schoolchild reading his homework. The biggest difference between then and now was he was no longer a child, and the loaded 30-30 rifle beside him was his only companion. He read for hours, learning more from his Dad's journal. He did not realize just how long he had been lying there. It seemed that when he sat and read, time really flew by. His eyes began watering from reading so much, but he just could not pull himself away from the journal. Though he wanted to continue reading, he went ahead and closed the book for a short spell. He sat pondering what he had to do about his problems back in New York.

Sam learned from reading the journal that Frank and Joe were up to something. They had been embezzling money through the law firm which Frank's oldest son was running. At last count they had taken over $10 million from the Simplicity company. They were transferring the funds to an account in New York. However, the real kicker was that the account was in Sam's name. At first, Dad thought it was just about the money, and that they had put it in Sam's name as a cover-up to prevent their scheme from unraveling, but he had put it together too late. Old ideals die hard for some, he said. They were planning a total, hostile takeover. It broke Dad's heart to know that was their plan, but at the same time he knew exactly who had taught them how to do it.

Remembering back, Sam could recall that his dad had told him that story before, but he knew his dad had withheld many important details.

Sam continued reading in the journal: "When the big showdown took place, and I had killed Bill (the man that was using my identity), there was a very short time span in which to work, so I took in Frank, Joe, and Molly. I removed $54 million in three days from the organization. Since the accounts were all in my name, it was a rather simple task to do. Once the transactions had taken place, Frank, Joe, and Molly worked as couriers to carry the money back to Arkansas. For their services, I offered them each $1 million in cash, and they could go their merry way, or they could invest their million dollars into Simplicity and stay on at the Broken R. They chose to hitch their wagons and invest in Simplicity, but now that greed had taken over they appeared to want it all."

Sam read for awhile longer, then slowly drifted off to sleep. He was sure he would have dreams of this not being real. However, his mind was full of possibilities if it were. He awoke early the next morning with new life in his bones, and an excitement for life that he had never experienced before; he really wished Tara was there next to him. She had been his life support for many years. Now he knew it was time to give back what he had taken so much for granted. At four in the morning, he dialed the Broken R and was surprised when Tara answered the call.

"Hello?"

"Tara, is that you?"

"Good morning. Yes, it's me, and just where are you?"

"Baby, I can't say too much right now; I just had to call and let you know how much I love you!"

"Oh my, you must be in more trouble than we thought. The phones are ringing off the hook, and it appears nobody can have a conversation without some type of interruption anymore."

"I figured as much. Is everybody okay?"

"Yes, we're fine. Ronnie is beside himself as to what he should do. He has riders running day and night around here. No one comes or goes without signing in and out. He told me if I heard from you, all you had to do was just say the word and he would be there; whatever is going on, you don't have to handle it alone."

"Tell him I said 'thanks,' but knowing he is keeping you all safe is the most important thing to me right now."

"All right, but you know you're starting to sound just like your dad—always have to do everything yourself."

"Come on, now. Have you talked to Cyndi?"

"Yes, she left yesterday. She said she might be gone for a couple of days.

"Damn it! I wish she had not done that! How are the boys doing?"

"They're having the time of their life, acting just like kids again. They're taking their shifts riding, just like everyone else. Rick has Ben and Sara riding already."

"That's great. Tell them all I will be back soon."

"You'd better, mister. Even Mike is starting to worry about what you're doing."

"Okay, I will try to hurry."

"You promise?"

"Yeah baby, I promise."

"Okay, I love you. Bye."

Sam hung up the phone and started another pot of coffee. Feeling exceptionally good, he ran to take a hot shower, singing "Living on Love" for the entire duration. After his shower, he went to get dressed. Looking through his clothing was like looking into somebody else's closet. After spending an hour or so trying to decide what to put on, he suddenly realized he was a born-again cowboy. After grabbing some pants and a shirt, he called a cab to take him into town. He went to get some new clothes and then, feeling more like himself, went to have breakfast. He walked with a new step, smiling and greeting people as if he had known them all his life. At the diner he noticed an older truck in the parking lot with a "For Sale" sign on it.

Sitting in a booth, he overheard two young men talking about selling the truck, and that when they did they would be able to enter the local rodeo. If they did well this year they were going to follow the rodeo circuit. Sam ordered his breakfast, drank his coffee, then turned and struck up a conversation with the two men. They were brothers who were full of energy, talking about trying to make it on the pro-rodeo circuit. Sam asked how much they wanted for the truck.

"Three thousand dollars," the younger one stated. Sam could see a sparkle in his eyes; he imagined what it was like to be nineteen or twenty and feel like the world was suppose to bow at your presence.

Sam asked, "Do you have the title with you?"

"Yes, sir!"

"All right. I will take it, under one condition."

"What is the condition, sir?"

"You two have to autograph my book here. That way, when you get rich and famous I don't have to stand in line."

They both laughed.

"I'm serious, gentlemen," he said, handing them a pen and opening his journal to the next clean sheet.

They asked for Sam's name, and the younger one wrote, "To Sam—a man with a plan; your new friend, Lance Polk." He passed the book to his brother, Brett.

The waitress arrived with Sam's breakfast. "These cowboys giving you any trouble?"

"No! It's kind of the other way around."

Brett took the journal from his brother. "What did you write?"

"Read it."

He did, and then wrote, "Sam, thanks for the support. Glad to count you as a friend. Brett Polk."

Sam counted out the money when Brett handed him back the journal. "All I need now is the title, and the keys."

Lance signed the title off while Brett separated the keys. They made the exchange and shook hands to seal the deal. The boys went to clean out the truck, putting everything from it into Brett's truck. By the time they were done, Sam had finished eating and was coming out the door. Lance hollered to him, "We're almost done, Sam; just need to pull the tag."

When he got to the truck and looked it over, Brett asked him if everything was OK. "Sure," Sam replied, climbing into the truck. When Lance came around to the window, Sam handed him the address to the Broken R and told the two boys, "If you're ever down in Arkansas, look me up." He started the truck; it sounded good. "Well, it was nice meeting you two, but I've got to get back on the road."

He heard Lance say, "Come on, let's get something to eat." As Sam drove off, he was feeling rather good about life, realizing for the first time that life itself had its own rewards. Unfortunately, it was time to get back to business. When he got back to the house and settled in, he picked up the journal and continued to read. Skipping through some pages trying to get to the meat of the information, Sam knew he would have to reread the journal properly, but he wanted to know as much as possible now before he faced any more surprises. Near the end of the journal was a detailed list of projects that his dad had wanted him to do. It was amazing how well the list that his dad made seemed to coincide with his own plans. There was a note at the top of the page telling Sam, "Hi, Son. If anything happens to me before the completion of the tasks on this list, I will need you to see that the items are accomplished. Sam, I need you to fly to New York and finish a deal that I had started." He had given Sam the name of a real estate agent to contact. Apparently, his dad was in the process of buying the mansion where everything had happened so many years ago. With Simplicity growing at such a fast rate, he wanted to set up a nationwide headquarters where it all started.

On the 400-acre estate would be a building for Simplicity, an orphanage, and a school. The rest of the items did not click in his head. However, the list left him with many questions. The last few pages told him just how much funding he had at his disposal in order to achieve the completion of the projects listed.

Sam's eyes were about to pop out of their sockets as he read aloud, "Company jet, yacht, motels and ranches." There was also a list of different companies that had been bought out by Simplicity, or had 49 percent in stock shares, and a list of mergers that were to take place or be worked on for the next two years. Sam skipped over some of the details, knowing it would be awhile before he understood what all this stuff was about and what he had to do to achieve it. He flipped to the end of the journal and found a Simplicity credit card with a note that read, "This is your ticket into the company world. If you run into any problems, just contact the following people and they will have you fixed up in seconds."

Sam closed the journal, thinking it was truly amazing that his dad had been able to keep up with all of this. He spent the next few hours trying to put a total plan together. Every now and then, he would refer back to the journal for more details. It became clear why he needed to keep a journal of his own. He dialed the number to get a jet; and found out it was already in Montana. It had arrived there yesterday, and the pilot was on standby. The lady on the phone asked for the number on the Simplicity credit card. After Sam read the number to her she came back with, "Good afternoon, Samuel, and where will you be flying today?"

"I'm heading to New York."

"Okay, we will get the flight plan and call the pilot. You should be ready for takeoff in approximately two hours."

"How long of a stay are you planning?"

"I'm not sure."

"That's okay. Just give us a call when you are ready to leave."

"Thank you." Hanging up the phone, he went and packed. When he was sure he had everything he needed, he turned off the appliances, locked up the house and headed to the airport.

Chapter 12

Taking Care of Business

Sam made his way to the airport with no problem locating where he needed to be. Arriving a little early for takeoff, he removed his suitcase from the truck and walked inside to see where he'd need to park it. Inside the office were two young women trying to wrap it up for the day.

The one named Terrie asked, "May I help you, sir?"

"I was just going to ask where I needed to park my truck."

"Are you Samuel?"

"Yes."

"Then just leave the keys in it, and we will have one of the men bring it in after you leave. How long will you be leaving the truck here?"

"I'm not really sure yet."

"Is this a personal car or a company car?"

"Personal. I just bought it today; it's not even tagged yet."

The other girl looked up with a smile and said, "You have to be Wild Bill's youngest son, Samuel!"

"That's right," Sam replied with an even bigger smile.

"It must run in the family. Do you have the title with you?"

"Yes."

"Do you want it registered as a company car, or personal?"

"Personal. You can register the vehicle for me?"

"Sir, we work for you."

"Yes, this is definitely going to take sometime to adjust to these changes." He pulled out the title, and Terrie showed him where he needed to sign the document.

Terrie said, "By the time you get back, we will have your truck tagged and registered for you. Oh, look, Erin! He bought Lance's truck."

"You know Lance?"

"Yeah, he and Erin have been going together since high school."

Sam pulled out his journal and showed Terrie where Lance and Brett had autographed his book.

"Wait until I tell them who you are! Them boys will be wishing they had asked you for your autograph."

Sam laughed, "Why would they want my autograph?"

Erin started laughing too. "Yep, it runs in the family. Sounds just like your dad."

"I've been hearing that a lot lately."

"Well, that's a compliment, Sam. Your dad was a dear, sweet man to work with. We are glad to meet you, and hope now that you're here, we'll not have such an empty spot. We all really miss him."

The pilot came in. Erin handed him some papers, and after signing them, he handed them back and asked, "Are we ready for our level-one bigshot to come in?"

Terrie shook her head. "Renny Worthington, please meet your level-one bigshot. Sam, this is Renny—same as Penny, only with a R."

Sam shook Renny's hand and said, "It's good to meet you."

Renny apologized for his rudeness. "I am sorry, sir, I did not mean anything by that. You've heard the old saying, 'Open mouth, insert foot.' I sometimes get myself in trouble for my spontaneous remarks."

"That's okay. Hell, you're the one flying the plane, and that makes you the number-one bigshot to me."

They all laughed. Erin told them they'd better get going before the tower started calling. Renny and Sam walked to the plane. Once on board, Renny gave Sam the nickel-dime tour. "Bed and bath back there; here is the bar and refrigerator. If you need me, all you have to do is just push this button and talk, all right?"

"Got it."

"Okay, looks like we are ready for take off." Renny disappeared into the cockpit, and within a few minutes the engines were roaring.

Sam could hear Renny barking out orders to the men on the ground, then switch channels and start talking to the tower. Sam was amazed at just how much Renny sounded like his dad when he was barking out orders to others. He thought it must be a natural instinct for people who are used to being in control of the situations at hand.

There were a few minutes of silence, then Sam heard, "Simplicity One, you're cleared for take off on runway three."

"Roger, tower," Renny replied. The plane started moving. "Sam, you might what to buckle up until we're in the air. This is a little different from flying the big jets."

Sam buckled his seat belt, hoping the differences would be at a minimum; after all, he thought, the big jets were bad enough.

The radio voice faded away, and Renny decided to have a little fun. He hollered out, "Hang on, cowboy; we're going for a ride."

In a matter of seconds they were off the ground and soaring high into the air. Sam, of course, felt like he had left his stomach back on the ground. Once Renny got the plane leveled out, he entered the flight plan into the system, then switched the plane to autopilot and left the cockpit to check on Sam.

"You're looking a little green there, partner. You think you're gonna be OK?"

"Yeah, as soon as my stomach catches back up with my body."

Renny poured him a shot of Crown Royal and handed it to him to drink. "This always seemed to cure that problem for your dad." Sam took the drink; sure enough, it helped. "All right. If you need anything else just let me know."

Renny headed back to the cockpit. Sam sat back with his journal, catching it up to the minute. He then started designing a plan for his arrival in New York.

It was 7:30 a.m. back at the Broken R when Ronnie received a call from Frank Jr. asking, "Hey, Ronnie, where would you like for us to unload the new stock?"

Ronnie, at a loss for words asked, "Well, where are you at?"

"We're about twenty minutes away if everything goes well."

"Who, may I ask, is 'we'?"

"Damn it, Ronnie, what's with all the questions? I didn't ask you a complicated question! All I want to know is where you want me to put the new stock that is on the truck. I'm tired, hungry, and I've been on the road now for three solid days, and I'm in no mood for fifty questions."

Ronnie was getting upset with Frank Jr. "Just answer the question: who is 'we'?"

"For the life of me I don't see what difference it makes, but it's me and David."

Ronnie's mind went into overdrive. "Okay, Frank, take the stock to the back gate. I will meet you two there. We have to quarantine all new stock for at least 30 days."

"Ronnie, is something wrong? You have been acting strange, and asking odd questions."

"Everything's okay. I will meet you two at the back gates."

After hanging up the phone, Ronnie called Mike on his cell phone. "We've got troubles. Guess who is heading to the back gate?"

Mike, who was already worn out from trying to set up a new security program, replied tersely: "Come on, Ronnie, I'm in no mood to play guessing games. Spit it out."

"Frank Jr. and David are bringing in some new stock."

Mike stuttered, "Da . . . did you say David? What in the freaking hell is going on around here?"

"I don't know, but I'm headed over there to meet with the two of them now."

"Okay. Meet me at the house as soon as you can; we have got to get to the bottom of this, fast."

"My thoughts exactly, Mike. I'll see you in about thirty or forty minutes."

Ronnie had four extra ranch hands meet him at the back gate. When Frank and David pulled in, there were four semi trucks following them. Ronnie gave orders to the ranch hands. "Separate the stock in these four paddocks, make sure they're fed and watered, and Stan, let's make sure the vet is out here tomorrow to check out each and every one of the new stock. Once that's done you can close off the north gate, and turn them out to pasture."

"Got it, Ron." Stan took over giving orders to the rest of the cowboys. "Come on, you heard him. Let's get these critters bedded down for the night."

As the trucks were unloaded, Ronnie confronted Frank and David. "Where in the hell have you two been?"

David, tired from their journey, snapped back, "What's your damn problem? Surely, you can see! We brought this stock in from New Mexico."

Ronnie saw that the confrontation was about to get out of control. "Okay, calm down. We've got a problem. I am just as confused as you and David are. The three of us need to get this job done, and go see Mike at the house. He is waiting for us there."

The trucks were just about unloaded. The drivers lined up to get their paperwork signed. One of the drivers, who had delivered to the Broken R before, asked Frank Jr. and David, "Could you fellows give us a ride over to town? We're going to spend the night there and head back out in the morning."

Ronnie overheard them as he signed the paperwork. "Town? Yeah, sure, we can do that." Then he remembered the fellow in jail over there. "Damn, I should have thought of that before now." As they finished up, Ronnie told Stan, "Take my horse back with you; I'm going to ride with the men into town."

Frank Jr. and David both waited for answers concerning what the big fuss was about when they arrived. With Ronnie deep in thought, it appeared they wouldn't get their answers any time soon. Figuring they would get their answers when they met with Mike, they just went along with Ronnie, who appeared on a mission to uncover something. "After dropping these men off, we will pick up a fellow that is already in town," Ronnie said. "I think maybe he will be able to explain to us just what in the hell is going on."

The town was still buzzing with riders.. People were roaming from place to place. Ronnie, Frank Jr., and David dropped the truck drivers off in front of the motel.

The driver that was familiar with the town said he could handle it from here; since he knew his way, he could give the other men directions to where they needed to go.

Ronnie headed straight to the jail. "You two wait here. I'll be right back." Ronnie stepped out and checked his guns, then walked into the jailhouse.

Frank and David both looked at each other. "Frank, what do you suppose is going on?"

"I haven't got a clue, David, but apparently it's serious. Ronnie had that look!"

"What look?"

"The one that says he wants answers, and he wants them right now!"

"Damn it, Frank, you've got a good memory. What's it been—four or five years now since that happened?"

"I was sixteen then, so it's been six years."

"Boy, I remember Ronnie was going to kill somebody over that prized bull of his."

"If it hadn't been for Uncle Bill, he probably would have, too."

Ronnie came back out, shoving the young man who was still in handcuffs. "Get in the car. Frank, we're going to the main house. Mister, I suggest that you think twice before you even blink out of turn. I'm not in any mood for any more bullshit, and I suggest you get ready to start talking, or—let me put it this way—you won't be needed anymore."

When they arrived at the house, Mike had already gathered everyone together. Everybody greeted Frank Jr. and David with hugs and welcomes, although they still didn't have any clue what was going on. Ronnie told the handcuffed young man to sit down on a chair. Mike started to say something to Ronnie, but after remembering the incident when Ronnie's bull went missing, he decided he wasn't about to butt into this conversation.

Ronnie said, "Mister, I'm going to ask the questions and you're going to answer them if you want to see another tomorrow, and you better hope like hell I believe what you say! Mike, I need you to take everyone into the other room; this could get nasty. Also, fill Frank and David in on what's been going on."

They all left the room. Ronnie sat back in the chair and started spouting out questions. "Just who the hell are you?"

"My name is Kevin."

"All right, Kevin, where are you from?"

"New York."

"You're doing well so far. Who do you work for?"

"My father."

"And that would be who?"

"Phillip."

"Now why would you try and kidnap a baby, then lie about another kidnapping?"

Kevin held up his hands, "Sir if you will take these handcuffs off of me, and let me have a cup of coffee and a cigarette, I will tell you anything you want to know; that is, if I can."

Frank, David, and Mike entered the room. "Do you think we can trust him enough to remove the cuffs?" Ronnie asked.

Mike walked to the door and locked it, then turning around slowly he reached out to Ronnie, "Ronnie, hand me your gun."

Ronnie handed Mike his gun. With the gun pointing at Kevin, Mike told him, "Mister, this is the only warning you're going to get: I suggest you make no mistakes. If you make one wrong move, I will kill you right where you're sitting. Okay, Ronnie, you can turn him loose. I believe he understands the rules. Now let's see if he wants to live or die."

Ronnie removed Kevin's cuffs, and Frank handed him a pack of cigarettes while David went to get him a cup of coffee. Kevin lit a cigarette, sucking hard on the first drag. When David came back with the coffee, Kevin took a few sips, and then started talking.

"As I said, my name is Kevin, and my father's name is Phillip. My grandfather was the next in line to run this giant organization in New York, sometime back in the 80s. Although I know nothing of what the organization did; my father learned everything he knew from his father. These are the facts that I do know about the organization: your father killed the man who ran the organization in the beginning. Your father had been able to bankrupt my grandfather before being discovered, and the organization did not want the risk of Mafia-type publicity, so they shut down everything and moved their headquarters to California. Even though my dad went on to do good for himself through the years, he always swore to my grandfather that he would one day right the wrong that had been done to him."

"What in the hell are you getting at here?"

"I'm trying to tell you this goes a long way back. Hatred, greed, murder—you name it."

"But what was your part?"

"My part was simple. As you can see, I am not important; no one has come looking for me. I was not supposed to hurt anybody; they just wanted me to get everybody worked up. That way, Sam would go to New York."

Tara, who had been standing at the door, was not able to hold back anymore. "I knew it! I knew something like this would happen. Ronnie, you go get as many men as you can gather up." Reaching to take the gun from Mike, she told them, "Both of you go find Sam, and bring him home. If this one comes up with any more useful information, I will send it along."

Rick came in with his 30-30 pointed down at Kevin, "It's okay, Mom, you can give Ronnie back his gun."

Mike and Ronnie were walking out the door when Mike said, "Ronnie, you get some men together and I'll make the flight arrangements."

Frank, David, and Brad were all ready to go. Ronnie headed to the bunkhouse; Stan stood outside. "What's up, Ron?" he asked.

"Look, see how many men we can get ready for a flight to New York tonight. Have them meet me at the main house within the hour."

"Sure thing, Boss. You want me to go?"

"No, I need you here to run the place till I get back."

Stan was about as easygoing as a turtle. "Okay, I'll see what I can do."

Mike was on the phone to the airport. A young woman told him, "The company had a jet coming in, but it was booked to shut down here."

"Change the plans; have it refueled, and the plane checked out, and find me a pilot to take her to New York now."

"I'll get on it, sir."

Mike hung up the phone. "Mary, would you help me get some of my things together?"

Mary knew that whatever the problem was, it had to be severe. Mike hated flying, yet he was fixing to get on an airplane. She wanted to ask, but figured this was something Mike had to do on his own. Therefore, she kept quiet and helped him to gather a few things, before she started to pack herself a few items.

Mike asked, "What are you doing?"

"Where ever you go, I go."

Back at the house, Tara was still talking with Kevin and trying to get information. "What is it they want with Sam?"

"Everything. They were planning a switch."

"What do you mean, to kill him?"

"That's what I mean, lady."

"Well, Kevin, you'd better hope like hell that doesn't happen."

"Why, lady, you all just don't get it; I'm dead already, and the rest of them are probably dead by now as well. This switch was for all the marbles."

Tara, feeling overwhelmed with an "all is lost" feeling, reached out and slapped Kevin. "Don't you say that! Hell, don't you even think it."

Rick put the handcuffs back on Kevin. "He's going with us. Tara said. Mister, you're right about one thing: if Sam dies, so will you!"

Tara ran to her room and packed a few clothes as fast as her mind would let her. When she came down, Haley was standing in the kitchen packed and ready to go. Tara was so upset she was trembling. Haley reached out to give her a hug. "It's going to work out. Try to have faith. Here come Mike and Mary now."

When Mike saw that Haley was packed, he told her, "You're not going, Haley."

However, she just put up her hand and said, "Don't bother. Our family is in big trouble, and I'm going."

Ronnie pulled up in the old rodeo bus. Ten men were already onboard; he hollered out to the house, "Come on! Minutes are ticking away!" They were just about to drive off when Rick came running for the bus, talking on the phone at the same time. When he stepped inside, he said, "Now look, little brother, somebody has to take care of things around here. We will keep in touch with you."

On the other end of the phone, Brad reluctantly agreed. Rick hung up the phone, and they were all off to the airport to get on a plane headed for New York.

Ronnie, who was driving, handed Mike his cell phone. "Look up the Bar S."

Mike handed it back. "It's dialing."

When John Redd answered, Ronnie, trying to save time, told him, "John, we're coming. Be ready for anything. I am bringing twenty men with me, and I will need as many riders as you can put together for me as well. The Broken R will pay $200 extra a day."

John acknowledged the information and said, "Call me when you know what time you will be arriving."

"Okay, will do."

When they arrived at the airport, one of Simplicity's airplanes was already in the hangar, with maintenance men working on it. Mike walked into the office; the man in the office offered no idle talk. He reported to Mike, "We need at least another thirty minutes, sir, to have her ready for takeoff."

Mike asked him, "Would you please look up on your computer and tell me were Simplicity One is, or if Samuel is flying anywhere tonight?"

Within a few seconds the man replied, "He left Montana this afternoon, and will be in New York by nine tonight."

"When do you think we'll be there?"

"My guess would be that you should be arriving around three or four o'clock in the morning, New York time."

"Thank you."

Mike walked out, telling everyone it would be at least 30 more minutes before the airplane could take off. He also told Tara and Ronnie that Sam was already in the air, and would beat them to New York. "At this point, we know he's okay, because he's still in the air, but he will land before we do."

Everyone started boarding the plane.

Chapter 13
Coming Together

Renny invited Sam to come sit up front in the cockpit with him. Once Sam got himself seated, Renny said, "You'll be a regular flyer by the time I get done with you. We're approximately one hour away from landing."

Sam thought about the kaleidoscope of events that had taken place since his return home, and the things he had learned since receiving his dad's journal (where he found the only real information he had uncovered). While things were in such an uproar, he hadn't had any time to sort through the questions of why things were happening, and truly find any answers to what was going on. Realizing that Renny had to have known his father very well, Sam started asking him questions. "Renny, you flew my dad around a lot, didn't you?"

"Sure did, just about everywhere that he needed to go. Why do you ask?"

"Well, we've got a situation in New York." Not wanting to reveal any major details to Renny, he tried a new approach to the problem. "Are you a vested member of Simplicity?"

"No, not yet. I don't think I will be for four or five more years."

"How would you like to help me, and I'll kick in that five years for you?"

Renny, knowing what that would mean to him, told Sam, "I hope I can do what ever it is you're wanting."

Sam explained, "I heard you barking out orders back at the airport, and it was amazing just how much you sounded like my dad."

"Yeah, he was the best I ever heard at it. But, what's that got to do with me?"

Sam went on to explain: "I was just thinking that when we get to New York, I want you to play the role of my dad."

Renny rubbed his face. "I don't know, Sam; I just don't think many people would buy it. We might sound alike, but we don't look alike."

Sam thought for a minute. "Well, maybe not. But if we dress you like a cowboy, and keep you in the shadows, I think it might work."

Renny told Sam, "There should be some clothes in the back. As far as I know, no one had cleaned out the closet."

Sam went to the back of the plane; sure enough, there in the closet were two sets of clothes with matching boots and hat. Laying out a set of clothes on the bed, Sam saw that the overhead compartment was locked. Pushing the intercom button, he said, "Hey, Renny, do you have the keys to this overhead compartment back here?"

"No, your dad was the only one to have a key."

Sam reached into his pocket and pulled out the key. "This looks like it. Damn, it works!" Inside was a matching set of Colt 45s just like at the ranch. "This is going to work," he said when he returned to tell Renny what he had found.

Renny was shocked. "What you want me to do—shoot somebody?"

"No. Not unless they start shooting first."

"Oh, shit! Boy, what are you getting me into?"

Sam swore Renny to secrecy concerning everything he was about to tell him. "No one can ever know what we are fixing to do."

Renny agreed to the five-year pay off, which would make him a vested member of Simplicity. After their meeting, Renny told Sam, "I think it's time for you to buckle up; we'll be landing soon."

Sam returned to the back of the plane and strapped himself in, after placing the journal into the overhead compartment where he had found the guns. He buckled himself in while they made a perfectly smooth landing. Renny pulled the plane all the way into the hangar and then shut the engines down. He gave instructions to the ground men: "I want her refueled and checked out. She is to be ready to fly at a minute's notice."

The voice came back on the radio, "Yes, sir. Also, we have a message up front for Mr. Samuel at the counter. Be sure you pick it up before you leave."

"Roger that!"

Sam told Renny, "Go get changed. It's getting late; we've got to get started. I'll meet you in the office when I'm finished."

"Okay. Better see what the message is about." Sam entered the office, on guard for anything that might look out of place.

The man at the counter asked, "Are you Samuel? I'm sorry, sir, but I have to ask for proof of identification."

Sam showed his ID, and the man thanked him and handed him an envelope. Sam read the note:

"Sam, sit tight. We are all on are way, arrival time should be about 4 a.m. Nothing is as it appears. Big trouble!

Mike"

Sam wrote down the address of the mansion he was fixing to buy. "Meet me here by 10:00 in the morning, and thanks for coming!" he wrote. He folded the note and placed it back into the envelope, telling the man to make sure Mike got the message.

"Will do, sir. I hope you enjoy your visit."

When Renny stepped down out of the airplane, the man asked, "Sir, who's that with you? You were supposed to be flying alone. Wait, it can't be—looks like Wild Bill!"

Sam watched Renny walk toward the office; anyone could tell it had been a long time since he had worn a pair of cowboy boots. "No sir, that's my pilot."

Renny was damn near limping in just that short distance. Walking in, Renny said, "Hi, Jack, how we doing tonight?"

"I'm fine now, but you damn near gave me a heart attack. I thought you were Wild Bill coming off of that plane."

Renny signed his paperwork and winked at Sam. They walked out and got into a company SUV. "I guess you were right. Old Jack and your dad were just like brothers, I guess, because they share the Robinson name."

Sam used Renny's phone to call the real estate agent. When Becky answered the phone, she was casual, not expecting a business call that late. "Hello?"

"Is this Becky?"

"Yes, may I ask who's calling?"

"You were working on a deal with my father to purchase an old mansion in upstate New York."

"This must be Samuel."

"Yes. I was wondering if it is still available."

"Sure—no one else has made an offer."

"How much are we talking about?"

"Five million, in cash."

"Sounds like my dad really wanted the property."

"Yes, he seemed really interested in it."

"Will you prepare the paperwork and have it ready tomorrow? I'll meet you there about 10 a.m. with a cashier's check."

"Sounds wonderful. I'll see you there."

"Good night."

When she hung up, Becky made a little war cry and danced in circles. "I did it, I did it!" Her kids came running to see what was going on. Hugs and kisses are always free, but when you make a million-dollar deal they're just a little bit sweeter.

Sam and Renny drove around town looking for the bank where the money was supposed to be. Once they spotted it, they got a room in a motel close by. After resting for awhile, they went through the plan again. Early in the morning hours, Sam had Renny drive him up to the backside of the mansion, just as Martha had shown him. They parked, and Sam pulled out the duplicate ID and gave it to Renny. "You know what to do now?"

"Yes, for the hundredth time, I know what to do."

"Okay, don't let me down, get the money and be here by ten. If anything goes wrong, and I don't make it, the other five million in the bank is yours."

"Everything is going to work, Sam."

Sam climbed out, and watched as Renny drove off. He took in a deep breath, and said, "Lord, help me!"

As he made his way around to the backside of the mansion, Sam counted at least ten men walking at different posts. His mind was racing for ways to get inside, wishing he had paid a lot more attention when he was a kid watching MacGyver on TV—that guy was a pro at this kind of stuff. Studying the layout was really no help, because he didn't know anything about the inside; no matter what, everything was a guessing game from here. There were several large trees spaced out along the back. He made his way slowly from one to the other, and was about midway when he spotted an open window. Surveying the area for a minute, Sam noted to himself that it looked almost too easy; the bushes should provide good coverage, but what if it was a set-up? Deciding to take his chances, he climbed up to the window; looking inside, he wasn't able to see much since the room was very dark. Carefully, he slid the screen out and slipped inside the window, putting the screen back into place. Using a lighter, he found the door and carefully opened it so he could see where it would lead him. It appeared to be a room right off the main entrance. He could see a light upstairs in one of the rooms, so he slipped off his boots, and quietly climbed the stairs, hoping nobody could hear his entrance. At the top of the stairs Sam heard voices, but they were hard to make out over the sound of his own heartbeat. His guess was that the balcony had a guard posted on it, so he slipped into the room next door.

Sam had just enough moonlight to see everything in the room. He sat close to the wall and pressed his ear up to it, but could still barely make out that somebody was talking. He tried to find a way to better hear what was going on in the other room. Sam started looking for a vent, or some other outlet that might lead into that room. While crawling on his hands and knees, he spotted a small beam of light under the bed; it led him to a vent that went from one room to the other. "Bingo, that's what I'm looking for," he said to himself. Now flat on his belly, he wiggled to get closer to the vent. Seeing feet, he was able to count at least four people sitting within his range of vision. The room was very quiet as he looked around at what little he could see from the vent.

When he heard somebody coming down the hall, he panicked. "My boots!" Stretching as far as he could, he pulled the boots under the bed. The door opened, and then slammed shut in the next room. "Well, well, just how are all my little pigeons doing today?"

Frank's was the first voice Sam recognized. "We need something to eat and drink."

"Why should I waste money and time to feed the dead?"

"You low-down dirty bastard."

Sam knew that voice; it was Cyndi's. She never held back when she was mad, but what was she doing here?

Molly never seemed to change. "Cyndi, don't fuss with this man, he is beyond human understanding."

Joe spoke up, "And that's what is going to get him killed."

Phillip was laughing. "Oh, don't worry, I sent out for some pizza. I am not going to starve you to death. I don't have that much time."

Frank responded, "You better believe you don't. You may think you have gotten this all worked out, but I am telling you, Phillip, it's not going to end as you think it is. Sam is not going to just waltz in here and give himself up without a fight. By now, he knows it was all a scam. Frank Jr. and David have both made it back by now; he knows we were supposed to be the bad guys. When he comes now it will be for revenge. Whether we live or die will not have anything to do with your faith. You wanted him so bad; well, you're going to get him, and a whole lot more."

"Shut up, before I shut you up."

"What's the matter, Phillip, does the truth scare you?" Sam heard a smack, and then Frank's laughter.

The door slammed again. Sam heard Phillip go down the stairs. He needed to get into that room. It was so quiet he could almost hear a pin drop. Sam whispered, "Sis, Sis! Can you hear me?"

Frank heard him. "Sam, is that you?"

"Yes. Is Cyndi alright?"

"Yes." Everyone started talking. "Quiet, I can't hear." Frank pushed the chair back to the wall. "Sam please don't tell me you're here all alone."

"Yes, I am, but the cavalry is on its way."

"Thank God. At least stay hidden until they arrive; surely you know what they want by now."

"Yeah, I've figured out most of it. But what is Cyndi doing here?"

"She came trying to find information, and she ran into John Jr., and he brought her here not knowing what was happening. Sam, I'm sorry."

"Tell her not to worry. Her big brother is on his way with help. You all try to relax; I'll try to figure out a way to get in there."

"Be careful, Sam."

The crew from the Broken R had just landed, and was trying to get themselves organized. Ronnie met John from the Bar S, and Mike was in the office with the pilot. Jack handed Mike the message from Sam, and after reading it, he took the message to John and asked, "Do you know where this place is?"

"Sure do. Can't be more than a couple of miles from the south gate of the ranch; better get moving, though, if we're going to get there by ten. Ronnie, do you still want us to go in on horseback?"

"Yes, the more the merrier."

John called the foreman at the Bar S. "Round up another twenty horses and have them saddled and ready to ride. Tell the others we will all meet them at the south gate."

"Okay, Boss, I'm on it," the foreman said.

A shuttle bus from the airport pulled up. Jack walked out and told Mike, "I could tell something was wrong, so I took it upon myself to call for the bus. You folks look like you're in a hurry."

The driver stepped out. "Who's driving?"

Ronnie took the keys. "Come on, we've got to get going."

They all loaded onto the bus. Jack told them, "You go on ahead and I will see the other fellow gets back to the main terminal."

"Thanks, Jack." Ronnie closed the door and popped the clutch at the same time. "Okay, John, I know it's by the Bar S so just tell me when we need to turn." Looking at his watch, Ronnie figured they should be able to make it by ten.

At five in the morning Becky was so excited she could not possibly go back to sleep. After two showers and a pot of fresh-brewed coffee, she was ready to do a dance down Wall Street. For once in her life, it appeared that things were starting to work out for her. Since her husband had died in that car wreck almost two years ago, she had barely been able to make a living selling real estate, and the life insurance money that he had left her was just about gone.

Bill had set Becky up in Simplicity; the only problem was, it would be years before she would see any type of profit from it. Becky vowed to herself though that if and when this deal was completed, she was going to get her children started early. She had already completed all of the paperwork, and all she had to do now was change the name of the agent for Simplicity. She would be at the courthouse as soon as it opened to record the sale of the mansion, leaving her enough time to drive to the estate to meet Sam at 10 a.m.

Renny awoke to the phone ringing in his ear. "Hello?"

"Sir, this is your 7 a.m. wake-up call."

"Okay!" Not being a morning person, Renny dragged himself out of bed and into the shower. A good hot shower always seemed to do the trick. By the time he was done, he felt good enough to whistle a tune while getting dressed. "I have to be at the bank when the doors open, make the transaction, and meet Sam at the mansion by 10 a.m.," he thought. Renny ran the plan through his head one last time, and subconsciously heard "Don't let me down" in the back recesses of his mind.

Looking in the mirror at his new Western-style clothing, he wondered if that was why his thoughts sounded like a new country hit in the making when he put the words to music: "Don't let me down, don't let me down baby, that's right nothing could get me down today." Renny packed the few things he had with him, and headed out for a good, hot breakfast.

Sam was still trying to figure out how to get into the room next door where everybody was being held. He was just as confused as before about what was going on, but didn't have time to think about it now. Cyndi was in there, and by God he couldn't let anything happen to her. Ever since they were little, his dad had always drilled into him and Mike that they had better look out for their little sister. After trying everything else, he figured the balcony was the only way he was going to make it into that room.

Out in the hallway, he could hear Phillip barking out orders from the foot of the stairs. Crawling along the wall as fast as he could, Sam made it to the door leading out to the balcony. After making a quick survey of the area he figured the time to act was now or never, so he jumped from one balcony to the other and slipped inside the door, holding his finger to his lips to keep everybody quiet. Standing in the room unsuccessfully trying to control his breathing, he made it over to Cyndi, gave her a hug, and whispered in her ear, "You hang on."

After searching the room to see if the key to the handcuffs were there, and not having any luck, he looked at Frank's watch; it was 9:45 a.m., and he knew he didn't have much time left. Unfortunately, at that moment the door flew open. Sam jumped, but he had nowhere to run. Phillip stood there pointing a gun directly at him, and said, "Just stop right there."

Cyndi burst into tears; she just wasn't able to control herself, and she started crying hysterically. Molly bowed her head as if to pray; Joe was fighting with the handcuffs in a last-ditch effort to try and save Sam, and Frank tried to plead with Phillip. "Please, don't do it!"

At the front gate, Becky undid the chain that held the gates locked, still humming a victory tune to herself. She noticed all of the horses coming, and thought, "Huh, there must be a parade going on!" Driving into the driveway and parking her car close to the front door, she checked to make sure she had the keys to the front door and glanced over the paperwork one last time, before stuffing it back into a big brown envelope with the name "Simplicity" on it. After hearing a war cry that scared her so badly she dropped the envelope, Becky turned to see that all of a sudden horses were everywhere. Riders with guns surrounded the mansion, with their guns drawn and ready for a fight.

"My God, what is happening?"

Up in the room, Sam and Phillip were having a stare-down. Hearing the ruckus outside put Phillip in a state of panic. He cocked the hammer back and pointed the gun at Sam. A gunshot rang out, knocking Phillip backwards.

A voice almost as loud as the gunshot came from the balcony. "Drop the gun or I'll finish you off right where you stand. Get the gun, Bean Head!"

Sam ran across the room, reaching Phillip just as he was dropping to his knees and grabbing the gun from him. Phillip passed out, falling face-first onto the hardwood floor. Sam raced to find the key for the handcuffs, in order to free everybody. He knew that others were probably on their way up to the room to check out what caused all the commotion. Ronnie kicked the doors open, and he and four other men entered the room waving their rifles. Ronnie said, "The cavalry has arrived."

Sam told one of the men, "I'm okay. Let everyone else know that I'm fine, and then help gather up the other trash." Sam threw Ronnie the key. "Ronnie, help them."

While Ronnie was undoing the cuffs, Sam pulled out the billfold with the fake ID for "Mr. Tim" and slipped it into Phillip's pocket before taking his true ID back and checking to make sure it was his. "There's your switch, you son of a bitch," he said. Cyndi grabbed him, stopping him short.

Frank, Joe, and Molly were all free now, and tried to say they were sorry for all that had happened and make their peace with Sam.

Sam just said, "Not now, we'll have plenty of time to talk later. Get them out of here, Ronnie." Pushing his way through the door, he ran to collect his boots.

Becky was in total shock, and had called the police. When Sam walked out the front door the sheriff was just pulling up.

Tara raced over to Sam, giving him a bear hug, "Are you all right?"

"I think so, but we're not out of the woods yet."

Becky, getting her nerve up, stepped from the car holding the papers in her hand. The sheriff was asking everyone, "Just who owns this place? Who's in charge?"

Sam thought to himself, "Come on, Renny, I need that check." Looking back, Sam saw Renny climbing over the brick wall. Renny ran while Sam waved at him to come on. Just as the sheriff made it to Sam, Renny reached out and handed him the check. Sam handed the check to Becky.

The sheriff said, "For the last damn time, who owns this place?"

Becky handed Sam the envelope, and said, "He does."

"Well, sir, do you want to explain this?"

"The company just bought this place and we were here to celebrate the purchase. We caught these people in the place, and there is one man upstairs who has been shot."

The sheriff called for a paddy wagon and an ambulance.

Upstairs, Molly had Phillip's shoulder wrapped, trying to stop the bleeding. She had given him some of those magic sleeping pills as well.

The sheriff checked his ID and said, "My God, do you all know who this is?"

"No, sir!"

"This is the fellow every cop in New York has been looking for. He is wanted for murdering a fellow right up the road here."

Sam knew that was supposed to be him. The ambulance came and they loaded up Phillip. The remaining men had an escort to jail. Once they were gone, when things began settling down, Renny walked over to Sam. "Man, I'm really sorry I was late!"

Sam thought to himself, "Then who was that on the balcony, and who shot Phillip?"

Chapter 14
Reunion at the Bar S

Even suffering from a lack of sleep, Sam couldn't help but notice the beauty of the scene before him. The old mansion looked good in the daylight, and with all the riders coming and going it was a sight only a true cowboy could appreciate. Taking his hat off and trying to dust himself off, he thought, "It is going to take some major cleaning up to get the place back into working order."

The last of the police finally pulled out around late afternoon. Breaking the silence, Becky said, "Samuel, I think it's been a day to remember, but I've got to get back to town and pick up my children. If there is anything else I can do to assist you, please feel free to give me a call."

Shaking her hand, he said, "I believe you did a fine job, Miss Becky. I hope the next time we meet it will be under better circumstances."

"Thank you. Me too," Becky said, then got in her car and drove off heading toward town. Even with all she had just witnessed, things couldn't have looked any better for her. Just glancing over at that five-million-dollar cashier's check brought a huge smile to her face; she knew deals like this came along only once in a lifetime.

John and Ronnie were doing a last sweep through the mansion, making sure there were no more hidden surprises. Mike was with Molly, and Cyndi found Sam and Tara walking around trying to put things back in some kind of order. When Mike caught up with Sam he asked, "Hey, Sam, how are you doing?"

Sam reached out as if to shake hands, but grabbed Mike instead, pulling him tight and giving him a bear hug. "I'm fine, and it's damn good to see you."

Tara was amazed at the change she was seeing in Sam; he seemed to be so much happier, and it appeared that he had found a new lease on life. Sam hugged Cyndi and Molly as though they had just returned from a long journey.

"I think we need to gather everybody up and head for home. You guys have got to be exhausted," Tara observed, and Mike agreed.

"Come on you three," Mike said, and they walked together just like the Three Musketeers, hugging and holding each other up.

Back in front of the mansion, Renny had brought the SUV around, and John and Ronnie were enjoying a smoke break. Seeing Sam, they hollered at Frank and Joe, "Here he is."

John asked Sam, "Are you ready to give it up and head over to the ranch, get something to eat and rest up?"

Sam didn't even know what he was talking about, but agreed with him anyway. John mounted up and hollered out, "Let's go home, men!"

Renny loaded up the SUV with Frank, Joe, Molly, and Cyndi. Ronnie and Haley rode up leading two horses. Haley told Sam, "Come on, cowboy—let's go for a ride."

Sam and Tara mounted up, letting every one else get out the gate, and then they relocked the front gates before leaving. On the way back to the Bar S, Sam could see the motel sign once they turned off the main road, and thought about how close he had been to help without knowing it was even there. When they came to the south gate of the ranch, it was a free-for-all ride across 100 acres of the finest-looking pasture one would ever see. The riders took the horses as Ronnie offered to show Sam and Tara to the main house.

For the next few hours, everyone enjoyed one of the largest cook-outs the Bar S had ever seen. Frank was trying to talk with Sam about the events that had taken place, but Sam would not discuss anything about the day on this night. Sam told him, "You go rest; I know enough to keep me happy for tonight. Tell Joe and Molly that we will all meet tomorrow before we all go home."

Frank walked away feeling a little better, and thought, "At least he said, 'before we all go home.'"

Sam and Tara ate their fill and visited with everyone they could. Later, while standing with John on the second-story deck overlooking the ranch, John asked Sam, "What do you think of the Bar S?"

"It's a great place you have here."

John shook his head. "You still haven't put it all together yet, have you?"

"Well, I guess not, since you put it that way."

"Where do you think the name 'Bar S' came from?"

Sam remembered reading in his dad's journal a list of ranches that Simplicity owned. "Well, probably from my dad."

"Sure enough, but the S came from 'Sam.' I know she doesn't compare to the Broken R, but she matched her dollar for dollar last year. Therefore, you, Sam, have a great place here."

"Me? Wow! Tomorrow we will have to take the grand tour, but for now I need to sleep for a spell."

John showed Sam and Tara to the master bedroom. "All right then, you two, rest up and I will see you in the morning."

The next day came with a touch of fall air, which made sleeping in easy. Sam might have slept even later if Tara had not woken him. "Come on, it's almost noon!" she said. "We have got things to do; you can't just sleep all day."

She led him to the shower. "Okay, I'm awake," he said.

They met everyone downstairs afterwards. Everybody seemed to be in good spirits, considering all that they had been through. John pointed the way to the kitchen and said, "Help yourself, boss! Jack is in there—he can whip you up some breakfast."

"Thanks."

Sam and Tara both walked into the kitchen. Jack was like a different person than the man they had met at the airport. Happier at what he was doing, Jack told the two, "Come on in here, and make yourselves comfortable." While talking with them, he poured the coffee at the same time. The kitchen was obviously set up for a working ranch, with two large picnic tables and the types of grills used for cooking larger meals. "You folks ready for one of old Jack's famous omelets?"

Sam, with a big smile, said, "Sure, give us the house's special." They ate and visited with Jack. Outside of a couple of hands who came through for coffee, but there were no other interruptions. Tara finished eating and dismissed herself to get things ready for the trip home.

Sam was sitting and enjoying the quiet of the moment. He knew he had to get with the program. He needed to settle some issues before he could leave. He hollered out to John. When John walked in Sam asked, "How long have you been running this place?"

"Over ten years now, but I worked it for five years before Simplicity bought it."

"Good, you know her well then."

"Yep, every square inch of her."

"All right, then, I want to take that grand tour you promised me before I leave. But first you need to find Frank, Joe, and Molly. We need to have a sit-down, and then I will be ready."

"Do you want me in this sit-down that you're planning?"

"Sure, if you don't mind. I might need to have a referee!"

John laughed and left to round up the other three. When John returned he told Sam, "Everybody is ready and waiting in the den." On their way to the den, John told Sam, "There is a bit of a problem with who is attending this meeting." When they got to the den there was Frank and Frank Jr., Joe and David, Molly and Mary, and Mike and Cyndi. John asked, "Do you still want me to stay?"

"Yes, and tell Jack to bring some coffee in here. I think this is going to be a two-pot meeting." Sam took charge without even thinking about it. "Now look, people, I know some of you do not like the idea of my being in charge of things; in fact, I am not sure that I like it myself. After all that has happened, either we will leave this room as family and friends, or we will part company as enemies. If I have learned anything from this whole ordeal, it is that we have enough enemies. When Dad used to tell me stories about his life, I did not always grasp the morals of them, but there's nothing like facing a Colt 45 and knowing you could die in the next few seconds to add new meaning to life or death. Now, I said all that so I could tell you where I stand, and then each of you can tell me where you stand. My place, as I see it, is to fill my dad's boots and take over his part of running the show—and thanks to Dad, he left me with help. Mike knows more than I will probably ever know about running Simplicity; therefore, anything to do with the business from now on, including myself, has to go through him—no ifs, ands, or buts."

Haley and Tara stuck their heads in. "Sorry, Jack sent us with the coffee."

"Come on in. Everyone help yourselves."

John slipped in, asking, "How is the meeting going? I heard almost everything from the door."

Sam sipped his coffee and lit a cigarette. "So far, so good. We'll give everyone a minute, then we will get started again. Where is Ronnie? We've gotten everyone else in here—why isn't he here?"

John said, "I will be right back, I think I saw him ride up just a few minutes ago." John ran to the back deck to look; sure enough, Ronnie was with some of the other

Bar S cowboys. "Hey, Ronnie, you're needed in the den. You need to get in here."

Ronnie said his goodbyes, then came over and said, "What's the problem?"

"They're having a meeting, and Sam just asked where you were."

"He wants me to be there?"

"That's what he said." John and Ronnie slipped back in just as Sam was calling the meeting back to order.

"Okay, since you all have other things you would like to be doing, and I do as well, we shall continue. Mike, would you like to say anything, since I started with you?"

"Not really, you're doing fine. Go ahead."

"Does anyone have a problem with Mike that they need to address?" No hand went up, but Sam saw Mary's face light up with a smile as though she wanted to say something. Since she refrained from it, Sam moved on. "Now for the Broken R. For her concerns and her needs, and to ensure her continued success, Ronnie will be in charge. Any business to take place on the ranch will go through him. Whatever he sees as fit will stand unquestioned. Does anybody have a problem with this?" Once again, nobody objected. "Anybody want to clarify anything concerning this with me or Ronnie?" Nobody had any comments or complaints.

"Now there's a matter between Frank, Joe, Molly, and me. I ask you three, because it does not matter to me, are you all comfortable talking in front of everyone else?" They agreed it would be OK. "Good, because this is a serious matter to be handled, and I think if we get it out in the open it will be easier to deal with."

Frank stood up and said, "Sam we talked about this before we came in here, and I'm going to speak on behalf of the three of us; then, if there is anything I have left out, or if there are any more questions, we will go from there." Frank looked deep into Sam's eyes while talking to him. "We know that somehow you found out a lot about our past, which is not important at this point, but you knew things that took us all the way back to when we first met your dad. That made us just as suspicious of you as you were of us, because you just came back into the family as though nothing had ever happened.

"We had been approached by Phillip approximately six months before your father's passing. Not wanting to upset him by bringing his past back to haunt him in his last days, we decided to try and handle things on our own, to save him the pain of facing a war with Phillip. The money we took was to try and buy peace between your dad and the organization Phillip represented, even though we knew there was no way we could come up with fifty-four million dollars. We figured that maybe we could persuade them to take payments of ten million a year. However, knowing what we did about how they tried brainwashing children years ago, we should have known it would never have worked. Phillip was totally controlled, even in his adult years; there was no rhyme or reason to him, or logic. They trained Phillip to take your place, and he was so obsessed with the idea that nothing short of what happened today was going to stop him. In addition, he would use anybody, as you know, in order to get to you. In the end, he knew we would cave in on him, and that is how we all ended up prisoners here when you found us. Now I have to ask you, do you want me to explain who Phillip is to everyone, or should I stop?"

Sam paused for just a second, putting everything together in his mind, before answering. Jack knocked on the door, interrupting his thoughts. "Hey, sorry to interrupt you, but turn on the TV; I think you might want to see this."

John pulled the TV remote out of a drawer and clicked it on. On the screen was a newswoman telling about the incident that had taken place at the mansion. She reported that Tim had died while in surgery, and that the other men in custody were being held pending further questioning.

Sam said to John, "Turn the TV off. I think we have seen enough. Frank, I think you have explained your actions well. Molly and Joe, do you have anything that you would like to say, or add to what Frank has stated?" They both agreed Frank had explained everything well. "Okay, I think some things are better left unsaid, and the less that is said about Phillip from here on out the better we all will be. However, from now on nobody in this room stands alone or tries to handle their problems on their own. We are a family baptized in blood. Whoever fired the shot that took Phillip's life saved my life, and others in this room. We are all, now and forever, indebted to you. I do not know who did it, and I do not want to know. Therefore, if you do know, you must carry your secret to the grave with you. Frank and Joe, I want you to find out as much as you can about this organization; we cannot afford not to keep our guard up. To all of you, if you are going to travel, try not to travel alone. Make sure somebody knows what your plans are before you leave, because you can rest assured these people are not just going to give up. We gave them a big whipping this time, but we have to prepare for future attacks, and if my guess is correct, there will be others! One final thing that I need to explain before we cut out of here: the mansion that I purchased yesterday was by request of our dad. He was in the process of buying it before he passed away. His wishes were to build an orphanage and school on the place. Frank, Joe, and Molly, I think you will be happy to know that regarding the money you were going to use as a payoff, half of it paid for the mansion, and the other half will go to run the place. In addition, if there are no objections, then Frank, Joe, and Molly will oversee the running of the mansion. Because this was a request from our father, Mike, Ronnie, Haley, Cyndi, and me will see to the financing aspects of building the orphanage and school. The rest of you may be asked later to help with other things as we need help. Are there any questions, or anything that needs to be brought up that I have missed?"

Mary pushed Mike on the shoulder and whispered, "I think this would be a really good time for our announcement."

Mike stood up rather slowly. Sam waited for him to speak, but it seemed as though Mike didn't know how to get started. So Sam jumped in and said, "Mike, why don't you and Mary come on up to the front here." As they walked to the front Sam said, "I think my brother has something he would like to share with all of you, at this time, and then we will end this meeting once he is done. Take it away, big brother."

Mike, holding Mary's hand, announced: "Mary and I would like to invite you all to attend our wedding. We have decided that we are going to be married on the fifteenth of next month, and the ceremony will take place on the Broken R."

The room broke out in cheers and tears. Poor Molly was beside herself. Mary was her only child and it was hard to tell if her tears were of joy or sorrow. Finally, she made it to the front, hugged them both and whispered to them, "May God bless you both, and just know you have my blessings as well. I know that if Wild Bill were here today, he would be standing tall at this moment with his blessings also."

Mike couldn't say anything to top that so, very gracefully, he just said, "Thank you."

As everyone was leaving, they voiced their congratulations to Mary and Mike. John's eyes were tearing up, so Ronnie asked, "John, would you like to go for a ride with me and Sam?"

Haley, crying, made her way up to Mike and Mary, and gave Mary a hug. Then she hugged Mike and whispered to him, "Way to go, brother, you did well."

Mike was fighting hard now to maintain his own emotions as he said, "Thank you, little sis. I think Mary has something she wanted to ask you."

"What?"

"I want you to be my bridesmaid." They hugged again, both crying.

Mike used the moment to make his escape to the men's room. Once he had regained his own composure, he returned and told Mary and Haley, "Ladies, I think I am going to join the others for a quick ride."

After everyone returned from the grand tour of the ranch, they saw that once again the girls had outdone themselves in the kitchen. The feedbag was on, and everyone was good and hungry.

John spoke up and ordered silence, "We here at the Bar S have been pretty relaxed about our praying, but having you all here has made me realize just how much we all have to be thankful for, so please bow your heads and let us give our thanks back to who is really in charge. 'Our Father in heaven, we bow before you knowing that all good things have come from you. We stop to give thanks for your protection, and may your hand guide each and every one of us to do our best. That we may always be known as your children, we ask for your blessing upon the food we are about to partake of and the hands that prepared it. For it is in the name of our Savior Jesus we ask these things. Amen.'"

Everybody sounded out with, "Amen."

They all joined in eating and fellowship long into the night. The next day they knew they would part ways, but would be forever bound to each other from the experiences they had shared.

Chapter 15
Back on the Broken R

With relationships mended and new friends made, the gang was ready to head home, if only for a short time. Sam knew he was going to miss the Bar S, but he missed the Broken R just as much, if not more. He could hardly wait to see Samson; he missed riding and talking with him. Sam had become so attached to Samson that he thought of him just like one of his own kids. Sam was planning to go riding with Brad shortly after returning home, so he could bring him up to speed on the things that had taken place while everyone was away. Sam took some time to catch up on his notes in his journal, and he read a little more of his dad's journal on the flight home. Somehow, in his mind, it made him feel just a little closer to his dad.

Sam could remember his dad telling him how lonely his life had been in his early years. Now he was able to understand just why his dad pushed himself so hard, trying to have a close family, and keeping everyone he cared for close by and all working together in harmony: because when you get to the end of your road, and death comes upon you, you don't want to leave this world alone.

The plane jerked suddenly, causing Sam to drop the journal on the floor, and snapping his mind out of his deep thoughts and back to the present. The turbulence didn't seem to bother Tara, so she continued to sleep right through it. Needing a break from the silence, he slipped up to the cockpit to talk with Renny. They hadn't had much time to talk, with everything else going on.

"Hey, Boss, what's happening?"

"Just thought you might like some company for awhile. It's pretty quiet back there right now."

"I'm glad you came up; it's always better if you have someone to talk with. Besides, there is something I needed to share with you, but I wanted to wait until the right time."

"What's on your mind?" Sam asked.

"Well, you know how crazy things got that day?"

"Yeah, it was crazy, all right."

"Well, when I was running from the truck, just as I got past the wall I saw someone drop something from a window into the bushes. I was in such a hurry that I didn't think much about it at the time. However, after things had calmed down later I went back. Somebody had dropped a briefcase into the bushes. There it is," he said, pointing to the briefcase behind the seat. "I do not have any clue as to what it contains, nor what the combination might be, but I figured whatever is in it, the contents belonged to you since it was on your property."

"Well, maybe so. But what if it's a bomb?" Sam asked.

"Holy sh . . . I didn't even think about that! But now that you've said it, don't try to open the thing here."

"It's pretty heavy. Let's just sit this baby back here until we get home."

"Good idea; we're only about an hour away," Renny said, then added,

"What about our deal? I know I was a little late getting the check to the mansion, but those people at the bank were just slow."

"You don't have to let that worry you. As far as I'm concerned, we did it! When we get home, I will have Mike transfer the money into your account. You know, even as a vested member of Simplicity, I want you to stay on with us."

"Sure, Boss, I'm not going anywhere. If I do, it will only be as a request to take a couple of weeks off and go home for a visit, but I'm content and enjoy my job working here, so just because I'm a vested member doesn't mean you'll get rid of me that easily."

"Good. Well, I guess I had best head back and check on Tara, while you prepare to take this bird down."

"Okay, Boss. See you on the ground."

Sam made his way back to his seat to find Tara already awake. "Where have you been?" she asked.

"I've been sitting up front talking with Renny."

"Oh! You really are a big shot, sitting up front with the pilot."

"Girl, don't you get smart with me! I'll tell you just what I told him for calling me a big shot."

"What was that?"

"I told him that as far as I was concerned, he was the big shot. After all, he was the one flying the plane."

Tara laughed. "Well at least you're developing a good sense of humor. Are we getting close?"

"Yeah, we shouldn't be more than twenty minutes away now."

Renny made the announcement over the intercom system. "We'll be starting our descent into Little Rock in approximately ten minutes; please make sure that everyone is seated, and buckled up."

After the plane landed, everybody exited the aircraft. As everybody else made their way to the bus, Renny ran into the office to sign off on his paperwork to complete the trip, and once that was done he rushed outside, hoping to catch himself a ride out to the ranch as well. Seeing the last few people were fixing to board, he hollered, "Hey, wait for me!"

Carrying the briefcase, he approached Sam. Renny reached out and handed it to Sam, saying, "I think you forgot something."

"Thanks, I think you're right. Are you coming out to the ranch?"

"Yes I will, if you don't mind."

"Mind? Of course not—jump on in. Actually, I am getting rather excited about being home. Besides, I think it's too damn hot to stand out here all day."

They both entered the bus just as Ronnie had turned the engine over. Reaching to turn the AC on, he told Sam, "Let's give her a few minutes to get cooled down, and then we will be on our way."

Everybody was excited about being home, and chit-chatted back and forth about all of the things that they needed to do now that they were back. Wanting to share in the excitement of being home, Sam tried to relax, clear his mind, and not dwell on the ordeal that he had been through. Not having any success at that, he laid back in his seat, closed his eyes, and allowed himself to drift off in thought. Pulling a photo from the recesses of his mind, he was able to see much more clearly just why his father was able to appreciate the simpler things in life so much. Knowing the years of hardship that he had suffered had done to him the opposite of the intended results. Instead of giving up on life and following a chosen path dictated by someone else, he had learned to treasure every moment of life that was simple and pure, without the hardship and despair.

Still deep in thought, Sam thought about questions that his father had asked him many years ago: "If you took the financial hardship out of life, what would you choose to do with your life, and what would be the most important thing in your life?" He tried to remember his answers, and realized his father was correct when he summed it all up with, "Most people lie to themselves, and embellish that lie with excuses as to why they cannot do what they want. They have lied to themselves for so long it just becomes a habit; instead of doing something to change their ways, they just continue on a path of self-destruction, making the same mistakes repeatedly. Leaving everything to faith for anything to change, some people do get lucky, but because of that they cannot see they also need to change. With 'luck,' it usually does not take long before they are right back where they started."

In his mind, still riding across the ranch enjoying the fresh air, Sam saw the answer to it all: "Whatever is most important to you at this time, that is what you will do." That is how humans think. It's just like the way Sam was daydreaming of doing just what he wanted; it was such a deep train of thought that it was as real to him as if he were there. Sam opened his eyes to the sound of everyone talking; coming back to reality, he wondered just how long he had been gone with his thoughts. Looking about with wide eyes and scanning his surroundings for a clue, he saw the front gates of the Broken R. With a new lease on life, a new sense of purpose, and excitement in his voice, he hollered, "I'm home, I'm finally home!"

It was not very long before everyone started going their own separate ways, hurrying to get their lives back to normal. Ronnie, looking like he was born in a saddle, had called ahead to have Stan get his horse saddled up and ready to ride. Within minutes, he had mounted his horse and told Sam, "I'll see you later," and rode off across the land toward his own home at the ranch.

Sam watched as Ronnie rode off over the hills, while Tara tugged at him and said, "Come on, and let's go inside ourselves."

Still holding the briefcase, Sam walked with Tara and Renny to the house, and everybody else went their own way, happy to be home.

"What do you think, Tara, does it feel like home to you?"

"Nothing ever looked better, and we are all here, so what else could you call it?"

Renny butted in: "It's been awhile since I've seen her, but the Broken R just has that way of making you feel secure, and always at home."

"Come on, let's get things in order, and then we'll go for a ride," Tara said.

"That sounds like music to my ears. I'm ready," Sam agreed.

"Do you want to go with us, Renny?"

"Sure."

"When we're done riding, we can all stop off in town, and I'll buy dinner for us all."

"Great!"

Sam slipped off into the study, and placed the briefcase, along with the journals, into the secret room. Once he left the room, he took a few minutes to wash up and then decided he was ready to go. As the three of them left the house and headed to the barn, they all looked like school kids running a race to see just who would get there first. Stan helped them all to get their horses saddled up, and then as they were riding off, he hollered out, "Y'all have a good time!"

They rode for most of the afternoon, then stopped over in town for dinner. Rick, Brad, and their families all met them at the diner. Sam sat proudly with his family and friends, enjoying every minute, laughing and rehashing the experiences they had gone through in New York.

Brad was very disappointed he had missed all of the action. He told Rick, "If there is ever to be a next time, I am going, and you will have to stay home."

Rick agreed, "If there are any more adventures, then yeah, Brad should be the one to go."

Sam, of course, silently hoped that they would have many more days like these to come, but with less "adventures," as his sons had called them.

The next weeks did bring more peace and quiet for the family. Sam had sent Rick and Brad to Montana to put the family affairs in order. Sam brought Kelsey into Simplicity, since he had been a good friend. Since Kelsey was renting and had a family to support, and as a token of gratitude for the help he'd provided in Sam's time of need, plus the friendship he had given without question,

Sam paid off his home in Montana, and then signed it over to Kelsey.

There wasn't much else going on, so Sam was free to ride and do pretty much as he pleased. Frank and Joe were making arrangements to move to New York; Molly, of course, wouldn't join them until after the wedding. Frank Jr. and David both had requested a transfer of employment to the Bar S. That way, they could be closer to their own families. Ronnie processed the paperwork, hating to let them go. He had watched both Frank Jr. and David grow up on the Broken R, from little kids to young men, and it broke his heart to have to say goodbye to them. But he understood their reasons, so he wished them the best and told them not to be strangers.

He called John at the Bar S to make the final arrangements for the transfer, and told him, "You make sure and take good care of them two men."

Cyndi and Haley were busy little beavers, helping Mary plan the wedding of the century, and Mike, as usual, was always busy with the new computer system, working long hours trying to get all the bugs worked out of it and get it functioning properly before his wedding day. Tara was getting acquainted with the Broken R. She had met most of the permanent residents in town; Sally, who ran the day-care center, had become a pretty good friend, and Tara spent a lot of her time at the center helping out since Ben, Sara, and Billy were there three days a week.

Patty and Donna were settling into the swing of things. In their free time they would work in the communications center with Mike, trying to learn everything. Sam felt a little lost, but realized there were still a lot of unanswered questions. However, he had chosen to seek these answers on his own. Once again, Sam found himself reading the journal over again, still looking for clues about the ring of power.

Getting up to leave the secret room, he accidentally knocked over the briefcase that Renny had found in the bushes. "Damn, I had nearly forgotten about this thing." Finding a screwdriver, he broke the locks and slowly opened the briefcase, praying that it was not a bomb or booby-trapped. "Whoa, what is all this?"

The briefcase contained a billfold with Phillip's driver's license, credit cards, and $1,000 in cash. Besides the billfold, there were tickets for a flight to Germany.

Sam said, "It looks like Phillip had a get-away plan."

There were also three packages wrapped in brown paper in the bottom of the briefcase. Tearing open one corner of the first package, Sam found five hundred cash bonds worth $5,000 each. He calculated that if each package contained the same amount, that would make the contents worth $7.5 million, give or take a few dollars. "God almighty help us! This has definitely got trouble written all over it." Sam went ahead and checked the other packages to see if he was right; sure enough, all three packages were just as he figured. Putting them back into the briefcase, he closed the lid and slid the case back under the desk.

"I wonder who threw this out the window? It couldn't have been Phillip. I had better call John." He picked up the phone, dialed the number and waited for John to answer.

"Hey, Sam, how's it going?" replied John.

"All is good, John, but I thought I had better give you a heads-up. Is Frank still staying there?"

"Yeah, he said he probably would be moved over to the mansion by the middle of next week."

"Well, tell him for me that he will need to keep extra tight security on the place."

"Why? Are we expecting more trouble?"

"Well, let me put it this way: there was a package found in the bushes, and I just got around to looking at its contents. I believe somebody might be very interested in finding it."

"Is that right?"

"Well, as far as I know, everyone they picked up is still in jail, but I'll tell Frank. Oh, by the way, tell Ronnie his two boys are doing just fine."

"Will do, and if I find anything else out I'll keep you up to date."

"Okay then, talk at you later. Bye!" Sam hung up the phone and then left the secret room.

Sam thought, "This can't be good; it looks like Phillip must have been involved with somebody else, and he was so sure he was going to take me out that he must have taken them out first. My God, these people must be crazy!" Walking out the front door, he lit a cigarette and was halfway to the barn before he stopped himself from doing something crazy. Scolding himself for allowing his thoughts to get the best of him, he convinced himself not to look for just the bad. They would just have to face whatever came their way—but he wasn't going to fret over what he couldn't see.

Regrouping his thoughts, he saw Ronnie. Riding up, Ronnie asked, "Is everything okay?"

"Yeah."

"You don't sound so sure to me."

"I've just got a lot on my mind."

"Got time for a ride? We could talk about it; besides, remember that surprise I told you about?"

"Well, I do now that you have brought it up."

"Come on, then, we'll go check it out."

Getting Samson saddled up, he asked Ronnie, "Where are we off to?"

"Up to my place, on the other side of the Broken R. You haven't seen it yet."

Sam mounted up. "That's right; I haven't been that far yet." Riding up over the hill, Sam asked, "What's the surprise all about?"

"It wouldn't be a surprise if I told you now, would it?"

"Okay, well, let me ask you something," Sam said, showing him the ring. "Do you remember when my dad started wearing this ring?"

"Yes, it was shortly after the original house was built. I bet you didn't know my place was the first home built on the Broken R."

"No, you're right, I didn't! So we are talking at least twenty-something years ago, or better."

"Sam, I know you're having a hard time trusting anybody with everything that has happened to you since coming home. I don't blame you; in fact, I would probably react just like you. But sooner or later you are going to have to learn to trust somebody. You said at the Bar S that we were family, and everything that had to do with running the Broken R was my responsibility."

"Sure I did, and that is the way it stands—even now."

"Okay, then, listen to me. I don't want to have to play guessing games. Between you and me, the only way the Broken R is going to make it is with you running the show. I am not sure myself exactly what the ring is all about, but I do know this: 'Whoever has the ring has her fate in his hands.' Now I can take care of running the ranch as it is, but her secrets now belong to you, just as they always belonged to your dad. So let's quit skipping around the problem, and get to working on them together."

"Sounds like a plan, Ronnie; what do you suggest we do?"

"Well, your dad always came up here and stayed while I was gone on trips; his personal mail still comes here."

Riding up to the house, Sam thought to himself, "This is more what I expected when I thought of the Broken R, before I had ever seen her. Just a plain simple log house with a matching barn—nothing fancy, but as pretty as a picture in a magazine."

They put the horses in the barn, and walked out the back door overlooking a paddock.

"Well, what you think of him?" Ronnie asked, pointing to the horse.

Walking closer, Sam could tell right off that the horse looked just like Samson. "Whoa, boy, come here and let me look at you."

"Could you tell he was Samson's?"

"Sure could, right when I saw him I thought he looked like his twin."

"Well he's yours. Still kind of jumpy under the saddle, but once he gets going he's fine."

"So this was the surprise?"

"Yeah, your dad had him pretty much ground broke, but all stock on the Broken R has to be two years old before anyone is allowed in the saddle. That is just the way it is, one of your dad's rules. The other rule is that it is time for Samson to go back to pasture with the mares."

Sam absently looked around. "Well, if those are the rules, I guess there is not a whole lot that I can say."

"If you are ready, we can do it together."

Leading the horse out to the front, Ronnie told Sam, "Hold Samson right here for just a minute." As soon as Ronnie pulled the first shoe, Samson started whinnying and throwing his head. "Hold him, Sam, we're almost done." When the last shoe came off, Samson started dancing. When they turned to walk away, Sam could see the mares coming in, and Ronnie ran to open the gate, hollering to Sam, "Take his halter off, and let him go."

When Sam slipped the halter off, Samson shot off like a bullet, racing to meet with the mares. Ronnie and Sam stood at the gate watching the horse strut his stuff. Just as they were about to leave they saw Samson stop and look back. It was as if he was saying "I'll see you later."

CHAPTER 16
BECOMING BROTHERS

As they walked back to the house, Sam couldn't help himself from turning and looking back, watching until Samson was clear out of sight.

"He knew the minute you started pulling off his shoes just where he was going, didn't he?"

"He sure did. Your dad has turned him loose every year around this time, so he could be with the mares. Hell, he probably knew on his way up here what was fixing to happen."

Sam looked at the house and studied it intensely. Ronnie broke the silence. "Come on, Sam, I want to show you something." Leading Sam to the back part of the house, he said, "This was your father's room." The only furniture in the room was a large cherry-wood bed, a matching dresser, and a large desk. "Now, I'm not sure just what we're looking for, but whatever it is, we start looking right here."

The two men started searching through everything, acting like detectives trying to uncover any type of clues to solve the mystery of what happened at the scene of the crime. Sam searched through the contents of the desk, and Ronnie started with the closet. After a short spell Ronnie asked Sam, "Are you having any luck finding anything?"

"Not really, I'm just about as lost as you are. I'm sure it would help if I knew what I was looking for, but unfortunately I don't. I guess I'm just hoping that when I do find it, I'll be able to recognize what I have found."

Sam found a bunch of odds and ends, but nothing that seemed to make any sense or offered any information pertaining to the ring. Ronnie had pulled a few shoeboxes out of the closet full of old papers, some dating back to the early 70s. However, like Sam, he was not finding anything helpful either. Nevertheless, time did seem to fly by, and Sam noticed the sun was setting on the backside of the house. He asked Ronnie, "Are you coming back down tonight?"

"No, I think I'll just keep looking for a while longer. Later, if I feel like it, I'll make a run over the back forty, and then I'll mosey on over to town and have a little supper."

"All right, sounds good; I guess I should head to the house. I'll meet you here in the morning, if you don't mind."

Ronnie walked outside with Sam and asked, "What are you going to name him?"

"You mean he doesn't have a name yet?"

"No, your dad said it was up to you to name him—of course, that is, if you stayed on at the ranch."

As they adjusted the saddle to fit, the horse hauled off and kicked Sam in the leg. "Damn Bean Head!" Sam limped around trying to walk off the pain from the blow.

Ronnie finished putting the bridle on the horse, laughing the whole time.

"What's so damn funny?" asked Sam.

"Bean Head! No matter what you name him now, he will always be a Bean Head."

Sam, realizing the humor in the situation, had to laugh himself.

After Ronnie was able to catch his breath, he told Sam, "When you mount him the first time, give him his head. Once he figures out where he is going, then slowly start taking over the lead, and giving him directions. You will both be just fine; two Bean Heads are better than one." Ronnie started chuckling once again.

As Sam mounted, he followed the horse's lead. After turning around three times, he finally came to a complete stop. Then Sam spoke to the horse, "All right, Bean Head, let's go home." He barely bumped his boots against the horse's flanks, and off they went. He waved back at Ronnie and hollered, "I'll see you in the morning."

"Okay, in the morning!"

The next morning Sam placed his dad's journal in the briefcase, and strapped the case on the back of the saddle. He turned and gave Tara a kiss. "Honey, I will be at Ronnie's if you need me."

"Okay. I think today I'll just hang out here at the house."

"All right. I'll see you later this afternoon. Maybe we'll go into Benton tonight, and catch a movie or something."

"You know what? That sounds like fun, and I'm going to hold you to that, mister."

"I'll see you in a bit," he said, waving as he rode off.

Sam had the feeling for some strange reason that he and Ronnie were just about to crack a great mystery.

Enjoying the ride over to Ronnie's, Sam talked to Bean Head for the entire ride. "Well, Bean Head, what are we going to name you? It seems we got off on the wrong foot, but you seem to be a little more sociable this morning."

The horse threw his head back as if he were agreeing with Sam.

"Well, your daddy is Samson, and the only other horse that's as strong as you are. What about Hercules; do you like that name?" Sam patted him on the neck, and when they reached the top of the hill he hollered out, "Let's see what you've got then, Hercules."

Taking off in a full gallop, Sam almost lost his hat. He let Hercules have the reins. Sam leaned to the left, and Hercules followed; when he leaned to the right, Hercules followed to the right. They were like two new dance partners learning each other's moves. "All right, boy; whoa!"

He gradually slowed back to a walk and snorted, blowing just a little bit. "I think we've got it down, big boy! You and I will be best friends, and if you do well, we might even get you a small herd of mares."

As they rode up to the house, Ronnie was on the front porch having a cup of coffee. "You two looked good coming across the flat lands there; pretty awesome sight."

Sam nodded. "Ronnie, I would like you to meet Hercules."

"Well, I'm honored to make your acquaintance, Hercules," said Ronnie.

Sam removed the briefcase, and then pulled the saddle and bridle off the horse.

"You think he's going to hang right here, and wait for you?" asked Ronnie.

"Well, you just watch this!" Sam started walking away, and he told Hercules, "Come on." Hercules turned and followed Sam to the paddock, just as if he knew what was expected. When they got to the gate, Hercules walked right in. When he turned around, Sam gave him a carrot. "Okay, boy, I'll see you in a little while."

When Sam returned to the porch, Ronnie was pouring him a cup of coffee. "That was all right; pretty amazing, for the two of you being together only one day. You are starting to show some of your dad's talents now—he sure liked working with the horses. Hell, you know that; look at Samson. Most of the time, it was like he was telling him what to do."

"I know, and that's just how I want him to be." Picking up the briefcase, Sam told Ronnie, "Grab my coffee, and come inside. I want to show you something. Once you look in here, brother, there will be no turning back! We have to be in this together all the way—good or bad."

"I hear you loud and clear all the way."

"Hand me that knife over there."

"Here you go," he said, passing it to Sam.

Popping the lock open was much easier for Sam the second time. Turning the case around where Ronnie could open it and see its contents, Sam said, "Here you go."

Ronnie opened the briefcase, looking it over without touching anything.

"Well, what's the matter?"

"Nothing, but I've got a bad feeling about this." He picked up one of the bundles and pulled back the paper. "Five-thousand-dollar bonds, how many are there?"

"Five hundred to a bundle," replied Sam.

"Holy smoke! That's over seven million!"

"Seven point five million dollars, to be exact."

"Well, what are you going do with it?"

"Oh no, it's not what am I going to do with it; it's what are *we* going to do with it."

"Okay, I'm with you. What are *we* going to do with the bonds?"

"Well, the first damn thing we're going to do is find a safe place for them."

Putting the bonds back into the briefcase, Ronnie saw the journal. "Hey, that's dad's journal!"

"Yeah, I brought it along to see if there were any clues I may have missed."

"Well, I can tell you this much: we have to be on the right track, because I've never seen that journal leave his room. It shocked me when I saw it; I thought it was still in here hiding somewhere."

"Well, then, let's put our thinking caps on and get busy."

"You know, Sam, last night I was thinking: it always seemed that when it got quiet at night, I could hear Dad in here late at night, and it sounded like he was moving the furniture around, but the next day everything was just like it is right now."

"That's it, then. Looking at the room, what would be the easiest thing to move?"

"Well, I thought the desk, but it doesn't move—it was built into that spot."

Sam was trying to place a picture in his head, and put his dad's words to it: "The best place to hide something is in plain sight."

"I think you might be onto something, Ronnie; here, start clearing the desk off."

Ronnie started stacking things into an empty box, and said, "Why would Dad keep so many outdated calendars? There has to be at least a dozen or more of them stacked on the desk."

Sam's mind was so deeply absorbed in other thoughts that he didn't hear Ronnie's question. However, Sam knew more about how things had been working with the secret room and the secret compartment on the plane.

"What are we looking for, Sam?"

With the desk cleaned off, there was nothing left but a nameplate with "Simplicity" on it, but the nameplate was not removable. "I think we are looking for a key lock, and with what you have told me it's on this desk somewhere. I can feel it in my bones."

"Come on, let's take a break and have another cup of coffee. Maybe if we study this a minute, we'll be able to come up with something."

Sam agreed, but kept his eyes on the desk. "It's here, I know it is."

Ronnie came back carrying the coffee. Handing Sam a cup, he said, "Damn, that's hot stuff." When he tried to set the cup down in a hurry, he accidentally spilled a small amount onto the desk.

Ronnie reached into an old laundry basket and threw Sam a towel. Sam used it to wipe up the spill around the Simplicity nameplate—and then it turned. "Ronnie, look!"

"What am I looking at, Sam?"

"The nameplate, it turned!" Sure enough, Sam saw a key lock. "There it is, I have been looking for this—see!

I knew it had to be here somewhere." Sam reached into his shirt pocket and pulled out a key. He inspected the key and the lock, trying to determine whether they would fit.

Ronnie stared at Sam with an odd look on his face, and asked, "Might I ask just where you got that key from?"

"It's a long story, brother, but one day when I'm not as excited, I'll tell you all about it." Placing the key into the lock, and turning it, he could hear the clicks. "Come here, Ronnie, and help me push on this side." With both men pushing on one side, the desk slid rather easily, revealing a set of steps built into the floor and leading to another secret room.

Ronnie said, "There she is!" and went down about ten steps to a solid metal door. "Holy Moses, Sam, we found it!"

"I know; it kind of makes you weak in the knees, doesn't it?"

"Man, I haven't had an adrenaline rush like this since I rode my first bull!"

Both men stood studying the door, seeing a combination lock and a slot for the "Broken R Brand." Sam, knowing the ring matched the slot, slipped it off his finger, and placed it into the slot. It immediately lit up the key pad waiting for them to enter the combination number.

"Damn it, we don't have the combination number, Ronnie!" Putting the ring back on his hand, they both climbed back up the stairs.

"It's here, I know it is, and it's right here in front of us. All we have to do is figure it out." As he sipped his coffee, Sam's brain was now working in overdrive. "Ronnie, do you have any cigarettes?"

"Yeah, just a minute. I think they're in the kitchen." Returning with the smokes, he said, "Here you go, what are you thinking now?"

"It's right here somewhere. Dad's favorite line was 'Simplicity is not always a sign of ignorance but wisdom in its purest form.' Dad lived it, breathed it and above all he believed it. The combination to the safe had to be on this desk somewhere."

Ronnie grabbed the box into which he had placed everything. He started laying its contents back out. "I'm not sure what we're looking for, but this is everything that was on the desk."

"What is unusual about all of this stuff?"

"I'm not following you, Sam; you've got to be more specific."

"That stack of calendars, you said something about them earlier."

"Yeah, I was wondering why he would have kept so many old calendars."

"Everything else looks like it belongs here. I think you might have been on to something, and didn't know it. It's got to be the calendars. Let's put them in order, and see if we can come up with anything."

Ronnie laid the calendars out from the earliest year to the latest. Sam was studying them as though he were looking over fine diamonds, picking up one and flipping through it, before turning to the next. Ronnie started from the other end, doing the same and asking, "What are we looking for?"

"A pattern; there has to be a pattern."

"I'm not seeing anything yet," Ronnie said. After placing the calendars in order once again he said, "There's no January on any of these so far, Sam."

"Ronnie, I think you're better at this than you know." Going back to the first calendar, Sam placed his back into order. "You're right; there's no January."

"Okay, then, what else is missing?"

Sam grabbed a sheet of paper and wrote down January. Ronnie flipped through the calendar, telling Sam each month that was missing as he flipped through.

"It looks like April is missing, June is missing and September is missing." Going through the others they discovered they were all the same; each calendar was missing the exact same months.

Sam was studying his list, "I think I've got it, Ronnie: One-Four-Six-Nine!" Running down the stairs, Sam placed the ring back into the slot. When it lit up he said, "Okay, here we go," and he typed the security code, 1-4-6-9 onto the keypad.

The door made a clicking sound, and opened slightly. Pushing the door the rest of the way open, the two men walked inside. In the room, they found a small roll-top desk near the front. On both sides of the desk were boxes stacked five wide and six high, and the middle of the room contained additional boxes.

Sam opened the roll-top desk, and there sat the journal his dad had told him about. "It's just as he had said, Ronnie, this is my father's adopted dad's journal."

"When did he tell you about this journal?"

"In his own journal. This one here is from his adopted dad. I'll be right back." Sam retrieved the briefcase and his dad's journal and came back down the stairs. He placed his dad's journal next to the other journal. "He told me this is where it belonged."

Ronnie was studying the outside of the boxes. Every box had been marked with a year. "What do you reckon all this is, Sam?"

"Well, I'm not sure, but here is a ledger; let's see if we can figure it out. First entry January 2005: 16 boxes with 2,000 savings bonds, $100 each." Each entry read the same with a different year, right up to January 2025.

"My God, Sam, you're good with numbers. What's that add up to?"

"When all these bonds mature that would be $80 million!"

"You've got to be kidding."

"No, I'm not kidding; unless I've made a mistake, that's what it comes up to. In addition, we are going to add $7.5 million to it. Our dad said the 'Broken R' was worth her weight in gold, but I had no idea!"

"Me neither, Sam."

While he flipped through the ledger, a piece of paper fell out of it onto the floor. Sam spotted the document and, bending over, he picked it up. "Hey what's this?"

"I don't know, but it looks like a letter."

> "Dear Sam:
>
> Well, Son, what do you think now? I wanted to let you know that I did all this for a reason. I am sure you have read the journal by now, so make sure you read my father's journal as well. Keep them safe, and learn who your enemies are. If you are not real careful, payback will come quick and hard. I did the best I knew how, to ensure the continued success of the company, and the Broken R. In time, you will do even better once you get the hang of it. The very fact that you are reading this letter means you are catching on really well.
>
> Good luck, and all my love,
> Dad"

"I think he is right, Sam, you're going to do just fine as long as you don't let anyone get the best of you."

"Well, with you watching my back I think we'll do just fine. By the way, since we have no more secrets between us: thanks for saving my life up there in New York!"

"What makes you think that was me?"

"I know it was you, so let's just leave it at that."

"All right, brother, let's do just that."

With a handshake and a pat on the back, they would now be brothers bonded in blood forever. Sam went about placing things back as they were upon entry, and said, "OK, let's go get us some fresh air. It will take more time to figure it all out, so for the rest of the day it will be business as usual."

"I agree. Besides, I need to get over to the north range, and make sure Stan has everything under control. They are supposed to be branding all of the yearlings today."

As they pushed the desk back into its natural position, they heard the lock snap into place, securing the passage. Sam scanned the room one last time and said, "Everything looks good."

As both men were walking out the door, heading to get their horses saddled up, Sam stopped and asked Ronnie, "Hey, would you turn Hercules loose on your way by the paddock?"

"Got it, and when I'm done this afternoon, I'll swing back by the house."

"That will be great, we'll see you then." Hercules came right to Sam; he saddled him up, and told him "All right, boy, let's go home!" With a little bump, they were off. Sam let him have total control, and without any hesitation Hercules headed straight for home.

CHAPTER 17
TAKING THE POWER

That evening Sam and Tara enjoyed a quiet meal at home, the first one since they had been on the Broken R. They both decided to stay home instead of going into town. Ronnie had stopped in for a short visit, but seeing that they both were relaxed, he didn't want to interfere, so he called it an early night and went home to let them have some time with each other.

Sam watched Ronnie ride until he was out of sight. He thought maybe he would sleep better, knowing he was sleeping on $87.5 million. Just thinking about it made Sam's head spin. When Sam found himself still awake after Tara had fallen asleep, he took out his journal and caught up on all of his notes. Then he started something new: making a list of the most important things that he felt he needed to do, noting them in order of importance. He wanted to stay on top of things, and by doing this, it seemed to bring a small amount of comfort to his mind, knowing that with it written down it would not get lost in the shuffle. He did this mainly because he had that gut feeling that did not seem to be going away: that there would be more trouble. Phillip had pretty much put a solid guarantee on that.

For the first time since Sam was a young child, he humbled himself in prayer, asking the Lord to see him through these trials. Sleep finally came, but his dreams were nightmares filled with violence. By the time daylight had arrived, Sam was ready to jump out of bed just so he did not have to see any more violent visions. He jumped into the shower as quickly as he could, hoping to wash away some of the bad dreams.

"Hey, are you going to stay in there all day?" he heard Tara holler.

With the steam already flowing into the bedroom, Sam stepped out and grabbed a towel. "Okay, it's your turn." By the time he got dressed, he realized that the shower had worked; he was feeling much better now, and almost ready to face a brand new day. Once in the kitchen, Sam poured himself a hot cup of fresh-brewed coffee and drank it alone, waiting for Tara to join him after she finished with her shower.

Cyndi walked in and poured herself a cup of coffee. "Good morning, Sam. How are you doing this fine morning?"

"I'm feeling better now, but I did have a rough night, though."

"What's the problem? Is it bad dreams?"

"Yeah, how did you know that?"

"Oh, it's a family thing; I have them as well. Daddy always referred to it as fighting our demons all night. Don't you remember?"

"Now that you've said it, yeah, I do."

"Anyway, I thought I had best come by and check in, make sure you were up to speed on the upcoming wedding plans."

"Damn, can you believe I had forgotten about that as well?"

"Well, we've only got a few more days, so we need to get started preparing the ranch."

"Sis, you've been talking with Mary, so you know what she wants, right?"

"Yeah, pretty much."

"Well, why don't you set everything up, and I'll pick up the tab. Does she want to have the wedding inside or outdoors?"

"She wants to be married outdoors."

"Then it needs to be here, where there is plenty of shade. We can decorate the meeting hall for the reception afterwards. Do you have any idea as to where they want to go for their honeymoon?"

"No, but I can find out and let you know."

"That will work. We need to make this a really special occasion, Sis; our big brother has never asked a thing from us."

"I know. I feel the same way."

"If you need anything just say the word; I'm going to get Tara to help you with decorating things, also, Haley said she would help too."

"Great!"

"Have you had breakfast yet?"

"No."

"When Tara gets down here, if you would like we can all go eat us some breakfast, and then get started. As I said, I want this to be a very special event, and at this point we have a lot of work to do."

As they were riding into town to go eat breakfast, Haley met up with them. She had gone out for an early morning ride. The town seemed alive with people—more so than what would be considered normal.

Haley said, "I wonder what's up. It seems like we have a lot more visitors than we normally do."

"I don't know, Sis. I haven't heard about anything special that's supposed to be going on."

Once they arrived at the diner, it didn't take long to find out what all the excitement was about. There was a movie producer visiting the town, looking for a new location to shoot a movie. That gave the women plenty to talk about during breakfast, mostly about what famous people they might possibly get the chance to meet.

Breaking into their conversation, Sam said, "All right, you gals get the stars out of your eyes. We have got far more important matters to discuss; for instance, planning the wedding of the century. I want this to be, not only the best, but also the most memorable event in our brother's life. If there is one thing I have learned from what all we have been through, it is that you have to grab hold and take the best out of life no matter what the circumstances are around you. Right now life is good, so let us not miss a thing. Cyndi is going to be the coordinator, so you'll need to work with her on what kind of decorating she needs to have done."

Haley broke into the conversation. "We've already sent out all the invitations. By the way, I was supposed to tell you Uncle Alan called and said he would be here for the wedding. He wants you to call him! I wrote his number down just in case you did not already have it."

"Man, I feel like a jerk. Things have been so crazy that I did not even think to call him."

Cyndi told Sam, "It's okay. I think we have the idea, so let us handle it. Surely, you have some other things to take care of?"

"Oh! I see how you are; trying to run me off, are you?"

"Yes, but only because we ladies are much better at this then you men."

"You're right again, and I know you will all do a fine job." After taking his last swallow of coffee, and kissing Tara, he said, "Well, I'll see you ladies later then; I have my own work to do."

Leaving the diner, Sam was just about to mount up when Ronnie hollered out to him. "Hey, Sam! Come here a minute—I have somebody here that wants to meet you."

Sam walked across to where the two men were standing. Ronnie introduced them to each other. "Trace, this is Sam; Sam, meet Trace."

Sam shook the man's hand. "It's nice to meet you," he said.

Ronnie bubbled with excitement when he asked Sam, "You do know who this man is, don't you?"

"Sure. I think everybody in town knows who this fellow is."

Trace spoke up: "Well, good, then; I don't need to beat around the bush with you."

"No sir. Ronnie is in charge of everything here on the Broken R; if you'll give him a rundown on what you're looking to do, we will see what we can do to accommodate you."

Turning to Ronnie, Sam said, "If you need me for anything I will be back at the house. I have some unfinished business to attend to. Trace, it was good to meet you. I hope you have a good visit, and feel free to call on us any time."

"Thank you. I appreciate your hospitality."

"Ronnie, you take good care of Mr. Trace here.

"I will, boss!"

"Maybe we can meet for dinner later?" said Sam.

"Sure, holler at me later."

"Okay."

Sam mounted up, tipping his hat as he rode off. When he got back to the house, he made his way to his journal. He added the wedding to his 'to do' list, and once he finished with his journal he called John at the law firm. "Hello? Yes. May I speak with John?"

"One moment please, may I ask who's calling?"

"Just tell him it's Sam from the Broken R."

"Yes, sir."

Within a few seconds John picked up the phone. "Hello, this is John."

"John, I've got a bone to pick with you."

"Yes, I'm sure you do."

"First thing I want to know: are you vested in Simplicity?"

"Yes, my father vested me when I was very young."

"Then I guess my next question is: who is your father?"

"You mean Frank didn't tell you?"

"Frank is your dad?"

"Yes, from his first marriage. They divorced when I was about ten."

"Then who are John and Martha in New York?"

"They would be my two children, Sam."

"Okay, this is starting to add up."

"Sam, I talked to Dad last night. I know what happened up there to a certain degree. Dad said some things are just better if I did not know. However, the day I came to the ranch, you probably don't remember the two men that were with me?"

"Yes, actually, I do."

"Well that was Phillip, and one of his men. I had my back against the wall, and I just didn't know what to do. When I talked to Dad, he told me to do whatever Phillip asked, and he would handle everything else."

"Well, John, tell me this: are John Jr. and Martha there with you now?"

"No, they're still in New York."

"Where do you want to be, John, here or in New York with your kids?"

"I would like to be with my family; Dad said he was staying up there too, running a new project for you."

"That's right, John, I'm going to do the same for you that I did for your Dad. You go ahead and make the arrangements to transfer to New York; you can all stay with your Dad if you like. Frank will bring you up to speed on what we are doing up there. John, you make sure everything is done on the up-and-up, though; I do not want any more problems! If you are ever approached again by anybody, I had better be the first to know about it! We as a family cannot survive if we can't trust each other. Now with all that said, do you need anything from me to make this transfer?"

"Mike will have to sign the transfer notice, since he's the CEO."

"All right, John, I'll have it done. Good luck to you all up there, and I'll be keeping in touch."

"Thanks, Sam. Goodbye."

Sam hung up the phone and made a note to have Mike send the proper paperwork. As he sat back and thought things through, he hoped he was doing the right thing. There was only one thing that he was certain about at this time: he would not let anybody else bullshit him around. If he made any mistakes, they would damn well be his own mistakes. That way, he would not have to second-guess himself. In his mind, Sam had already started making plans on how he was going to double the money that was in the vault. He was going to build his own bank on the Broken R, and it would sit right in the heart of town. He would meet with the lawyers to see what he needed to do to get the ball rolling on construction.

Mike came in, hollering, "Is anybody home?"

Coming out of the study, Sam replied, "Yeah, bubba, what's up?"

"Nothing. I just had to get away from the com center for a minute. I think we finally got the new system running."

"Good, that should take a huge burden off your shoulders."

"Yeah, I think it will work out better now that Eric and Bryan have a better idea of how it works. They shouldn't have to call me every time they need to do something anymore."

"Mike, I have been meaning to have you sit down with me and explain to me just what Simplicity is all about."

"It's pretty simple, really; that's how Simplicity got its name. It started as a simple man's investment company. When a new member joined he agreed to pay in a dollar a day or 365 dollars a year. If you stuck to the plan, in twenty years you would be a vested member. On the other hand, you could do an automatic buy-in for one million dollars, and be vested."

"Now that makes sense, but the dollar a day thing doesn't sound right."

"Well, that's what makes it simple. We have right now 2.5 million members, that's not counting the vested members, but I'm not sure of the exact number right now. I can tell you that over half of everybody on the Broken R is a vested member. What you do not see is at a dollar a day, Simplicity takes in a quarter of a million dollars a day just from new members. Our older members are doing just what Dad did for us, vesting their children at an early age, so by the time they are grown they can take full advantage of their options. Nevertheless, to me that is what made Simplicity grow so fast. People made so much money they just kept buying their families into the company. With that said, that is not counting anything which Simplicity owns—that is just members. That's right; to know what each investment made last year and how much we made all together as a company will determine how much interest we pay each member on their money. The cut off is, once you made a million dollars you become vested, and then you can roll the money over or you can take a hundred thousand a year and retire."

"Well, you do make it sound simple."

"It really is."

"Now, I've got a couple of things I need you to do for me."

"Okay, what do you need from me?"

"You know Renny, right?"

"Sure—one of the pilots."

"I need to know how much he has left in order to be vested in Simplicity. I am going to pay whatever he has left to make him a vested member."

Mike started jotting things down. "Okay, what else?"

"John, the lawyer here in Little Rock, wants to transfer to the New York office; I told him I would have you send the transfer papers."

"Is that it?"

"Yeah. I hope I haven't forgotten anything. No, wait—there is one more thing: where would you like to go on your honeymoon?"

"What? You think I am going to make that decision? We are going wherever Mary wants to go."

"Well, has she decided?"

"Yes, she wants to go to Jamaica."

"Have you already made the arrangements?"

"No, I figured I had plenty of time."

"Well, you don't have plenty of time. I'll take care of making the reservations, and you take care of those things for me."

"Damn, you don't have to do that."

"Look, Mike, I want to do this, and I want you to promise me you're going to have a good time."

"I'm going to do my best. Speaking of best, would you like to be my best man?"

"That I would consider an honor."

"Okay then. Go take care of those reservations." Mike walked to the door, then turned. "Thanks, Sam!"

When Mike left, Sam realized that was probably the longest conversation they had ever shared with each other.

For the next few days, the air held an extra tinge of excitement. A new look was taking over the Broken R. She looked like a beauty getting dressed up for her walk down the runway. There were flowers, ribbons, and lace everywhere. Ronnie had set up a small gazebo where the lucky couple would stand to say their vows. Mike, of course, was a wreck, almost depressed—mainly because he was so worried that things would not be perfect. Trying to maintain his composure and make it through to the big day, he decided he knew one thing for sure: he only wanted to go through this once.

Tara stood looking over at all of the beautiful work they had done. The setting was absolutely picture perfect. She got her video camera out to take some pictures, and caught Sam and the kids running and playing. Haley, Cyndi, and Mary were doing a mock rehearsal. She thought to herself, "Things should always be in such order." However, the truth was: without conflict, how could anyone learn to enjoy these moments, and treasure them, as they should be enjoyed and treasured? Everyone gathered close to the house to watch the sun set, and after all the good-byes and good-nights, Sam and Tara retired for the night, knowing that tomorrow would bring a big day.

Chapter 18

The Wedding

The early morning light gave way to a very unusual August day at the Broken R; a nice cool breeze in the air made it feel more like an early spring day. It was as if God himself was planning to spend the day at the Broken R and govern the events of the day. Sam could feel it in the air and see it in everyone's eyes. Although it was only 5 a.m., the women were up and hard at it trying to finish with the last-minute details. Not that the place wasn't perfect already. The Broken R was a picture in itself, but when the festive decorations were added, it just brought out the pure beauty for the occasion.

They all felt that this was going to be a great day—one of those rare days when nobody has a cross word to say against anybody else. They planned the wedding to begin at 9 a.m., in order to avoid the heat of the day. With all of the excitement, no one was able to sleep, so they all visited and helped each other with any last-minute details that they felt needed to be done.

Sam stood in the background studying everyone working so smoothly together; it captured a beautiful picture in his eyes, reminding him of the long-lost years with his family that somehow went bad. He thought to himself, "This must be what the old man had in mind—everyone together, having such a good time and enjoying life for what it is. When a truth is revealed, and you allow your eyes to stay open to it, then your heart is more apt to allow you to accept the truth. Accept your shortcomings with no remorse, but grasp the truth with the expectation of holding on to it, and keeping it from slipping away again."

These soul-searching moments seemed to be coming much more frequently to Sam, as he thought once again, "I've got to remember to write some of this stuff down."

There was a knock at the door. Alan and Robin walked in. "Good Morning!"

Sam walked into the kitchen to see who had arrived, "Uncle Alan," he exclaimed as he hugged him. "Man, how have you been doing?" He reached to give Aunt Robin a hug and said, "I can't believe it! I'm sorry that I haven't called, but things have been crazy; I'm still trying not to let it get the best of me. Come on in, and have a seat."

Alan took a seat at the kitchen table, and Sam asked, "Would you like a fresh-brewed cup of coffee?"

"Sure, that would be great."

Tara had already poured the cups, and was ready to serve them.

"We heard about what's been going on," Alan said. "We went by the old house in Bryant, thinking you were going to be there, but you had already left. The day of the funeral, we just slipped out, figuring you all were going to need a little time alone. I wish I could have been more help to you, but to be very honest with you, your dad never shared anything about the business or his problems with me. The Broken R sponsored me for the first five years when I started pro fishing. I did well enough that I became vested in Simplicity at the end of the fifth year."

"So you're still fishing?"

"Not as much as I used to, but I do still go out once in a while. Your dad and I used to try and sneak off as much as we could. Hey, you have a wedding to get ready for. Don't let me hold you up."

"No, don't worry; everything is under control."

Pastor Phil walked in with a great big smile. "At least one person in the family is full of confidence this morning." Then he turned to Alan. "Hi, Alan, how are you doing?"

"Just fine. How about you?"

"I believe this is going to be a day to remember, and what a beautiful day it is."

"I'll take that as, 'you're doing great'."

"You know it. I have got to chase down the groom to see if we're on the same page."

"Okay, maybe we can visit after the service."

"Yeah, let's do that."

Robin had slipped off with Molly, Cyndi, and Tara to help get the bride ready. Sam suggested to Alan that they go for a short walk, checking things out one last time before the wedding ceremony started. Ronnie was busy getting the riders prepared; the buggy was ready with its "JUST MARRIED" sign and tin cans tied on the back. "Okay, men, everybody knows what they are supposed to do?"

Stan answered for them. "Yes, Ronnie, we will all be on our best behavior."

"That's good, but be on time as well. 9:15!"

"All right, all right—we've got other things we need to do in order to be ready. You go make sure you're ready," said Stan.

Ronnie looked at the buggy. "I am ready. Guess I'll go check on the camera crew."

"That's a good idea. We will see you at 9:15."

When Ronnie caught up with Sam he said, "Hey, I need to talk to you."

"Sure, have you two met?"

Ronnie reached out to shake his hand, but got a hug instead. "Hi Uncle Alan."

"Hey, Ronnie—you're looking well, all decked out today."

"Thanks."

"What's so important that you need to talk to me about this morning?" Sam said.

"Well, I wanted to let you know Trace is going to be here today with his film crew. He should be here just about any time to set up his equipment to film the wedding."

"You're kidding?"

"Nope. He said he was really interested in using the Broken R to film his next movie. He thought if he did this as a favor for the family it might persuade you to make a favorable decision, and let him make a movie on the ranch."

"Ronnie, I left that decision up to you."

"I know you did, but he doesn't know that!"

"You are one sly fellow, Ronnie."

"I know. Mike and Mary will love having the wedding recorded—especially from a movie-making crew."

"Look, here they come now. Okay, I guess I'll catch you later!"

"Sam, you reckon he's just a little bit excited," asked Alan.

"Yeah I think so. What time is it getting to be?"

Alan looked at his watch and said, "Gosh, it is already a quarter to eight."

"No wonder there is so many people here. I guess I had better go locate Mike and Brother Phil," Sam said.

"Go, go. I know my way around the ranch. I'll catch up with you a little later."

In the house, the women were busy putting together their last-minute details. Sam found Mike and Brother Phil in the kitchen, "Are we all ready?" he asked.

Mike just nodded his head; Brother Phil was trying to reassure him that everything would go just fine.

"Yeah, Bubba, it's going to be great. Try to relax for a change, and enjoy the moment. Before you know it, it will all be over with. Come on, let's go ahead and walk outside—it's a beautiful day. Besides, you look like you could use some fresh air."

"Okay, I think maybe you're right on that one."

As they walked around to where the crowd was gathering, Mike almost lost it. "Oh, my God! Look at all of this! And what are those cameras for?"

"Just relax; it's not a big deal. We figured about six months from now when you're just an old married man, you might want to see what all took place on this special day."

"Yeah, I'm sure you're right!"

As the time came to get the wedding started, Brother Phil stepped up onto the gazebo. He picked up the microphone and tested it to see if it was on; when he was content that everything was working he said, "I would like to thank you all for coming today to be a witness to this very special occasion. If everybody would please take a seat, I have an announcement to make, and then we will get started. Due to the filming of the wedding today, I have to ask you to refrain from taking snapshots until after the ceremony. We will allow time for a photo session afterwards."

Brother Phil motioned for Mike to step forward and stand in front of him, with Sam and Ronnie beside him. Then they turned to face the back as the music started to play. Little Ben, looking rather handsome, led the way bearing the rings, followed by Sarah tossing rose petals onto the rolled-out red-carpeted path leading to the gazebo. Once Sarah had made it halfway up the aisle, Haley then started her walk, with Cyndi following. As they got to the front, Ben stood to the right and Sarah to the left, with all of them facing the front. For a second the music stopped, and the bridal party all turned to face the back.

A moment of silence took place; then the music started again, and out stepped Mary to make her walk down the path that would place her forevermore into the arms of the man she loved. With grace and precision, she made each step count, while every fairy tale she had ever heard danced in her head. Today she was a princess just about to marry her prince. To Mary, the trip down the aisle seemed so magical: this was the day she had dreamed of for as long as she could remember. She made that last step up to stand beside Mike, knowing her dreams had come true. Once again, the music fell silent.

Brother Phil broke the silence. "Before we get started, Mary and Mike would like to say their personal vows to each other. Mary, you will go first."

"Mike I've known you for a long time now; I just knew in my heart that one day we would be standing here face to face. I want you to know: today you have made me the happiest woman in the world. My vow to you, Mike, is to bring you as much happiness as you have brought to my life."

Mike responded, "Mary, in my heart I have known too that this would one day happen. My vow to you is from this day forward never to forget: my heart is now joined with your heart as one, for the rest of our lives."

Brother Phil gave them both an "Amen," and carried on with the ceremony: "Brother Mike, do you take Mary to be your lawful wedded wife, to have and to hold in sickness and in health, for richer or poorer?"

"I do."

"Sister Mary, do you take Mike to be your lawful wedded husband to have and to hold in sickness and in health, for richer or poorer?"

"I do."

"The rings, please." Ben stepped up. Brother Phil took the rings and handed one to Mary and one to Mike. He continued, "The ring is a symbol of your commitment to each other to remind you of this day that you stood before God, and all of these witnesses, and were joined together in holy matrimony."

Placing the rings onto each others' fingers, they each said, "With this ring I thee wed."

Brother Phil said, "And that what God has joined together, let no man put asunder. I now pronounce you husband and wife. Mike, you may now kiss your bride."

As they kissed, the music started; out from the front of the house, in two rows, came riders all carrying American flags. Parting at the gazebo, they encircled the crowd as Mike and Mary both walked down the path showered with rice and best wishes as a newly married couple.

When the horses parted at the end, there sat a horse-drawn buggy waiting to escort Mike and Mary to the reception hall, with none other than Ronnie waiting to be the driver. Sam helped them both to get into the buggy, and once they both were seated Ronnie drove between the riders. One group of riders rode in front, and the other group rode behind the buggy as it headed for the reception hall with a camera following.

Sam stood watching as they all rode off. What a sight! He felt confident that they had been able to do a good job, keeping the service simple, but very memorable. He explained to the other guests how to get to the reception hall. Then he made his way to the barn, and stopped in to check on Hercules. "Hey there, boy, how are we doing?" Hercules was glad to see him, throwing his head back and stomping. "You want out, don't you?" Sam could not help himself; he saddled up, and rode to the reception hall.

Everything was already in full swing when he arrived. The first person he ran into was Trace. "Hi, Sam, we are just loading up; we'll be out of here in a few minutes."

"Trace, I'm glad I caught you; I wanted to personally thank you for what you did today."

"That's quite all right. I think it worked out for the both of us. We got a lot of great footage in the can; the movie that we are wanting to film here has a wedding in it. Therefore, if Mike and Mary don't have any objections we'll be able to use a lot of this in our film."

"That's great! I don't think they will mind at all."

"Well, I gave Ronnie a rough draft of what we're offering to run by you. If it's possible, we would like to start shooting in two weeks."

"All right. I'll make sure he has things in order for you."

"Okay, then, you guys have a great day."

"Thanks again." Sam waved as they drove off. When he got inside the music was playing softly, and everyone was eating and visiting. The hall looked like they had done a complete facelift on it. A band was playing on the stage; down in front they had a section cleared off for a dance floor. The tables went all the way around the room, with the wedding couple seated in the center. Joining in, Sam sat with Ronnie, Cyndi, and Haley. Then he motioned for Tara to join him; they were having the time of their life just sitting back and watching all of the festivities.

Sam was having a hard time trying to keep up with everything, but he knew somewhere along the way he was supposed to propose a toast to the couple. He was wracking his brain trying to think of an appropriate toast for such a special occasion, when Cyndi tapped him on the shoulder. "You're up, brother."

Sam stood holding a glass. "If I could, I would speak great words of wisdom that would open the doors to heaven and let the light shine down on earth to protect and keep you safe, but since I have no power over these things, I turn to Him that does, and ask that He bestow these gifts upon you: a long prosperous life filled with the love you two have displayed here today; joy in having one another to share your triumphs; and the strength to carry each other through life without fault. May our Lord walk with you and keep you safe, so that we will all be able to share many memorable times together. Cheers!"

The crowd resounded with, "Cheers!" in response.

The band picked right up, and started playing again. Sam took the first dance with the bride, and then visited with Mike for awhile. "Well brother, I told you it would all be over before you knew it."

"It did seem that way, once we got started."

"I'm really happy for you guys, and remember: you promised to go and have a good time."

"I think everything's going to be okay now, and by the way, thanks!"

"You're more than welcome, but you better thank little Sis—she really did most of it."

"Okay, I'll be sure and do that." Walking away, Mike joined Mary on the dance floor.

Renny came in and caught Sam by the arm, "Hey, big shot, how have you been doing?"

"Good. What on earth are you doing here? I thought you were going to take some time off."

"No rest for the vested, boss. I got a package here for you from Frank. I was to make sure I placed the package in your hands only. After handing you the package I'm supposed to pick up the wedding couple, and wherever they're going, I get to stay until they decide to come back home."

"You know what to do, right?"

"Sure." He showed Sam the envelope. "Got this with the flight plan; it was from you, right?"

"That's it. We can't be too careful; you keep a close eye on them."

"Will do, boss. Food looks great; reckon I have time to eat before we have to leave?"

"Sure, you should have plenty of time. Go ahead."

The day was rushing by, but everyone was having such a great time, being caught up in the moment. Sam saw a group of people line dancing; Haley and Ronnie were looking good on the dance floor, as if they knew each step the other would make. It made Sam notice for the first time that they were about the same age. "Lord have mercy on me . . . I had better keep an eye on that situation. I think we might be doing this again sooner than I thought."

Molly walked up behind Sam and touched him on the shoulder. He jumped.

"What?"

"I'm sorry. You would think by now I would have learned not to do that."

"Hi, Molly. Is everything okay?"

"Sure is. I just wanted to thank you for making this day so special for Mary and Mike. It was just splendid.

Every move seemed to fit like a glove. It was an absolutely flawless wedding."

"Molly, I've never said this before to anyone, but I believe I had a lot of help from up above on this one."

"Well, thanks for your part, anyway."

"You know I believe He's watching over you as well."

"Make sure and send me a copy of the wedding tape, would you?"

"No problem."

"I think Frank and Joe will enjoy watching it as well. They are doing a real good job up there, still trying to forgive themselves for the mess we all made. I feel bad, too; I hope you will find it in your heart to forgive us."

"Oh, Miss Molly, come here," he said, and gave her a hug. "Don't you know I already forgave you guys? I know all this was my fault. If I had been where I was supposed to be, and kept up with what was going on, this would have never happened. The only reason you three are in New York is because it was my dad's wish to see this job done, and he would have been just as proud of you guys trying to defend him in his last days. I know you all had to be close, or you wouldn't have gone to such extremes to try and protect him. When things settle down here at the ranch, Molly, I'll come to visit as often as I can, and just because you are in New York doesn't mean the three of you can't come back here for visits. We are going to do as much as we can to see that the memory of my dad lives on. I hope that one day even his great-great-grandchildren will be able to look back and remember how all this got started. You tell Frank and Joe there are no hard feelings on my part. I thought we had worked all this out before I left, but with time I'm sure we will learn that forgiving each other will be easier than forgiving ourselves."

"Sam, you're going to do just fine; I've seen a great change in you since the first time we met." With another hug, she wiped her eyes. "I didn't think there were any more tears left. You run along, you have other guest to attend to, I will be okay."

"You be good, have some fun, I'll talk with you later."

"Okay, and thanks again."

Sam caught up with the newlywed couple. "Okay, you two, I can see you are having excessively too much fun, but the time has come for the both of you to offer your thanks to your friends that have come to this wonderful occasion, and your goodbyes. Your pilot is waiting on you."

"Okay," Mary said, "but I need to change before we leave."

Mike was feeling good, high on life, and all he wanted was to be with his bride. At this time the world really just revolved around Mary, so he asked, "Sam, you're getting rather good with words. Why don't you let us slip out of here, and you take care of the thanks and goodbyes for us."

"If that's the way you want it, Bubba, you got it."

While Mary was changing, Sam called security and rounded them up; Renny and Mike were in the SUV waiting for Mary. When she came back out of the hall carrying her wedding dress, Sam stopped her. "They're waiting for you," he said.

"But I've got to give this back to Mom."

Sam took the dress. "I'll make sure she gets it. Come on." He slipped Mary out through the back door. As she started to get into the SUV, Sam stopped her and kissed her on the cheek. "Now you take care of him. We will all be waiting on you two to get back, but for now go and have some fun."

Sam watched as they drove off. "Be safe" was all that went through his mind.

CHAPTER 19
THE RING OF POWER

Sam started back down the hall, heading to the back room to get the wedding dress from the table he had placed it on for Molly. As he bent down to pick up the dress, a cowboy bumped into him. Apologizing to Sam, he said, "Sorry, sir, I needed some fresh air." Sam barely got a look at him. He could tell that he was an older man, and that his hat stuck out, due to its being old and worn out. As the man walked out of the room, Sam just brushed it off, thinking that he'd probably had too much to drink, and got lost inside the hall. Carrying the dress to Molly, he had a hard time shaking off the feeling that he had seen that man before.

Once he turned the dress over to Molly, he slipped out the front door. As he walked around outside in the dark, the buildings kept him hidden in the shadows. He spotted the old man in the corral standing up and talking to Hercules. Sam quietly eased his way as close as he could get, trying to see if he could figure out who the man was without giving himself away. The man patted Hercules on the neck, saying, "You're a fine piece of workmanship. Your daddy would be very proud of you." Reaching into his pocket, he pulled out a carrot, and handed it to him. "You take good care of Sam now; I've got to go for now." He gave the horse a kiss on the nose.

Sam was just about ready to speak up, when the man mounted his horse and took off like lightning.

Running toward the corral, Sam could see the man riding over the flat lands heading toward the hill that led to Ronnie's place. "Sam, you've got to get a grip, don't do this." His mind was running wild. "Just breathe." Looking over at Hercules, he saw the horse, too, was standing at the fence watching the rider as if he wanted to go after him. Walking over to him, Sam whispered in his ear, "I know, but we can't, her secrets are now our secrets. We must protect them."

After Sam gathered his thoughts, he rejoined everyone in the hall. Uncle Alan and Aunt Robin had already excused themselves and returned to the main house. Sam was surprised when John from the Bar S hollered out, "Hey, I know you're not going to leave without having a drink with us first."

At the table sat Jack and some of the other Bar S cowboys. "Damn, guys, you all blend well. I didn't even recognize you."

"It's all these fancy duds you made us wear. They make us all look the same."

"Well, for a bunch of cowboys, you sure clean up good," said Sam as he took a seat at the table and visited with the men. For a short time he became a part of their gang, if only for just a little while.

Talking and having a good time, Jack jumped into the conversation. "Hey, Sam, John has a plan that he wanted to discuss with you."

"Not now, Jack."

"Why not?"

Sam looked at John. "Why not? Now is as good a time as any," he said.

"Okay, if you say so. Do you know where the motel and store are located on the back side of the ranch?" John asked.

"Yeah, I remember."

"Well, it has been put up for sale. I checked it out, and it would add another one hundred acres to the Bar S. I would like to buy it, and put in our own little town like here on the Broken R."

"That sounds like a very big plan. How much are you willing to give up accomplishing this?"

"We don't have enough cash, if that's what you mean."

"How much do you calculate that it would cost?"

"My guess is approximately four million dollars to make it operational. Then we could add to it as we can afford it."

"It sounds like it could be arranged. I will call Becky up in New York, and have her meet with you to see about buying the property. I am assuming that the Bar S is really owned by Simplicity."

"Yes."

"When Mike gets back from his honeymoon, I'll have to discuss this with him as well, to see how it needs to be done, but you should be able to go ahead and start getting a blueprint drawn up. We will make it happen."

John grinned, "That was simple enough. Jack, you were right; nothing to it."

"What were you expecting—some kind of fight over it?"

"No, not really; I just didn't know if you would cotton on to the idea."

"It's your plan; you're the one that's got to make it work. I think you can do it, so all we're really discussing is the money."

Ronnie came in, whooping and hollering, "I did it! I closed the deal with Trace. Sam, you are not going to believe this; a hundred thousand a week and they figure at least ten, possibly twelve weeks. That's going to look good for an old cattle ranch's income."

"Settle down, Big Man, and have a drink. We were discussing business as well; you might want to put your two cents in on it, too."

They carried on until late evening—just a bunch of cowboys talking big ideas. When they finally gave it up for the night, everyone else had already left. Sam closed up the reception hall and turned out the lights, then he remembered he had a package delivered to him by Renny from Frank. He grabbed it as he walked out the door.

Ronnie had already left to drop the cowhands over to the motel in town. John stayed behind and walked with Sam to the main house.

John asked, "What's the package about, Sam?"

"I don't rightly know yet, John. I just got it earlier today, and I haven't had time to look at it."

"I hope it isn't more trouble."

"Well, me too, but you know, John, I don't see any way that we're going to be able to avoid it. In my opinion, it is just a matter of when, where, and how. These people aren't the type for forgiving and forgetting."

"I know what you mean, but no matter what, we'll be there. All you have to do is say the word."

"I know, and I really appreciate it, too."

As they walked into the house it was quiet. "I guess everyone has already gone to bed," Sam said.

"Sounds like a good idea to me."

"Here," said Sam, checking the spare room, "you can sleep in here."

"Good deal. I'll see you tomorrow before we cut out for home."

"Okay. Good night."

Sam crawled into bed, tired from the long day. He was thinking of Mike and Mary, and hoped they would still enjoy their honeymoon once they found out he had changed their plans. Sam knew at this time they just could not afford to take any chances. He wondered what the family would have to face in times to come, if things continued the way they were going. He lay back and opened the package. There were several photos of men, and a letter from Frank.

"Dear Sam:

Just wanted to bring you up to speed with what we have going on here. We found two cars parked in the

> garage; we have been able to find out they were registered to a company out of California before the police confiscated them. John Jr. is running a check to see what else he can find out. The pictures you have are four men that showed up claiming to be FBI agents at the mansion. They searched the place inside and out. When I talked to the police, they did not know anything about the FBI being involved.
>
> When I called the local office here, they claimed they had not sent anybody out. I figured they were looking for something, but I don't have a clue as to what it is they were looking for. By the way, Sam, thanks for arranging for John Sr. to be with us here in New York. We are a lot like you and your dad, and I am glad we are going to have a chance to spend some time together. Well, I guess that is it for now; we will keep in touch if we find anything else out.
>
> Frank."

Sam put everything back into the large envelope, placed it under his pillows and called it a night, hoping sleep would come easily tonight, but without the nightmares.

The next morning came with rain showers, making it easier to sleep in. Sam awoke late, and as he'd hoped, he did have a peaceful night. He was looking forward to another full day, but soon found out the rain was not letting up. He visited with Uncle Alan and Aunt Robin for a short time before they had to leave for home. John had left him a note saying his goodbyes; they had cut out at daylight for the airport. With all of the kids at their own places, and everyone gone, Sam and Tara found themselves all alone.

They had grown used to the full days and busy schedules, and now, sitting alone with each other, they were not quite sure what to do with themselves. Walking into the family room, Sam realized he hadn't sat down and watched any TV since he had been back. Looking through the DVD collection, he spotted *The Lord of the Rings*. Sam hollered to Tara, "Sweetheart, do you want to watch a movie with me?"

Tara must have had a similar thought, because she came from the kitchen carrying a large bowl of popcorn. "Sure, what are we going to watch?"

"*The Lord of the Rings*. Have you ever seen it?"

"Gosh, a long time ago, and I think we've only seen the first one."

"Well, it will be like the first time for me; I don't remember it."

They spent the rest of the day watching all three parts of the movie, breaking only to get something to eat and to see if it had quit raining. At the end of the movie Sam was finally coming back to full speed, thinking to himself about the ring his dad had left him. The ring of power had to be destroyed in the movie. Maybe that was what his dad was trying to tell him about the ring: they will attempt to destroy him to get to the ring. The idea fit, whether it was true or not.

Sam was sharing his thoughts with Tara about the ring. "Oh! Sam, surely you don't really believe that, do you?"

"Well, sure I do. Look at all that's happened in just the last few weeks."

"Then all I can tell you is, you need to get rid of that ring."

"I can't."

"You can't, or you won't?"

"Both!"

"Samuel, you are really starting to worry me. Please don't tell me anymore. It was just a movie, and let's leave it at that."

A knock on the door interrupted their conversation. Ronnie and Sally entered the room.

"What's going on? Are you two enjoying this fine rainy day?" Ronnie said.

Sam hardly recognized Sally; she looked a lot younger to him than when he had seen her at the boarding house. "Yeah, we're doing just fine; we just finished watching *The Lord of the Rings*."

"Sam here thinks now that he's the 'Ring Bearer of the Broken R.'"

Ronnie smiled. "You just figured that out."

Tara said, "Oh my God, not you too. Come on, Sally, let's me and you go in here and visit. We will leave these hobbits to figure it out on their own."

Sam and Ronnie stepped outside onto the porch. "Man, what did you tell her?"

"Nothing really. I just made a comment about how the ring had to be destroyed in the movie. That maybe that was the message from Dad—that people would try and destroy me for the ring."

"Well, frankly, it sounds to me like maybe you're on the right train of thought. I can at least tell you this much: that is where the idea of the ring came from. Your Dad referred to it many times as 'The Ring of Power.'"

"Ronnie, did you ever meet my mother?"

"Yes. She would come out sometimes and spend the weekends with your dad, and there were times when your dad and I would drive down to Bryant and stay a day or two at a time. At that time, there wasn't much to the Broken R; just a lot of open land, and we were running three times the herd we're running now. I think your mother would be totally surprised if she could have seen the place now."

"What did she think of dad and his ideas of the ring, and all that went on?"

"Sam, your dad never mentioned a word to your mom about it. He made me swear never to tell her anything.

He said when you really love someone you have to protect them, and I believe he would have done anything to keep her safe. He didn't want her sitting around worrying about him, or thinking that someone might kill him."

"Well, what did you think of my mother?"

"She was always good to me, and I tried my best to be good to her. She was the complete opposite of your dad—a very quiet and reserved woman, but she wasn't afraid of anything, or at least you would not have known she was. She never backed down from your father, either. If she had something to say, she didn't hesitate to say it. I guess the only time I can recall ever hearing them argue was over you."

"Really? I can't imagine why they would argue over me," Sam said, starting to laugh. "Well, it sounded good."

Ronnie laughed too. "Yeah, you bet."

"Hey, not trying to change the subject, but what's going on between you and Miss Sally?"

"Well, we're not sure. We've been kind of dating for a while now, but it's nothing serious at this point. Speaking of such—the reason we came by was to see if you two wanted to go into Benton with us; maybe grab a bite to eat, and just kick around for awhile."

"Let's go see if Tara would like to go!"

Tara was ready to run; as much as she loved the ranch, she liked the idea of some time away from the house. All four of them spent several hours walking around, shopping, laughing, and carrying on, enjoying the night out just like back in the good old days.

Sam and Tara reminisced about the days when they were as young as Ronnie and Sally. Sam, of course, had a hard time remembering when he was ever that young. It seemed like such a long, long time ago at this point, but they had fun on their trip, buying a few trinkets just like they were on a fancy vacation from some place far,

far away, where they had to have at least a souvenir in order to be reminded of the trip later in time.

Upon arriving back home at the ranch, it was rather late, but Sam asked, "Hey, Ronnie, would you mind dropping me off at the reception hall so I can ride Hercules back home?

"No problem, brother."

Upon arriving, Sam jumped out of the car and went straight to Hercules. He mounted Hercules, and they both were on their way home. After placing him into his stall, Sam gave him an extra ration of grain, and saw to it he that was bedded down for the night.

Stan came walking into the barn, and commented, "You know if you spoil him too much he won't ever amount to anything?"

Sam laughed. "Is that true? I guess, Hercules, like it or not, you are going to be just another old Bean Head like me." Sam caught himself reaching out and patting Hercules on the head. "But I want you to know that will be okay with me; I will still love you anyway. Hey, Stan, have a good night; I'll talk at you later."

"Good night, boss."

Sam started walking to the house; rain had started to sprinkle once again, so he walked slowly in order to enjoy the cold drops that fell onto his face. Thinking of what he and Ronnie had talked about, he decided that sharing some of his personal thoughts might not be such a good idea. Tara had enough to worry about without him adding to her worries, and she had plenty of things to take care of without adding more to her plate. Spinning the ring on his finger, Sam did feel a sense of power, but the thing that affected Sam the most was that he knew his dad had entrusted him to carry on in his place. If there was nothing else to it that was enough for him, because deep down inside all he had ever wanted from his dad was for him to believe in him.

Chapter 20
The Honeymoon is Over

The next two weeks passed by quickly. Sam had been busy setting up arrangements with John for the Bar S project. Frank, Joe and Molly had flown in for a couple of days, and now that all of the past problems were resolved, they were all able to start on a lasting friendship with Sam and his family. They were now on a set time schedule for the completion of the New Simplicity national head office, and orphanage and school as well. Frank was back to his old self, all business and no play. He was sure that they could have the job completed within the projected time span of two years.

Sam had also begun making his own plans. He was working on a scheme to build a bank on the ranch. He had construction scheduled to begin within the next two weeks, but today was a very special day: Mike and Mary would be returning home from their honeymoon. With that in mind, Sam was trying to put business off for the remainder of the day, but it seemed as though that was going to be an impossible task.

Rick and Brad approached Sam. "Hey, Dad, we need to talk with you for a minute. We met an old man up on the south end of the ranch, and he was telling us that the next ranch over was going up for sale. It has approximately eight hundred acres. Since it joins the Broken R on the south side, we thought it might be a great investment!"

"Well, boys, I have to say that sounds like a good deal, but you will need to find out more about this property before we can make a final decision. Your Uncle Mike will be home later today, so if you two can get a plan together with all of the information, then we can present the plan to him and see what he says."

"But why do we have to run everything by Uncle Mike?"

"Because that's the way it works. Mike is in charge of Simplicity."

"So, what you mean is we really don't own anything?"

"Well, that just depends on how you look at it, I guess. Simplicity may own everything, but that is how we all got rich. Simplicity pays us. I guess we need to start taking night classes so we can learn all about this stuff."

"So what do we need to do?"

"Boys, don't over think this; just find out how much land is there exactly, and how much money they are asking for it. You will need Ronnie to look at the land, and he will decide whether it would be a good investment for the Broken R. If he thinks the land is good land, then we will all take it up with your Uncle Mike.

"All right, Dad, we'll talk to you later."

"Okay. You two be careful."

Tara overheard most of the conversation between Sam and the boys. "Well, it sounds like they're trying to fit in. At least they're thinking about business matters."

"Yeah, and after a while they will get a lot better at it. What time is it?"

"About noon. Mike and Mary should be getting here at any minute."

"That's good; maybe we will see things settle down just a bit. I've got some last-minute paperwork to do; would you holler at me when they get here?"

"Okay."

Sam left and went to the study, where he worked on catching up on his journal. He thought it was a good thing that he started this journal. It seemed to have been a perfect way of keeping up with everything. Feeling that brief moment of peace, Sam felt himself drifting off in a deep moment of thought. He pictured his dad standing right in front of him, telling him one of those short sayings that he never seemed to understand: "I have about fifteen perfect minutes a day, where all is well, nobody needs me, and everything is in the right place."

Sam answered him, "I have finally figured out just what you were saying. I've got a long way to go, and a lot to learn." The image faded away, and Sam opened his eyes. He was thinking about the last conversation he had had with his dad, and recalled him saying, "By the time you figure out life, the best part of it has already passed you by; and believe me, what you wouldn't give to be able to change it. Unfortunately, it's usually too late for most."

Talking aloud to himself, just as if his dad were standing right in front of him, Sam said, "Well, Old Man, I hope I'm not too late; I'm making you a promise that I will try to do my best." Getting up to leave the study, he turned at the door and said, "If you're listening, I just wanted to say thanks one more time."

When Sam returned outside, a group of people had gathered. A big "WELCOME HOME" banner had been stretched out between two trees in the yard, and Cyndi and Haley were just finishing tying it off.

"Tara, do you know all these people?"

"No, not very many of them."

"We are going to have to start making time to get around and meet these people."

"Cyndi said something about a family reunion sometime at the end of September."

"Well, that will be something to look forward to."

One of the riders hollered out, "Here they come!" The SUV came into sight and everyone started cheering. When it came to a stop, Renny jumped out and opened the door.

Mike stepped out and helped Mary out of the car; both waving to everybody as they walked up onto the porch. Mary stopped and looked dead straight at Sam.

"Well, sis, what did you think of Big Sky country?" he asked.

"You. I knew it had to be you." Mike stood shaking his head; it was obvious that he was not going to take part in this conversation, defending Sam's actions. Then Mary smiled at Sam, reached out and gave him a big bear hug, and said, "Big Sky country absolutely took my breath away; it was such a beautiful, awesome place, and we had a wonderful time." Mike went around shaking hands and thanking everyone.

Renny finally made it around to Sam. "Hey, boss, has everything been well around here?"

"Yeah, we have had a pretty good time. I trust everything went well with you three."

"As smooth as silk, once I explained to them why you went through the trouble to change their original plans. They seemed very relaxed and content with the change. I also believe that they really enjoyed themselves. I didn't do so bad myself; I actually started to like having my feet on the ground—at least for awhile."

The girls invited everyone inside; they had put together some snacks just for the occasion, so everyone headed into the house taking turns trying to visit with one another.

Sam stopped to talk with Mike for just a minute, asking, "Did you live up to your promise, and have a good time?"

"You know what, little brother? I really think I did. For the first few days it was hard to keep my mind off of business, but once I really got focused on having fun, and enjoying our time, we both had a blast."

"Good! I'm glad to hear it." Sam reached to give Mike a hug and said, "Welcome home."

They visited and talked for a couple of hours, then everyone started drifting off about their way. The sun was starting to set, and once again a peaceful day was about to end on the Broken R. Sam saw Ronnie riding over the hill leading two young colts, but he could tell right off that they were not everyday quarter horses. These horses appeared to be some type of special show horses, the kind of horses he had only seen in magazines. Trying to remember just what type of horse they were, he blurted out, "Arabian horses."

Ronnie rode up. "Are they back yet?"

Sam hollered inside the door, "Mike, Mary, come outside here for just a minute."

When they came outside, Ronnie presented the colts to Mike and Mary as their wedding gift.

Mary squealed with delight, and turned and looked at Mike. "Now you will have to start riding more often."

Mike stood petting the colts. "He sure is a pretty thing."

They both hugged and thanked Ronnie. He took the colts over to the small paddock by the side of the house, and turned them loose. Standing and watching them run and jump and kick, Mary laughed. "They're just like kids loose for the first time."

Ronnie had already made it inside and grabbed a plate of food. "Man, I'm starving to death; I haven't eaten a thing all day."

"Would you like me to make you some sandwiches to go with the finger food that you are eating?" asked Haley.

"That would be great. What do you think of them little colts?"

"They're beautiful! Where on God's green earth did you get them from?"

"They came all the way down from Kentucky. I have been hiding them for about a month now."

Looking out the window, Mike and Mary stood there watching the colts run and play. "Well, judging by their reaction, I think you really surprised them."

"I hope so. I want them to be happy; they both deserve it."

Cyndi and Sally walked into the kitchen, "Well, stranger, just where have you been?"

Haley answered for Ronnie. "Come here and see for yourself. Look what he brought for Mike and Mary's wedding present."

They were both impressed and gave him a hug. "You did well."

They went out to get a better look at the colts. Ronnie finished eating, and then went out to join the others. After visiting awhile, Ronnie asked Sally if she wanted to go into town with him for awhile. She spoke up quickly, saying, "Sure, I would love to."

When they rode off, Sam laughed and said, "If that boy isn't careful we're going to be having another wedding real soon." He thought to himself that he was glad to have been wrong about Ronnie and Haley.

Mike and Mary both responded with, "It could be."

Haley and Cyndi said, "We hope it won't be too soon," as they gave everyone a hug and called it a day.

With Sam and Tara following right behind them, Mike told Mary, "It's good to be home. Come on, we'd better get these two pretty things something to eat, and see to it that they have fresh water."

When they were finished and walking back to the house, Mary turned for one last quick look and said, "They sure are a pretty pair!"

Mike was never that good at being a romantic, but responded with, "Just like us!"

"Yeah, just like us!" Mary stopped and gave Mike a hug and a kiss

Sam had already closed his journal, and was fixing to give it up for the night when he found the envelope he had put under his pillow. Removing the envelope and placing it with his journal, he turned out the lights, kissed Tara goodnight, and said, "It's been a good day, but turn out the lights; the party's over." His body was tired, but his brain did not want to shut down. "I need to see what I can find out about those men in the photos," he thought. "I wonder how John is doing with his project on the Bar S? The bank, I cannot believe it, who was the old man the boys said they had talked to? Mike and Mary looked so happy to be at home. Ronnie sure outdid himself; those were the prettiest horses I have ever seen. Tara must have been tired; she's already soundly sleeping. Concentrate, Sam, and breathe, just relax; go to sleep." Somewhere in between these thoughts, sleep finally did come.

The following three days were extremely busy for everyone. They were all constantly coming and going, so much that it seemed like there was a revolving door at the ranch for a short spell. For most it was just a routine day, but for Sam it was pure excitement. He had fallen in love all over again, and when time permitted, he rode about helping the hands move the cattle across from one pasture to another.

He and Tara rode up to the south pasture to check on Samson, and while they were up there, they decided to ride across the land that the boys had told them was up for sale. Sam and Tara both took it easy; they were laid back and trying to enjoy the pleasure of time. It seemed time had become the most precious gift of all. Sam found himself happy with just about everything around him. His anger didn't even seem to be an issue with him anymore. He felt like he was in total control of it now. Trying to define that thin line between right and wrong, he studied it hard until he almost felt bad for feeling so good. They were on their way back when Rick caught up with them.

"Hey, Mom and Dad, are you guys having fun?"

"Hey, Rickie!"

"Dad, how many times do I have to ask you not to call me that?"

"I am sorry, Son, but at least it's not Bean Head, Jr."

"You're right; that makes Rickie sounds good. Anyway, we wanted to know if you are busy this evening?"

"Not that we know of. Why, what's going on?"

"Well, I met the people that owned the next ranch over. They are real nice people; they would like to meet you and discuss a deal."

"Okay, Son, did you get some names for these nice people?"

"Amanda and Paul. And they have one son, Gabriel."

"That's good. Have you talked to Uncle Mike yet?"

"Yeah, he said this evening would be okay with him, but I need to track down Ronnie; Uncle Mike said he has to be there."

"Sounds like you have a plan; get with your brother, and you two make sure you're there as well—after all, it was your idea."

"All right, Dad, we'll see you later."

"Come on, Tara, let's go get something to eat. All this work is making me hungry!"

"Boy, are you getting spoiled! All this hard work!"

"I guess so, because I'm powerfully hungry."

Taking off on a run, Tara hollered, "We better hurry then; can't have your mind starving. Let's go eat!"

Back at the house, Haley and Cyndi were being creative in the kitchen. "Some things never change, Haley. In a little while we're going to have a bunch of hungry people riding in here."

"Sis, why do we seem to be the only ones always in the kitchen?"

"Girl, that's a damn good question, but the truth is, we like to eat just as well as everyone else. I get tired of the same old choices, so this way we can make our own menu."

Haley sampled the chili. "Ah! Well, let me be the first to tell you: that is the best damn chili I have ever tasted."

Cyndi laughed. "Well that's because we added two giant spoonfuls of LOVE into it!"

They laughed together and continued making sandwiches and cutting fresh vegetables; it was a table even Grandma would have been proud of.

Haley, looking out the window, said, "Well, if that's not perfect timing! Here they come."

Before long the whole family was gathered together again, laughing and eating.

Haley, watching everyone eat, looked over at Cyndi and said, "I think you're right: It's that **LOVE** we put into it."

CHAPTER 21
SHOWDOWN ON THE BROKEN R

That evening, Rick brought Amanda, Paul, and Gabriel to the Broken R. By the time they had arrived, Sam, Tara, Mike, Mary, Ronnie, Brad, Cyndi, and Haley had all gathered for the meeting. After all the introductions, Sam called the meeting to order.

"We are all happy to meet you. We have heard that you might be interested in selling your ranch, and the reason we are here tonight is to see if we can make a deal. So, Paul, do you have a figure in mind?"

Gabriel spoke first. "Please, Dad, don't do this!"

"Son, we have already discussed this; please don't make this any harder than it already is." He looked at Sam. "We are asking three million."

"It's plain there is some conflict here; are you selling because you have to or because you want to?"

Paul explained that because they had had two bad years in a row, they had taken out a loan on the property, and with tough times, they stood to lose it. Sam could see Gabriel biting his tongue, trying not to say anything.

"Gabriel, you obviously don't want to sell," Sam said.

"No, sir! And you can just call me Gabe."

Sam couldn't help but smile as he looked at Rick. "Okay, Gabe it is. Let us take a deep breath here; I think we have a clear picture of what has happened. Old story with new people, and I never did like that story. Therefore, I am not going to beat around the bush. I think maybe that we can make everybody happy. Mary, you might want to write this down, just for the record. Here's the best offer: we'll go two mill in cash."

Paul stood up. "I think we're done here; there's no need for us to waste any more of your time."

"Whoa! Paul, would you please sit back down? You came this far—at least let me finish."

Amanda reassuring him, said "It doesn't cost anything to listen."

Paul shook his head, but sat back down. "Okay!"

Sam started over. "We will go two million in cash for you, Paul and Amanda. The other million will go to Gabe—if he wants to invest in Simplicity. That would make him a vested member and you could stay on your land." When he said that, Gabe actually started listening.

"What now, we can stay?" asked Paul incredulously.

"That's what I said."

Paul and Amanda were lost. "We are selling you the land, but we can stay?"

"There's more to it, but you've got the basic idea. Gabe here, as a vested member of Simplicity, would have equal say in the company. He would receive $100,000 a year, as long as he stays a vested member in the company. Then you could live on the land. Simplicity would own the place, and it would become a part of the Broken R. Anything you wanted to do from here on would have to be a company decision, so if you decide to accept our offer, these are the people you will be dealing with," he said, signaling around the room. "We will give you a few minutes alone to discuss it among yourselves."

After Gabriel shook their hands and thanked them for their time, everyone left the room.

Within a few minutes, Paul called them back in and they accepted the offer. However, they wanted to know more about Simplicity and how it worked.

"It's better if you hear it from my brother. He's in charge and will be left with the final say," Sam advised.

Everyone in the room welcomed Paul, Amanda, and Gabe aboard, and left to let Mike have his say. They later celebrated the moment with their new family members. Gabe had a smile on his face as he shook Sam's hand.

"Thank you, sir!" he said. "That was worth it."

"You don't have to 'sir' me; we're family now."

As a family, they visited and shared some history on both sides. When they parted, Rick was full of questions; Mike did his best to explain how it all worked and remarked that Sam had made an excellent deal for both sides. Sam had a full day and was ready to call it quits.

"You guys fuss and discuss all you want, but I'm going to give it up for the night."

The next day showed promise of being another beautiful day on the Broken R. Sam and Tara were in town watching everyone getting ready to start filming. Trace had people everywhere. It was amazing to see how much work and detail really went into making a movie. One of his assistants, Stacy, brought Sam a boxful of videotapes.

"Mr. Trace said to give these to you; they're for Mike and Mary."

"Make sure you tell him we said thanks," said Sam.

"I sure hope they like it, because it sure was a beautiful wedding."

"I'm positive they will. Thanks."

Stacy ran back and told Trace, who turned and waved. Looking into the camera to see if it needed a last-minute adjustment, he hollered out, "Quiet on the set, and action."

Sam and Tara watched a few minutes, then eased off and headed back to the ranch to give Mike and Mary the tapes. They were just outside of town when they heard three shots go off. At first they laughed, thinking it was part of the filming. But all of a sudden, Ronnie and a bunch of riders were busting toward the house. Sam and Tara joined in the chase. Looking around, Sam saw riders coming from every direction; he hadn't a clue as to what was going on, but he knew it couldn't be good.

Handing the box of tapes to Tara, he then turned the reins loose on Hercules, hollering at him, "Catch them, boy!" Hercules was young and strong, and within seconds he caught up with Ronnie and the other riders as they came into sight of the house. It looked like an all-out brawl was taking place. There was a blue sedan parked behind the house in the road, and there were two black SUVs coming up the road. No one was supposed to be driving on this side, so Sam knew now that trouble was at hand. Still riding hard, he told himself, "Remember to control it." But the blood was starting to rush to his head.

Coming to a stop just a few feet away, he saw Mike face-down on the ground with his hands cuffed behind his back. The other riders circled around the disturbance with their rifles pulled. Mary was screaming and kicking at one of the men, and Cyndi and Haley were pushing and hitting another. The other two were trying to get Mike into the car. Another shot rang out; Sam saw a man standing on the catwalk of the barn. He waved, and Sam waved back.

"Stop!" Sam hollered out as he grabbed one man by the arm. "That was your last warning shot." The man turned like a caged animal and took a wild swing at Sam before he could even react. Ronnie dived in and took him to the ground.

Mary screamed again; the man had her by the hair. Sam turned and lost it this time, swinging the butt end of the rifle and knocking the man upside the head. He dropped to the ground in a heap. He fired off a shot in the air, hollering one more time for everyone to stop. Mary made it to Mike and helped him to his feet; two big men from security had hold of the other two. Sam walked back to where Ronnie was holding one man down. "Okay, Ronnie, let him up," he said.

Sam placed the rifle barrel to the man's head. "Nice and easy now," he advised as Ronnie pulled the man to his feet. "Make sure he is clean. This is about to get out of control." Sam pointed over to the security men. "Hey, guys! You got everything under control?"

"Yes, sir."

"What are your names?"

"Connor Hilton, and this is my brother Cyler."

"Well, glad to meet you; now bring them two over here. Ronnie! Throw some water on that one; see if he is still alive. Mike, are you all right?"

"Yes; nothing but my pride hurt."

"Hell, Bubba, don't look down. From where I was standing you were doing pretty good." Looking at the man again, Sam recognized him from one of the photos Frank had sent.

"Give me the key to the cuffs!"

The man started talking. "We are FBI agents, and you are interfering with federal officers trying to serve a warrant for this man's arrest."

Sam pushed the barrel of the gun closer to his head. "I said, give me the key!"

The man slowly handed it over. Sam passed it over to Mary. "Let's get those handcuffs off of him."

Mike rubbed off the sting. "What are you going to do now, Sam?"

"I'm thinking, Bubba. What do you want me to do?"

"Hell, don't listen to me, because if I had my way we would be digging graves for the rest of the day."

"Did you hear that, mister? The boss just signed your life over to me."

"You'll all go to prison for this!"

"We're not going anywhere. You can save all that big FBI talk for someone that's going to believe it. You see, I know you're not from the FBI, and that warrant for income tax evasion is worthless." Sam turned to Ronnie. "Ronnie, is that one dead?"

"Well, not quite; he still has a pulse, but he has one hell of knot on his head."

"Okay, let's get him in the car. I don't want him to die here," Sam said.

Stepping back, with the gun still pointing at the man, Sam said, "Open the trunk."

When he had, Sam commanded them to strip down to their underwear and put their clothes in the trunk.

"Are you crazy?" they demanded.

"No crazier than you idiots, coming in here playing cops and robbers. Now, do it before my friends here have to help you! Okay. Connor, Cyler, make sure those guns are unloaded and throw them in there."

When the men were done stripping and were sitting in the car, Sam called Connor and Cyler over to the back of the car and pulled out the pager. He asked them if they knew what it was.

"Sure, it's one of our tracking devices," Cyler said. Taking it, he turned it on and slipped it into a nook by the spare tire. "We can track them anywhere they go now."

"Very good, and that's just what I want you to do. I want to know everywhere these guys go; but most of all, I want to know who they're working for."

"How far do you want us to go?"

"As far as you have to; if you need more help let me know. All our resources are at your disposal."

"Just a minute, then," Cyler said. Reaching in and removing the pager, he slipped it into a briefcase that was in the trunk.

"Good! Just follow my lead now."

Closing the trunk, Sam walked around to the side of the car. "All right, men, here it is; the best deal of the day. You get to live, and I hope your friend back there makes it too. You go back and tell whoever the hell you're working for that we're done playing defense. You have invaded our home and crossed the point of no return. You tell them we're coming after them now, and we will see how well they like it. When you leave here, there will be an escort to Little Rock; don't make any stops before then. Men, make no mistake: if you come back to the Broken R there won't be a next time. We will be digging those graves that we talked about earlier."

Connor got into one SUV to lead them out. Cyler followed behind in the other. The riders spread out and followed them until they were off the Broken R. Everybody else was busy checking on each other to make sure nobody was hurt. Then, without warning, they were caught by surprise when they heard Trace holler out, "Cut and print!"

Sam turned around and shook his head. "I don't believe it—and you've got it all on film."

There was much excitement in the air over the next few weeks. Sam thought they were close to putting an end to the war. Connor and Cyler left the security team at the Broken R and became licensed private detectives. They followed and tracked the four men for months until all four had met with a sudden death, leaving them with no real evidence as to who hired them to invade the Broken R. Things just seemed to come to a stop with that situation, but Sam kept Connor and Cyler searching for clues through their family and friends.

Life went on. Sam stayed busy with all his projects, hoping for the best, but deep down he knew this was not the end. He kept Connor and Cyler on his personal payroll and made sure they kept him up to date if there were any changes. Mike was so busy, what with all the new developments and preparing for a massive overhaul in the communication's center, he had no time to think of anything else. As for the rest? Well, time heals all wounds, and Ronnie and Sally had run off to New York and got married. Before long, it was just a faded memory.

Chapter 22
Kevin Returns

A lot of time had passed, with many hours of exhausting labor, and nothing concrete had been uncovered since the deaths of the men who had posed as FBI agents. It appeared that each time they got a good lead, the outcome always turned into a dead-end. After pursing the enemy for close to two years, they still had no idea who was behind the incident that had taken place on the ranch, and it didn't appear that they were getting any closer to knowing who it was or why they were trying to get to Mike. Sam figured that whoever it was had maybe given up after the last failed attempt.

These were thoughts that haunted Sam as he rode into town. Sitting tall in the saddle, he had matured into a full-blooded cowboy. It was more than a feeling now; it was a way of life for him. As he rode down the street, he tipped his hat to say good morning to the people opening up their shops for the day. As he got closer to the bank, Sam could not help feeling a little bit prideful. The bank had been one of his greatest accomplishments—not only because it had been his idea, but also because he had turned it into a very profitable business for Simplicity. Rick and Brad were now running the bank with the help of their wives.

Entering the bank, Sam hollered out, "Good morning!"

Rick stepped out of his office. "Hi, Dad, how are you this morning?"

"I'm good, Son, I just wanted to stop by and see how you are all doing. I didn't want to leave without coming by and checking on you all."

"What's up?"

"Nothing. Your mother and I are flying up to New York for the grand opening celebration of the orphanage and school. Your uncle Mike is also making the final changes this week, in order to convert Simplicity over to the new national headquarters as well. My guess is we will be gone for a couple of weeks, and I have to tell you, I'm rather excited about seeing the finished product after all the hard work, the many hours of sweat, and the millions of dollars that have been poured into this project. I think it is going to be an exciting event.

"Well, I hope you and Mom have a good trip. Don't worry about us, we are doing just fine. We haven't run into any major problems, and you know we love it here."

"I know, Son, and that's the reason for my visit. Things have been good here for some time now, but remember to never let your guard down. I need you to keep a close eye on everything while we are gone."

"Dad, you are going to have to learn to trust us. We will be just fine, and I will keep a watchful eye out for any sign of trouble."

"Thanks, Son. I know you probably think I'm just a paranoid old man, but one day you will understand where I'm coming from. Okay, let me get out of your hair; I believe you have work you need to get done."

Saying his goodbyes to everybody else, Sam left the bank and made his rounds throughout the town. He and Hercules were just about to pass the cemetery, so they stopped for a glimpse of his father's grave. It seemed as if three lifetimes had passed since they had buried the old man; Sam was still having a problem believing that his father was gone. The scene that lay before him brought back memories of him lying in the casket, and because he had not seen him physically since the burial, it made it easier, when he came to the cemetery, to believe that he was gone.

Talking to Hercules, he said, "Well, boy, they say in life as long as somebody remembers you in their heart when you die, your memory will always live on. I reckon the old man will live on forever, because he touched a lot of people in his lifetime."

They made their way across the open flat lands, stopping only to take a good look at the herd. When they arrived at Ronnie and Sally's place, they found Ronnie outside in the barn doing a few chores.

"Hey, brother, it's break time."

Ronnie was already breaking a sweat from working. As he threw the last bale of hay into the feed room he said, "I believe you're right. Come on up to the house, and we will get us something to eat."

Sally stepped out the door, hollering, "Ronnie, breakfast is ready."

"Well Sam, I'm not sure if it's you or my wife who has perfect timing, but I don't think either one of you could have timed that any better."

"I'm not sure either, but breakfast does sound good. I left the house early this morning before anyone else was up, so I haven't eaten."

"All right, then, let's eat. I'm sure you didn't ride all the way up here for breakfast, though."

"Well, no, but it's those little extras that make life worth living."

As they were eating, Sam explained the purpose of his visit. "Ronnie, I came by to let you know we are gonna be gone for a couple of weeks."

"I'm glad you came by, then. I thought that was supposed to be next month. Man, how time flies. I guess I've been pretty busy, and time has gotten away from me. You be sure you tell everyone on the Bar S that we said hello, and that we send our best wishes."

"No problem. I'll be sure and tell them."

"I bet they're still talking about that wedding that you threw for us up there last summer."

"Well, that's what it's all about, creating memories that last a lifetime."

Sally came into the kitchen carrying an oil painting. "Look here, Sam, John sent this to us."

Looking at the painting, he commented, "My goodness gracious! Now that is one fine keepsake! That needs to hang over your fireplace mantle; you two never looked better."

"Thanks, Sam." Sally took the painting back to the living room, and hung it over the fireplace.

"Ronnie, I've got to get going; you two take care of each other."

"Okay, Sam, you too. Have a safe trip. I'll be sure and make my rounds, and keep an extra eye on things here."

"Thanks, brother." Sam walked outside and hollered, "Hercules!" He mounted the horse and waved at Sally and Ronnie, who stood on the front porch waving back.

"It appears time is getting away from us, Hercules; let's head home." They rode as fast as they could until they topped the hill, and then slowed to a walk for the remainder of the way, giving Hercules time to blow out. Sam was feeling better about things at the Broken R, and was now ready to make the trip.

At the house, Cyndi and Haley were helping Tara get a few things packed. Sam called Renny to make sure he was going to be on time, then asked the women, "So, are you all ready to go?"

Tara answered, "Yes, but I think Haley wants to ask you something."

"Well, go ahead, ask away."

"Do you think it would be okay if Gabe went with us?"

"That's it? That's all you needed to ask?"

"Yeah."

"I don't see a problem with it, if he wants to go."

"Thanks," she said, giving him a big hug. "What time are we going to be leaving?"

"In approximately one hour. That should give us plenty of time to make it to the airport."

"Okay, I'll tell him to hurry up."

Tara handed her the telephone as they both walked into the kitchen. Cyndi and Sam carried the suitcases to the SUV waiting to take them to the airport. Once Gabe showed up, everyone was ready to leave. Haley had apparently fallen head over heels in love with him, and she could only see the good in life; no evil could touch her—for the time being. Sam sat watching the two lovebirds; he could not help but wish that life would always be so good for them.

"All right, folks," Tara hollered. "Let's load 'em up."

They headed for the airport, driving down Interstate 30. Sam's thoughts had lapsed back in time, as they drove past the places where he had spent his childhood years. He wondered who would ever have believed he would have made it this far. He still tried, at his age, to understand life, which never seemed to add up for him. As they passed Bryant, Haley pointed out to Gabe the old house where she had grown up.

Sam was still in his daydreaming state, thinking, "I need to go by the old house and check on everything." Before he knew it, they had arrived at the airport.

Renny was there with his warm welcoming smile. He greeted each one, reached out and gave Tara a hug, then slapped Sam on his shoulder. He said, "Okay, big shot, let's load this old tin bucket up and we'll be on our way."

Sam and Tara had both been up since dawn, so they took advantage of the private bedroom and slept through the entire trip. Everybody had become a pro at flying by now, with the exception of Gabe; this was his first time in the air. Renny took the time to fix him a good stiff drink right after take-off, just as he had done for Sam on his first flight. It was a good flight for Gabe.

Sam, now rested, made the drive out to the mansion. When they pulled up to the gate, they had to use the new intercom system that had been set up. They pushed the button and a voice came on, asking, "How may I help you?"

"Hello, this is Sam; we are expected."

"Yes sir, you sure are," the voice responded, and the gates parted.

Frank, Molly, and Joe were all waiting at the front entrance for them. Sam and Tara—and even Cyndi—were amazed at what they had done to the place. It was just beautiful, and the fall colors on the trees made it look even more spectacular. The hugs and welcomes went on for some time, but when they finally made it inside, they all stood in awe. The outside was something to admire, but the inside literally took their breath away; they had truly created a work of art.

"My God," were the first words out of Sam's mouth. "Tara, can you believe this?" Cyndi stood speechless. "Haley, what do you think?"

"I think you all need to get a grip; it looks just like I thought it would," she said, winking at Molly. "I knew all along they would do a fantastic job."

That evening, everybody sat remembering the old times, and what the possibilities were for the future.

To the surprise of Haley and the rest of the group, after dinner but just before everybody was about to leave, Gabe stood up and asked, "Could I have everyone's attention for just a few minutes?" Pulling a ring from his pocket, he knelt down in front of Haley and asked, "Haley, will you marry me?"

Sam, along with everybody else in the room, stood silent, waiting to hear her answer. After what seemed like an age of pure silence, she whispered, "Yes."

Frank hollered, "Hey, Henry, grab a bottle of champagne and have Vera grab some glasses. We need to prepare a toast to Haley and Gabe. He just proposed to her."

Molly, of course, was hugging Haley's neck, and asked, "Can we have the wedding here at the mansion?"

"If Gabe doesn't have a problem with it, then I don't see why not."

Gabe answered, "I don't care where we get married as long as you will marry me, Haley. You get to make that decision, but if you want my input, I think it was this place that gave me the courage to ask you, so maybe this is where we are destined to be married."

Cyndi was already crying before she made it around the huge table. Hugging Haley, she said, "Oh, Sis, that was just beautiful. I wish for you nothing but joy and happiness. I just wish Mike and Mary could have been here for this one."

Mike and Mary had actually arrived in the meantime, and upon entering, they started toward the dining room when they heard Gabe making his proposal to Haley. Stopping just short of the entrance to the dining room, Mike hesitated before entering. He was happy for Haley, but sad for himself, hating to face the fact that Haley was grown now, and he had to let her make a life of her own.

Upon getting his emotions in check, they both finally walked into the dining room. He walked up and grabbed both of his sisters, and said, "Who said wishes don't come true?" They all visited and celebrated while talking about the grand opening events the next day.

The opening ceremony started at 10:00 a.m. Frank gave his welcome speech and then turned the floor over to Mike.

Mike walked up onto the stage, waving to the crowd as he made his way to the microphone. "On behalf of my family I would also like to extend our welcome. On this special day we have taken a tremendous step toward fulfilling a vision of my father's; he had foreseen this structure as being a great facility in meeting the need of orphans—for housing as well as education. For those that did not know it, my father was an orphan as well, and he always had a vision that some how or in some way, he would do the best he could to try to protect and help as many orphans as he possibly could. His vision did not stop just here in New York; his vision was to aid and assist orphans all around the country. It was our father who started with just a simple idea." Stopping for a moment, Mike asked his family, "Please join me up on stage." When all were beside him, Mike continued: "We may have contributed the money for this project, but we owe our deepest respect to the people who have actually made this project happen." Pausing once again, this time Mike asked Frank, Joe, and Molly to get up on the stage. After introducing the three individuals, Mike said, "These are the three people responsible for making my father's dream a reality. We extend our deepest gratitude and thanks to you."

As Mike was shaking their hands one by one, Sam walked up to the microphone. "We couldn't have asked any more from Frank, Joe, or Molly. They were our father's closest friends. We commend you for the fantastic job that you have done here. We set out to preserve the memory of our father, and you have done just as requested. Thanks so much from all of us. You have filled our hearts with joy. Now I would like to invite everyone to stay and check out the facilities, and have lunch with us. Once again, thank you, Frank, Joe, and Molly, and thank you all for taking time out of your busy schedules to come out and support this celebration, acknowledging the opening of the orphanage, school, and the new headquarters for Simplicity."

For the rest of the afternoon there were many questions to answer: people wanting to know more about the school and the orphans, and others that wanted to know about Simplicity. Sam was tired from answering questions, and telling some of his dad's old stories to so many people.

In the late afternoon, a young man approached him. "Sir, you may not remember me, but if it's not too much to ask, I would like just a few minutes of your time to speak with you."

"No problem. Have you had any lunch yet?"

"No sir."

"Well, come on, then. We can talk and eat at the same time."

"Sir, I was really hoping for just a one-on-one visit."

"Very well, walk with me to the dining hall, and if you can convince me that what you need to discuss with me needs to be said in private, we will take our food elsewhere and talk."

"Sir, my name is Kevin, and I just got out of jail last week."

"Okay, Kevin, my name is Sam, and what is it that you want to talk to me about?" The name Kevin was not registering with Sam; it appeared time had blanked out that memory.

"Sam, are you sure you don't remember me at all?"

Sam was thinking hard, but he just could not place the face. "I'm sorry, Kevin, but you're gonna have to jog the memory banks for me."

"Well, approximately two and a half years ago, your grandson was kidnapped."

Sam stopped immediately and looked hard at Kevin, "Are you trying to tell me that you are that Kevin?"

"Yes, sir, that's exactly what I am trying to tell you."

"Apparently, you've got a lot more guts than common sense, to come waltzing in here. You're damn lucky I don't shoot you right here, in front of God and all of these witnesses."

"You're probably right, but you see, I don't have anywhere else to go. My dad has made it impossible for me to go back home. In fact, I am surprised that I am still alive today. I figured a hit man would take me out the day I got out of prison."

Sam's memory had come back in full force by now. The cash bonds that he had locked away must have been what Kevin was referring to when he said he was surprised that he was still alive.

"Well, Kevin, you have convinced me; let's get something to eat, and we will continue this conversation alone in another room."

The two sat for over an hour, covering a lot of questions to which Sam had long searched for answers. Phillip, Kevin's dad, had indeed tried to do a double rip-off. He had stolen the 7.5 million in cash bonds from the organization, and when the switch was officially completed and he had taken over Sam's identity, Phillip planned to set himself up in Germany, run Simplicity, and convert all of the organization's monies into the Simplicity bank accounts.

"Damn it, Kevin, why would you want to come back and tell me all this?"

"Sir, I have already told you why; I am lucky that I have made it this far. I do not know what it would take to prove to you that I am on the up-and-up with you, but the truth is, I came to you to ask for a job. I am clean of the drugs that they had me on, and I can now think straight. I believe that, if given a chance, I could be a great asset to your team, and besides, I don't think they would ever think I would come back here, so maybe I would have some element of safety."

"Very well-spoken, Kevin. I admit it all adds up, and I can't help but feel that you're being sincere, but I'm telling you: we are going to have to do a lot of really hard work to make you fit in with the others. I like you, and think you could be a real good asset to us. You have already provided me with details that I have long wanted to understand, and I'm sure there will be more that you can clarify for me in time, but make no mistake—I don't think the others in the family will be as understanding. Here is my plan for what we are going to do: I'm gonna make some phone calls . . . by the way, you haven't told anybody else your name, or who you are, have you?"

"No, sir, you're the only one I've talked to."

"Good. Start thinking about what you would like to be called. Keep quiet, and hang out here for a while; I need to put some ideas together. I will meet you back here in about an hour."

Sam left to take some time to think things through. He called John and they met out in front of the school. Explaining his plan to John, he asked, "John, do you think you could turn him into a ranch hand in two weeks?"

"Hell, that's a tall order, Boss, but I guess if he's willing to try, we will damn sure give it our best shot."

"That's the spirit! I really do appreciate this. When you get ready to leave, give me a buzz and I'll bring him out to meet you."

Sam met back with Kevin. "All right. First of all, did you come up with a name?"

"What about Jason?"

"Sounds good to me. Here's what we are gonna do, Jason. You are gonna spend the next two weeks on the Bar S and learn how to become a full-fledged cowhand. When I get back to the Broken R ranch, you will transfer down there to work. If you do well, then we will go from there."

"Okay, sir, I'll give it my best."

Chapter 23

Mike Has A Plan

Sam spent the rest of the day visiting with the new staff members and guests, never missing a chance to boost Simplicity's membership although it was an easy sell. At this meeting, he had already signed up fifty new members, and handed out over 100 new-member applications. When John called, Sam found Jason and took him to meet John before they headed over to the Bar S. When they got in the SUV, Sam introduced them.

"No one knows anything about this except the three of us, and I want to keep it that way. Is that all right with you, John?"

"Sure, boss, I understand."

"Jason, is there any chance someone here would recognize you as Kevin?"

"I don't think so."

"Okay. Remember you only have a couple of weeks, so pay close attention to John, and when you are around the other hands, make a mental note to be sure and pay close attention to the lingo they use. John, I want you to put ten thousand dollars on a card for him, and make sure he is outfitted right."

"Got it. I'll see that it gets done."

"Okay. Well, you guys better get going; I need to stay here and finish out the day. I'll be over later tomorrow, and that way I can see what all you have done to the ranch."

"Great! Then we'll see you tomorrow."

Sam returned to take the tour through the new Simplicity headquarters. Mike was just finishing his little speech. "As of an hour ago, we are fully functional, and the system is now downloading information from Arkansas. By tomorrow, everything will be running from our new national head office. I extend my personal welcome for each of you to join us on our tour, and if you are not a member of Simplicity yet, we hope to convince you to join us today. Thank you."

Mike led the group on a full-fledged tour of Simplicity; Sam stayed near the back and enjoyed being just one of the guests for a while. Besides, he was lost once Mike started talking about computers, but, like everything else he had witnessed today, it was top of the line, and very well presented. The place alone was enough to dazzle him, even though he did not understand how it worked. When Mike concluded the tour, there were several of the new staff waiting to sign people up, if they chose to join. When Mike was free, Sam chatted with him for a short time.

"Well, brother, that was really something. And I might add, you did a fine job as well."

"Thanks," replied Mike, looking over to see that several more people were signing up. "That is what tells the story. Hey, by the way, Tara told me you signed up 50 new members today yourself."

"Yeah, that's not too bad for a dumb old country boy like me, is it?" said Sam.

"Don't sell yourself short, little brother; that's quite an accomplishment. By the way, come on into the office here; there's something I think you need to see."

"Sure, what is it?"

Pulling out some files, Mike laid them on the desk. "Do you recognize the names of any of these companies?"

Sam looked closely at each file, and picked three out. "These here I remember from Connor and Cyler's reports, but if I recall correctly they were dead ends, 'cause they were dummy corporations."

"Exactly, but do you want to hear something that will blow you away?"

"What are you trying to tell me?"

"Simplicity now owns all of these companies."

"How can that be, Mike? And how come you didn't say something sooner?"

"Well, mainly because I didn't know until the other day, and when we started doing the change-over we uncovered this. You know that gut feeling you are always talking about?"

"Yeah, Mike, I'm having it right now."

"Good, because the best I can come up with after running the hard copy is that all these transactions took place just two weeks ago. The final kicker is that they were supposedly done by Dad!"

"What the hell did you say?"

"Well, at least the transactions were done in Dad's name."

"Mike, do you believe there is any way possible it could have been Dad?"

"No, Sam; Dad may have convinced some people that he was bigger than life, but he was just another man, just like you and me, with the foresight to never give up."

"What makes you so sure?"

"Sam, I was there, remember? I sat with Dad for hours during his final days. Besides, Dad never logged a thing in the computer system. He always brought everything directly to me."

"Okay, Mike, I believe you, but ever since I have been back, somebody has gone through a lot of trouble to try and convince me that somehow, some way, Dad is still alive."

With a little bit of a grin, Mike continued, "I remember you telling Cyndi you had had a conversation with Dad in the old house in Bryant. I didn't think much of it back then, because I knew you were going through some tough emotional times then, but remember a couple of years ago when those phony FBI agents tried to kidnap me out at the ranch?"

"How could I forget that?" said Sam.

"I know, but my point is, I thought I'd seen Dad that day myself," said Mike.

"Oh my God. Don't tell me: the old man on the cat walk of the barn," said Sam.

"Yeah, you're right. So you thought it was Dad too, didn't you?" said Mike.

"I sure did."

"Well, little brother, I've got some ideas, but they're pretty bizarre. I wouldn't want to mention them to anyone else; they might want to lock me away, thinking I had lost my mind."

"I know, Mike; that's exactly how I have felt for a very long time, but I remember one time Dad said the reason God gave him two sons was because he knew it would take two men to replace him. So with that in mind, I guess we are going to have to start working together and find out just what the hell is really going on."

"My feelings exactly; that's why I'm showing you all this."

"Then there's something I need to share with you, Mike."

"What is it?"

"Earlier today, I was approached by a young man who said his name was Kevin—the Kevin that had kidnapped Little Billy. He swears his loyalty to us because he is afraid the organization will have him killed because of what his father did. You remember Phillip, don't you?"

"Yeah, that was his father."

"Well, I found out today that what I had suspected was true. Phillip had tried to do a double take on both the organization and Simplicity. Apparently, he had planned to incorporate the two."

"What did you do with Kevin?"

"Well, he's at the Bar S learning how to become a cowboy. John is the only one I have told besides you. We are working him in under the alias of Jason."

"What makes you believe him, Sam?"

"When everything went down with Phillip, Renny found a briefcase that someone had thrown out of a window. There was 7.5 million dollars in cash bonds, along with a ticket to Germany. His story matched up; he just didn't know the dollar figure."

"Okay, but what do you think he's gonna do for us?"

"Mike, do you ever think about what Dad told you?"

"Sometimes, but what's that got to do with anything?"

"Well, Dad used to tell me when I was just a kid, 'keep your friends close, but keep your enemies even closer.'"

"Oh, I get it. So you're thinking he can give us insight to the enemy's camp. Now I think we are on the same page."

Mike and Sam worked for hours trying to devise a plan, when Tara interrupted their thoughts by hunting them down. "Don't you two think you ought to give it up for the night?" Tara asked.

Looking at his watch, Mike could not believe it was 8:30 already. "Okay, tell Mary I'll be right in, and Tara, if you don't mind, I still need Sam for just a few more minutes."

"No problem."

Sam gave Tara a kiss and said, "I will see you in a moment or two."

Mike turned back to Sam and said, "Well, what do you think?"

"Frankly, I think you're right; they will have us both locked up in the funny farm if this doesn't work, but let's give it our best shot."

Calling it a night, they headed off to join the rest of the family. They would spend the rest of the evening together reminiscing about the day's events, and how many new additions they had added to the Simplicity family.

The next day brought everyone together at the breakfast table. They made their plans for the day over one of the biggest country breakfasts they had ever seen.

Sam backed away from the table, patting his belly. "My compliments to the chef. I could not eat another bite if I tried." He drank his last swallow of coffee, and excused himself from the table.

"Come on, Mike, I'll walk with you over to your new office."

Mary waited until they were gone, then asked Tara, "Do you know what's going on with those two?"

"No, but it's got to worry you."

"What's that supposed to mean?"

"Oh, I didn't mean it like that. I just meant I'm used to worrying about Sam; Mike has always been very level headed."

"Well, all I know is, they're spending a lot of time together and that can only lead to more trouble."

Tara agreed. "But we could always hope they're just learning to work together."

Mary smiled. "I think I'll hold on to that idea; it sounds good and it's a more suitable thought than the others.

"Sam, are you sure you want to go through with this?" Mike asked him when they were alone.

"Look, big brother, this was your idea; we are in this together, or not at all."

"All right. I am behind you 100 percent. Give me a layout on what you have planned before we head back to Arkansas."

"No problem, I'll keep in touch. You just work on your part, okay?"

"Yeah."

"Okay, then I'll see you later. Tara and I are going to head over to the Bar S and check things out over there."

Mike waved as Sam walked off, and wondered if they could really pull this scheme off. He had to laugh at himself and his thoughts. He was thinking, "I wonder what Dad would have to say about this: his two boys conspiring together on such a devious plan." Mike spent the rest of the day running through comparison reports to see if any other transactions had taken place of which he was unaware. Thinking of his plan to reveal who and why, he now had to make a decision on who in the family he would trust to let in on their plan.

Sam and Tara had spent the day at the Bar S, feeling more at home as they took their tour through the new town. Even though it was not completed, it was still amazing. On the main road side, it had all the look of a modern strip mall; facing the ranch side it was completely western, and favored the Broken R almost to the letter.

"Well, John," Sam said, "it looks like you're well on your way here. Where did you come up with the idea to give it the double face?"

"Believe it or not, that was Frank Jr. and David's idea, Sam. They said we should encourage the public to drop by."

"Well, who said those boys were gonna make you good cowhands? By the way, how is our new cowhand working out?"

"They're running him through the mill today. He probably won't be able to walk in the morning. That is when we will start his training."

"Sounds like you got the ball rolling. Let's find Tara and try out that new diner. It has been quite a day, and from the looks of it, you are doing a fine job here. By the way, how is the money holding out?"

"To be honest with you, I way underbid the project; we are almost broke, but we are working on some ideas to raise the money to finish the project."

"Well, let me know; maybe I can work something out at the bank to loan you the money."

"That sounds good, because they were kind of excited about getting her finished."

"Hey, there's Tara." Sam called out to her. "Tara, come on; we are gonna get something to eat at the new diner."

In the diner they ran into Jack, a cowhand who gave the impression that he had been out riding fences too long. Jack was one of those people that just could not help himself; he loved to talk to people. It was as if he had not talked to anybody in a month, so he never shut his mouth, but they all had a lot of fun during the meal. Sam laughed, and cut up right along with Jack just as if they were brothers, but deep down inside he was practicing for his new role that Mike and he had devised.

Back at the Broken R, things seemed to be in running in perfect order. Rick and Brad had to work a little late, so they were on their way to the diner to meet with their families.

Ronnie and Sally were taking their evening ride around the ranch, just trying to keep an eye on things and make sure everything was in order. "Everything looks good, Sally. Do you want to run into town, and maybe grab a cup of coffee or something?"

"Baby, that sounds good to me; let's kick up a little dust." They rode hard up the back roads until they got into town, then slowed the horses to a walk until they had made it to the diner. Tying their horses off, they went inside to get a drink.

Rick hollered, "Uncle Ronnie!" just as they walked in. "You two come on over here and join us. What have you been up to?"

"Hi, Rick, we were just out riding, checking things out, trying to make sure everything is all right. Have you heard anything from your Mom or Dad?"

"Mom called this morning, said everything went really well, and that they were going over to the Bar S today to see what all they had done there. They must have had a good time, because I haven't heard a thing this evening."

"Everything seem to be going okay with you guys?"

"Yeah, it's been business as usual; nothing very exciting, just your everyday run-of-the-mill business transactions. I must confess, though, I am looking forward to my next day off. I am missing the freedom of being able to jump on my horse and go for a ride in all that fresh air. You don't realize how much you miss it until you're stuck in an office. Yep, I can't wait for that next day off."

"I know what you're talking about. I never cared much for being shut in an office all day myself, but you like working in the bank otherwise, don't you?"

"Oh, yeah, I didn't mean for it to sound that way; I had just gotten spoiled having a lot more free time, and I used to take long rides around the ranch. It gives you a sense of freedom like nothing else I have ever experienced."

"Well, Brad, you're the quiet one tonight. Is everything okay?"

"I'm sorry. I guess I was paying more attention to the food. I didn't have any lunch today."

"No problem. As a matter of fact, I think we are going to head on out to the house and get ourselves settled in for the night. You two take care; if you need anything, just give me a holler."

"Okay, Uncle Ronnie, we'll see you later."

Ronnie and Sally took the short route out of town and cut across to the house. By the time Ronnie got the horses put up and made it to the house, Sally had already fallen asleep on the couch. Ronnie stepped back out onto the porch to smoke a cigarette. Standing there in the quiet of the evening, he couldn't help thinking of Wild Bill. In his younger days he remembered him standing right where he was now. Bill would look over at him and say, "Well, Son, we got quite a lick of business done today." Now Ronnie's thoughts drifted to wondering if one day he might have a son himself. If everything could always be this peaceful and happy, he would like to have a dozen children. The Lord knows best, though, he thought. He finally gave it up for the night, and counted it a good day.

Chapter 24

The Plan Revealed

Sam and Mike met early the next morning, before anyone else had awakened. They continued to work on polishing their plan.

"Well, Mike, the way I see it, everyone in the immediate family is going to have to know about the plan, or it isn't going to work."

"I know, I have been thinking the same thing. If we tell them what we are up to now, it might blow their minds, but at least it won't screw up our plans after the fact."

"Have you talked to Trace yet?" asked Mike.

"Yes, I have a meeting with the make-up artist tomorrow afternoon. I will become Dad sometime tomorrow afternoon. Therefore, we need to have that meeting tonight."

"Okay, Sam, I'll have everyone meet with us together about seven tonight, but you're much better at explaining things than I am, so you get the job of explaining everything."

"I think that's a fair deal," he said, shaking his brother's hand to seal the deal.

That evening the family sat in suspense, wondering what in the world was going on now. Mike would not tell them a thing while awaiting Sam's arrival. When Sam walked into the room and took a look at the people he had grown to admire and respect, he was starting to get cold feet, and wondered if this maybe wasn't such a good idea after all.

When Mike called the meeting to order, everyone sat quietly. Sam knew it was too late to turn back now. He stepped in, trying to take on his dad's confident personality, and looking at this as a job, with nothing personal about it.

"All right, I know all of you are anxiously waiting to hear what this is all about, so bear with me for a moment and I will try to explain everything in complete detail. That way, there won't be too many questions for Mike to answer when we are done. First, there are some strange dealings going on in the Simplicity system. Mike has discovered that we are taking on a numerous amount of new businesses that we know nothing about, but the real problem is that these deals are indeed taking place right under our noses, and they're being done in our father's name. Now, just briefly, that leaves the door open for numerous problems, first with the IRS, and second with countless future problems if we do not catch who is doing this. Mike and I have created a plan which we hope will draw out of hiding the person who is responsible for this data manipulation. My role in this plan is to become Dad, and see if I can cause enough commotion to get our computer snitch to come out of hiding. The reasons are obvious as to why we are letting you know what we are doing. We do not want you to freak out and go nuts on us when Dad appears. You may all have conflicting views of what you think about this, but apparently, we need Dad to help us fish out the traitor we have on the inside of Simplicity. Your role will be to help us watch everybody closely, to notice any strange behavior, or any parties overly interested in the fact that Dad is still alive and kicking. We have put a great deal of thought into this, and we want everyone's full cooperation. We all know the problems we have had to face in the past with not being completely honest with each other, so whether you agree with us, or disagree with us on this decision doesn't matter, but as a family we need your absolute total support. We are dead serious in trying to get to the bottom of this problem, and we are going to do whatever it takes to protect you, and our father's name.

"Let us take some time, and all of you think about what I am telling you. We will all meet back in here in about an hour, and we will discuss any questions that you might have. Now, I do have to ask that you tell nobody else about this plan. Just for the safety of the plan, we are the only people that need to know what is really going on."

Everyone separated in different groups to discuss their opinions.

Sam pulled Tara to the side to explain to her how all this was to play out, so as things started to happen she would be able to explain to the children what was taking place.

"Sam, I can't believe you're doing this!" she said. "What is even harder for me to believe is that this was Mike's idea. You two don't have a clue to the Pandora's Box you're fixing to open up."

"That may be so, but Tara, we cannot just sit back and watch someone steal everything right from under our noses—or worse yet, land us all in prison for tax evasion for revenues not paid on companies we knew nothing about. We are not talking small figures here."

"Well, I can see you're dead set on this plan. Let's hope that's not how you end up. You know they wanted your dad dead a long time ago, and if you're not careful, that's exactly what's going to happen to you."

"Come on, Tara; try to have a little confidence in me."

"Oh, believe me, I am trying." She gave him a hug and a kiss, then whispered, "I am trying."

Mike and Mary were in the other room having the same conversation, only Mary was more concerned about the unborn child that she was carrying; a fact that she had just unveiled to Mike. "I didn't want to say anything until I was absolutely certain. I got the call from the doctor's office this afternoon, and with all that has been going on, we haven't been able to talk to each other, but: you are going to be a daddy. You need to grow up and quit playing secret-agent games with your brother."

Mike's emotions were jumping as if he were on a roller-coaster ride. He was excited, but scared at the same time. Despite having mastered the art of controlling his emotions, Mike was having a tough time at this moment. "Look, Mary, I understand what you are trying to say, and I would have expected no less from you, but you cannot see the world through my eyes. Nothing could make me happier than knowing we are going to have a child, but at the same time I wouldn't want my child to grow up thinking I was a coward, and tucked tail and ran from trouble just because it was the safe thing to do."

Mary broke down and, with tears in her eyes, knew that Mike was right. Turning to hug his neck, she said, "Well, you just make damn sure you make the right moves and take care of yourself."

Cyndi had slipped off, but nobody knew where she had gone. She returned just before the meeting was to restart. Once everybody had returned, Frank spoke up first.

"Sam has laid out their plan. Molly, Joe, and I agree that we should pledge our support; we are not sure just how much help we can offer, but whatever we can do to help, we will do it."

Mike stood up to take the floor. "We are happy to hear that, Frank. I just want to make this perfectly clear, so that there are no misunderstandings. This was my idea, and if anything goes wrong, I will take full responsibility for it."

Sam chose to close the meeting with the final details: "Tomorrow, 'Sam' is leaving on an extended trip back to Montana. By the end of the day, 'Bill' will return here for a welcome-back party from an overseas trip that he has been on for almost three years. Does everybody understand? It is imperative that we all use the same story if you have anybody asking."

Everybody agreed, and swore they would do their best.

Mike took the floor one last time. "Before we all part for the night, I would just like to share some good news with you," he said, motioning for Mary to stand with him. "We are going to have a baby."

Everyone seemed to be frozen in time for the next few minutes; after all they had discussed about the plan (which was tough to swallow), they finally had some good news as well. Once the news actually sank in, they all lined up to congratulate Mike and Mary. The family spent the rest of the evening polishing up the plan and celebrating the news of the new addition they would soon have.

The next morning, Sam and Tara slipped out just before daylight and went to the Bar S. They had a special breakfast fixed just for them, and Jack was like his old self; he could put a smile on anyone's face just by being around him. After breakfast, they went riding to share as much time as possible together before Sam had to go into the city.

"Sam, I know I can't change your mind about this, but you have to promise me to try and be careful."

"Well, darling, I give you my word: I will be careful. I promise you I don't have a suppressed death wish."

"Well, maybe not, but you're stretching that neck out and putting it right on the chopping block, just to see who is going to step up to try and take it off of your head."

"Okay, babe, I see your point. That's enough graphic details, I don't want to start this all off on the wrong foot."

They rode up to the barn, put the horses up, and got ready for Sam to leave to have his makeover. John was the only one from the Bar S who knew what was going on, and had shown up to run Sam into the city. As they were heading for the house, Sam had seen Jason riding out with a young woman.

"Who is that? Jason is riding with John?"

"Her name is Ashley. She showed up here this morning looking for work, said she moved here from Michigan to try her luck in the big city, but things weren't panning out for her. She said her grandfather had taught her to ride when she was just a kid and she loved it; she didn't care what kind of work we gave her, as long as she could ride in her off time."

"Today is Jason's day to stay in the saddle and ride the ranch, so I guess the two have paired up for the day."

"Well, now, did you hire her?"

"Yeah, a good-looking cowgirl like that? I couldn't let her just get away; besides, Jack has been hollering for help in the kitchen for months. If I had not hired her, I believe old Jack would have paid her out of his own pocket."

Sam laughed. "I can just imagine; he would have done it, too."

"Well, let's hope our boy there don't get no romantic notions. He will be pulling out soon to go to the Broken R. How's he been doing?"

"I think he will pull it off; he spent two hours in the pool trying to soak off them saddle sores last night, and you see he's right back at it today, so he's at least making the effort anyway."

"Good."

"Tara, would you like to ride with us into the city, and do a little sightseeing?"

"Yeah, I'm going to be without him for awhile, so I need to spend as much time with him as possible."

They all loaded up and headed into the city. After they dropped Sam off, John took Tara sightseeing.

As Sam entered the room, Stacy welcomed him and made the introductions. "Sam, this is Barbara; she is the best in this business."

"It's nice to meet you, Barbara."

"It's a pleasure to meet you. You did remember to bring some photos with you, didn't you?"

"I sure did," he said, reaching in his pocket and handing the photos to Barbara.

"Okay, then, best of luck, and I hope everything works out," Stacy said.

"Thanks, Stacy."

"We will see you in about four or five hours; you're in good hands."

Barbara was already studying the photos and looking at Sam. "I don't think it's going to take us as long as we thought. There's a strong family resemblance. Come with me, Sam, and we'll get started." Barbara led Sam to a room, and told him "Get comfortable; you're going to be sitting for awhile."

Sam removed his hat and shirt, hung them up, and then climbed into the chair. "Okay, I guess I'm ready," he said.

"Good, then let's see what kind of magic we can do here."

Barbara went straight to work. She placed the photos up on the counter so she could look at them periodically, and hollered for Andy to come look at his hair. She worked while Andy studied Sam's hair.

A few minutes later Andy replied, "I don't see a problem, Barb; I will have it ready in about an hour, and I'll leave it a little long. That way, you can dial it in."

"Thanks, Andy, I will see you then."

Sam leaned back in his chair and closed his eyes as though he were preparing for a long winter's nap. His mind drifted off, wondering if he could really pull this off. He was thinking of his dad and trying to remember details of things he had said and done. To this day, no one had totally convinced him that his dad was gone. There was something his dad always said, "If you're the only one that believes something, whether right or not, it leaves room for a one-percent doubt." They spent the next three hours doing pretty much the same thing, except sometimes Barbara would ask him to move, or she would ask a question that he needed to answer. After he'd spent a little over three hours in the chair, Barbara asked, "Sam, are you ready to take a look at Wild Bill? Mind you, I still have a few more last-minute touch-ups, but this should give you a good picture at this point."

"Not really, but let's get on with it," he said and turned to look into the mirror. Not meaning to verbally express his feelings, he still blurted out, "Oh my God! This is unbelievable!" Drifting with his thoughts, it was as if somebody had turned on a light switch in his head. Sam was looking in the mirror at the man with whom he had held a conversation just a little over two years ago. He did not realize then just how much older he looked until he'd seen himself in the mirror. He thought to himself, "I know he is alive now. That could have been me in that damn coffin."

Barbara called Stacy in to check out her work, and Andy followed right behind her. All three of them, talking, seemed to jar Sam back to the present. Putting his shirt and hat back on, he took another long look into the mirror. He turned, and hollered, "What the hell are you all gawking at?" All three jerked back in shock.

Sam said, "I am sorry." Reaching out, he touched Stacy on the shoulder. "I am so sorry, but that's why they called him 'Wild Bill!'"

Reassuring him that everything was okay, Stacy said, "But you damn near gave us all a heart attack."

He thanked Barbara and Andy, emphasizing what a great job they had done. Stacy walked him back up to the front where John and Tara were waiting to pick him up. When Sam entered the room, Tara stood in shock, and she had been expecting to see the change. John stood laughing; he had heard the prank that Sam had pulled in the back room. There would be no doubt that Wild Bill was back if Sam continued to perform as well as he had in that room. Sure enough, they had done a fantastic job. To anyone who didn't know better, "Wild Bill" had returned. With another round of thanks, they headed back to the Bar S.

Everyone at the Bar S was in total awe to see Bill again, but they were not sure just how to handle the situation in approaching the extent of his disappearance. Of course, Jack took it right in stride, and jumped in by saying, "Well, Boss, this comes as quite a shock, and I hear Sam left just a short time ago, and per my understanding, he is supposed to be gone for a while. It is apparent that you two just cannot seem to get on the same wavelength, but let me tell you up front, the boy has been doing a fine job in your place. You will have to get John to show you all the improvements that we have made since you have been gone, and before you head back to the Broken R, that old mansion deal looks like it went over big. You will not believe it unless you go by and check it out yourself."

"I will make it a point to check it out," he said, afraid to say too much at this point. Sam could not believe no one has questioned his reappearance; it was as though they knew all along he really was not dead, but also knew they would no longer get to see him anymore. "Maybe I am reading too much into this," he thought, "but there is definitely something fishy going on here. What the hell, here I sit thinking, and I just spent a small fortune to change myself to look like my father, so I could take his place. For the most part, it appears to be working, so I had better get my head screwed on, or I am likely to lose it!"

Chapter 25
The Bank Robbery

Sam immediately found a flaw in their plan. While talking with Jack, he could not keep up with the conversations. When Jack started reminiscing about the good old days when they both ran the herd together, Sam knew they had to do something quick. He asked Jack, "Hey, Jack, if you don't mind, would you walk outside with John and me? We need to ask your opinion on something."

"Well, sure." Jack followed the two men outside, and Sam and John attempted to explain to him what was really going on, and why.

Jack took a step back, looked hard at 'Bill' and said, "Well, I don't believe my eyes then, because I would have sworn it was Bill in the flesh. You should not have any trouble convincing anyone else. Your dad and I were real close back in the day, and you sure fooled me."

"Then maybe we can talk awhile, and you can kind of give me some history to work with."

"Sure thing, Sam. Come on, let's go into the study; I've got some old videotapes that you might want to see, and I'll rustle up some grub."

They were off on a journey into the past, and Sam was getting more information than he had bargained for, but he enjoyed every minute of the films. He thought that by morning he should know everything he needed in order to make their plan work.

When daylight came over the Broken R, it seemed as though another normal day was fixing to get started. Everyone was hurrying about to get things underway. Rick and Brad met each other riding into town; they were going to open early today, since they were expecting a big shipment of government bonds to arrive.

"Good morning, little brother, you're looking mighty spiffy this morning with that new Stetson hat on."

"Well, thank you, big brother, and what would be on your mind that you would start my day with such a compliment?"

"Can't really describe it, Brad, but for some strange reason my soul is in tune with everything around me today. I feel like, for once in my life, there is nothing I could do or say that would make life any better. I have reached the top of the mountain, and I am looking down, and all is well with the people I care about the most, but there is this feeling that there is more required of me."

"Boy, are you becoming quite the philosopher; you had me hanging on there like I was fixing to be enlightened myself."

"Okay, brother, if you didn't want to hear it maybe you shouldn't have asked."

"No, it's not that; I really enjoy talking with you. I just never knew you had such deep thoughts."

"Well, ask Dad; it runs in our blood," said Rick.

"Sure enough, then maybe there's hope for me too," said Brad.

"Come on, little brother, let's get to work. I am already longing for quitting time to get here; I have big plans for this evening."

They left their horses at the livery stable, and walked the rest of the way to the bank. When they arrived, they locked the front doors behind them and headed straight for the back door. Rick had just gotten the vault doors opened when the back door buzzed.

Brad asked, "Do you want to get that? And I will start pulling the cash out for the day."

Rick just nodded, and headed to open the door. There were two armored trucks backed up to the dock. One of the drivers said, "Good morning, Rick, and are you ready to get started here?"

"Sure, fellows. Just bring the delivery in, we are ready."

They started stacking the packages of bonds on dollies, to roll them into the safe. They had been going through this routine once a month now, for as long as the bank had been open. No one had to ask questions; there was very little time for talk, due to the vault's being set on a time lock. Rick had never let the vault go past its 30-minute window, mainly because it was a real pain to reset if you messed with its schedule. When the delivery was completed, Rick closed the door with only a minute to spare. He signed off the purchase order for receipt of the bonds, and the security team was saying their goodbyes when they heard the vault door click back into the locked position. Rick expressed his thanks, and then locked the back door once again. Walking back to the front of the bank, he asked Brad, "Do you need any help getting the cash drawers ready?"

"No, I have it under control. Go ahead and open the front doors."

Rick pulled the shades open and then unlocked the front doors for business. "Okay, little brother, we are officially opened. I hope it is a quiet day. When the girls get here, we need to get this shipment logged in."

Brad pushed the last cash drawer into place. "I hope you're right, brother, and I sure could use a quiet day. I've been having a hard time keeping my mind focused on business here lately; maybe it's time for a vacation or something."

Before Rick could respond to Brad's comment, the front door opened and four young men bolted inside with guns drawn. One of the men yelled, "Get your hands up in the air where I can see them. You behind the counter, fill these bags with money." He threw the bags onto the counter. "Okay now, nice and easy, and nobody will have to get hurt."

Brad was placing the cash into the bags steadily, but not too fast. He had tripped the silent alarm during the process. Therefore, red searchlights were circling from the rooftop of the building, signaling to anyone that could see them that they were in trouble.

Ronnie and Stan were the first to notice the lights, since they worked the holding pens that were located almost straight out in front of the bank. Having the other hands ride to gather everyone else, Ronnie told Stan to follow him, and they would enter town from the south side so they would have both ends covered. Riding hard, Ronnie pulled his Winchester, expecting the worst.

In the bank, Brad had the moneybags full. "All right, hand them bags over nice and easy." As Brad started to hand the bags over, he stumbled, and the gunman raised his pistol to shoot.

Rick hollered, "Noooo . . .," then jumped between the man and his brother, taking the bullet almost dead center in his chest.

This sent the four robbers into a dead-for-all panic. They grabbed the bags and ran for the door. Brad jumped back to his feet with a Winchester of his own. Seeing his brother on the floor bleeding, he hollered, "Stop, or I'll kill you!" and the last man at the door turned to shoot once again. But this time Brad shot first, sending at least one of the robbers to the promised land, as the bullet took him right off the front porch.

Ronnie heard the gunshots and saw two men running to get away. Taking no time to think, he shot both men before coming to a complete stop in front of the bank.

Stan saw another man running down the alley between two buildings, but he didn't want to shoot for fear of hurting an innocent person. Pulling out his rope, he chased the man out into an open range, where he was able to lasso him. The gunman was trying to take a desperate shot at Stan, but when Stan kicked his horse into a full gallop, and what little slack there was came out of the rope, it almost snapped the man in half, and his gun went flying. Stan slowly dragged him back to the bank, where his partners in crime all lay dead in the middle of the street.

The sirens were blasting; Ronnie was waving everybody in, first the ambulance, then the police. When the medics ran toward the men lying in the street, Ronnie hollered, "Get inside, those men are dead; come help the man inside."

They turned and ran into the bank, where they found Brad holding onto Rick. Trying to be strong for his brother, he said, "Everything is going to be all right now, help is here, you just hang in there."

The medics went to work on Rick, trying to stabilize him enough to transport him to the hospital. Brad made the phone call that nobody ever wants to hear. When Tara answered the phone, Brad could hardly speak, "Mom, Mom,-get home now. Tell Dad to hurry, we were just in a hold up at the bank, and Rick has been shot."

Panic filled Tara's heart, but she had to ask, "Is he alive?"

"The medics are trying to get him to the hospital now, but it does not look good. Hurry! I will call you back. I have to go; we are heading to the ambulance, and I am riding with him."

"Okay, bye."

The police car pulled out in front to escort the ambulance to the hospital; the ambulance driver sped off, knowing that they were fighting a race against time. Time was of the essence; if Rick was to have any chance of living, they had to get him to the hospital very quickly.

Ronnie was talking with his old friend James Ostrom, who was now sheriff of Faulkner County. When he saw Donna and Patty barreling through town he told him, "James, you are gonna have to handle this; if there is anything else you need from me, just let me know. You know where to find me." Turning to Stan, he said, "Stan if you don't mind, please stay here and help them with whatever they need.'"

Mounting up on his horse, Ronnie headed the girls off. "Come on, I will try to explain everything on the way."

They took the shortcut across the open pasture to Ronnie's place, putting the horses up as fast as they could, and trying to talk at the same speed. Ronnie hollered, "Patty, go grab the keys to my truck; they're hanging right inside the kitchen door."

Grabbing the keys, Patty told Sally, "We have to get to the hospital now!"

"Where are the kids?"

As they were all running for the truck, Sally met them and Ronnie said, "I'm really sorry, honey, but I've got to go. Pick up the kids, and meet us at the hospital."

Sally just nodded and ran for her car. She could see the panic in Ronnie's eyes, and she knew without asking that it had to be a matter of life or death.

Sam and Tara sat holding hands on the plane, praying that God would spare their child's life. Mike and Mary sat in silence, knowing there were no words to comfort them; just being there was all that they could do.

Tara was crying, remembering when they first brought Rick home from the hospital. Sam was trying to hold it together for the both of them, and he said, "Come on now, be strong and think positive, he's a healthy boy, and he's gonna be just fine."

Tara, with a half-smile on her face, and tears rolling down her cheek, said, "I know, he's going to be just fine."

They sat back in silence holding on to that hope, and continued praying, asking God to be with Rick and to give him the strength to fight on.

By the time the plane had landed in Little Rock, everyone had pretty much forgotten what the plan was. They were too busy thinking of Rick and the problem at hand. Ronnie was waiting at the airport to rush them to the hospital; they had flown Rick to the Baptist Medical Center in Little Rock, which meant they were only twenty minutes away. When they started disembarking from the plane, Ronnie pulled the SUV as close as he could get.

Tara was the first to speak. "Ronnie, please tell me. Is he still alive?"

"Yes, he's holding on, and should be out of surgery by the time we get there."

Sam was beside himself in his thoughts; he had jumped into the car without a word. Ronnie could see Mike was just full of questions. "Don't bother asking, brother. I will bring you up to speed on the way."

Mary and Mike got into the SUV, and they drove off toward the hospital. At the hospital, they found Brad sitting in the ICU waiting room with several others from the Broken R. They had all shown up to donate blood. Even though Brad knew about the plan, he was still shocked to see his dad. He hugged his mother's neck and whispered in her ear, "Am I supposed to call him 'Grandpa'?"

She could hardly speak, so she just nodded yes.

Brad turned and hugged his dad. "Hi, Grandpa, I'm glad you could make it."

"How you been doing, boy? Long time no see."

"Okay, I guess, given the circumstances," said Brad.

The family reunion was quickly broken up when the doctor came out to speak with them. "Hello, I'm Dr. Chakalas," he said, shaking hands with Tara and Sam. "Your son is now in stable but guarded condition. He is young and strong, and I believe in time he will make a full recovery. I do not foresee any further complications, but it will take him some time to recuperate from a blow like this."

"Can we see him?"

"Sure, but we have to ask that you keep it down to just two people at a time, and limit your conversation for the moment. It's okay to let him talk, but we don't want to rush him into remembering everything too fast."

Sam almost slipped when he reached to shake the doctor's hand. He was fixing to introduce himself, but the doctor cut him short by grabbing his hand and saying, "You must be Grandpa."

"Yes, and we want you to know how very thankful we are for your care in taking care of our boy."

"No problem; I will keep you posted as the treatment progresses. You all go have a good visit now."

Everybody breathed a sigh of relief just from the news. Tara and Patty went inside first to visit with Rick. Sam sat back for the moment, willing to take a few precious minutes to thank God. The waiting room was starting to empty out, with all the cowhands leaving and going back to the ranch. Mike and Mary were feeling better now that they knew Rick was going to be okay, so they decided to get something to eat. Ronnie and Sally joined them. If the family had not been so distressed, they might have noticed the extra gleam in Eric's eyes, and the unusual excitement he seemed to have from seeing the reincarnated Wild Bill. At this time, Sam was not even concerned with the plan, and didn't give it much thought, but it seemed to be working without anyone helping it along.

Tara, knowing how jumpy Sam could be, spoke before touching him on the shoulder. "Hey, are you ready to see your grandson?"

Sam was not even trying to act out his part, but moving very slowly, he pulled himself to his feet. "Sure, how is he doing?"

"Well, he seems to be fine, he's kind of talking about off-the-wall things, but I figure that's because of all the medication they have him on."

Sam and Brad entered the room slowly and sat down by the bed. When Rick opened his eyes and saw his Grandpa sitting there, he was taken by surprise. Sluggishly he asked, "Gran-Grandpa, how are you doing? Have you seen my dad?"

Trying not to upset the apple cart, Sam played along with Rick, not knowing for sure if Rick knew anything, or if he just did not remember. "I'm doing pretty good, and yeah, I've seen your dad in New York."

"That's good. You know, Grandpa, we never told him our secret."

"Which secret are we talking about? I'm sure we had several."

"Yeah, you're right; you know, about when we would sneak off to see you when you came to Montana."

Sam turned to look at Brad and saw his face turning beet red; he did not have to ask if it were true or not. Rick faded back out for a short time, giving Sam a chance to regroup his thoughts. They visited a short while longer before the nurse interrupted them and asked the family to come back later. They needed to check the bandages and make sure everything was in order before the doctors made their evening rounds.

As everyone joined back together in the waiting room, Tara told everybody Rick seemed to be doing okay, but she would stay at the hospital with Patty, and everybody else should go home and get some rest. Sam would have argued, but he knew it would have done him no good. He just gave Tara a hug, and followed the rest of the family out the door.

Everybody seemed very quiet on the ride home, but Ronnie and Brad kept them busy thinking as they went on about all that had happened. Sam was in shock all over again when he found out Brad had actually shot one of the bank robbers. His boys were grown up now; that was nothing new to him, but maybe only now he was accepting it. Catching a glimpse of himself in the mirror, he forced himself back to reality. Those were hard blows to Sam's ego, knowing that his children did not need him anymore, and that his wife and children had kept secrets from him for all these years. When they arrived back on the Broken R, they said their goodnights and parted ways. Sam could not explain it, nor did he understand it, but everything all at once had taken on a whole new look, as if he were really seeing things through his own dad's eyes.

Chapter 26
Wild Bill Returns to the Broken R

Even though Sam was dead tired, sleep would not come to him. His mind was working overtime on the things that had already taken place, and the things that still would probably happen. He climbed out of bed and began pacing the floor, trying to figure out what it was that he seemed to be missing. He had that odd feeling, like déjà vu, that he was missing something important, something big, but he couldn't seem to pinpoint the source of his distress. He had a hard time explaining why or how he was feeling this way, but he knew something was definitely not right. Before he knew it, he had gotten dressed and was heading for the study. Sitting behind the big oak desk somehow made him feel as though he was still in control of things. Taking out his journal, Sam began to enter the events that had taken place. A sudden thought came to him, and everything seemed instantly to be clear to him. It was as if the clouds had rolled away, and for the first time since he had been back, everything made perfect sense.

He had been played, manipulated into every move he had made since his return to the ranch, even whether he should stay on when he first came back for his dad's funeral. As he turned back to the beginning of his journal and the letters from his dad fell out, he put them in the order he received them. He studied them as if he had just uncovered another secret treasure. He leaned back in the chair and closed his eyes; his brain was playing like a videotape, but he wasn't sure whether it was from lack of sleep, or all the stress he had been under. Everything played out crystal clear. Mike had played all of this from the beginning, and knew a lot more about what was going on than Sam had ever dreamed of him knowing. He had been the one sending the notes, all the while telling him Dad was gone. He was the one who had been trying to make Sam believe their dad was not dead, and look at where it had led him: straight into another mess.

Whatever it was, Sam knew now that his time was short, and he didn't have many aces left in the hole. He spent the next few hours explaining everything in great detail in his journal, then writing out his last will and testament. He did not realize that time had slipped by so quickly, and daylight was only a few hours away. Taking off the ring, he placed it into the box, right beside the journal and his will. He took the time to lock the box inside the desk drawer.

Sam then went to take a shower, getting himself ready for what he figured was going to be his last rodeo. It is strange how he saw things so differently when he wasn't sure there would be another tomorrow. He caught himself seeing minor details in a different light. With his fate hanging in the balance, he seemed to be more alert to the things that he would normally have taken for granted—especially since he was looking death in the face. Things mattered to Sam now; he noticed every detail of the clothing he wore, making sure the shirt buttons lined up with the button on his trousers. He even took a minute to shine his boots. Looking out the huge bay windows that overlooked the Broken R from his room, Sam remembered seeing this sight in front of him for the first time. Oh, what a beautiful sight she was, too! Today he saw her from a different perspective; without peace, she was just a fancy rich man's prison.

After he was completely dressed, he returned to the study and entered the secret room. He strapped on the gun belt, then checked each pistol, making sure that they were fully loaded. He took off his new Stetson and put his dad's old hat on, thinking it was more fitting for the occasion.

Checking the monitors, he reset the security cameras inside the main barn, zeroing in around Hercules' stall. If things went the way he had foreseen, he would have it all on videotape. After securing the secret room, he stopped to look in the mirror, adjusting his hat and then the gun belt. Then, as if he were in some kind of trance, he began to have a conversation with his dad—besides, that is, who he was looking at in the mirror.

"Well, Old Man, you're looking rather good this morning."

"Well, thank you, Son, and might I say you're looking pretty spiffy yourself."

"Are you ready for this showdown?"

"Just another walk in the park, my boy."

"How do you stay so cool under this kind of pressure?"

"It's like this, Son: once a man accepts the worst that could happen, he then has nothing to fear."

Then, all at once, it clicked in Sam's mind: that is why his dad was so confident. These weren't just quick-witted answers; he really believed the things that he said. Still looking in the mirror, he nodded. "Okay, then, let's get this over with."

He headed for the kitchen like a condemned man going for his last meal. He had a ham sandwich and a cup of coffee. Laughing to himself, he realized he had not even smoked a cigarette since he had left New York. Taking his coffee, and grabbing an apple for Hercules, he stepped out onto the porch. Sitting in one of the big rocking chairs, he fired up a cigarette.

Still talking to himself, he said, "Sam, you almost had it all."

Daylight could not be far off, and it had been a long hard night. Finishing off his coffee, Sam started his walk to the barn. He took the last puff of his cigarette, stepped on the butt, and continued walking toward the barn. He thought to himself, "Maybe I'll have time to say goodbye to Hercules before anyone shows up."

He walked slowly, and with a slight limp, it was as if he were still in some kind of trance. Everything was moving in slow motion, just like a bad nightmare, but he was trying his best to not let his fear show.

When he entered the barn the motion lights came on at the door, giving enough light to see down through the barn. He stopped for just a minute. Everything looked quiet. He continued his slow walk down to Hercules.

"Good morning, Big Boy," he said, reaching to scratch his ears.

Hercules responded with a little nod, then put his head down, as if he knew what was next. This caught Sam's attention, just as other things had. Hercules responded to him as if he recognized the old man, and Sam was not surprised to see the response.

"Well, boy, I want you to know that if I don't make it through this, you were the best thing that has happened to me since I have been here; you have been a true friend." Taking the apple out of his pocket, he gave it to the horse. "Here you go, my friend."

"Well, now, isn't that something? A man with everything calls his horse his best friend."

Sam did not recognize the voice, and found himself caught completely off guard. Drawing his gun, he expected to be dead before he could turn around.

"That's it, Wild Bill, turn around. If you taught me anything, a man should always look into another man's eyes when he's talking."

Now he was in a staredown with Eric and a double-barrel 12-gauge shot gun. Sam almost choked, because at this range he knew it was over if Eric pulled the trigger.

Cocking the hammer back on the .45 pistol, and trying very hard to stay calm, he said, "Big hole, little hole; looks like we're both gonna die."

"Good God, that's it, an old movie line. Somehow, I expected so much more from you."

"What? Surely you weren't thinking I was gonna beg for mercy, did you?"

"No, but I did figure you would want to know why."

Eric couldn't help but want to explain why. After all, he had dedicated most of his life just for this very moment.

Sam knew every minute from this point on was precious, so he went ahead and encouraged him to talk. "Well, I figure I know why, but what I can't figure is, why you?"

"You would if you had studied your family trees a little better. What in the hell did you think you were going to do, save the world? Hunting down the poor little orphans and building this ranch for them? Living like you're all one big happy family? Did it ever occur to you that when you killed my adopted father, we might have been a happy family?"

Sam was lost for most of the conversation, until that moment when everything his dad had told him rushed into his head. He knew he had to try to keep Eric talking. If he had any luck, maybe somebody would come along soon. "When you say we, are you trying to tell me there are more here that want to see me dead?"

"Oh, they're not here yet, but they will be soon. You see, we figured out that you faked your death; that Sam couldn't keep his month shut about having talked to you when he first came back. Just as we thought, we figured that if we threatened your boys enough, you would finally come out of hiding. It damn near took killing your grandson to get you to come out of your cave; well, you won't be saving anybody after I get through with you."

Sam's blood began to boil, knowing Eric had something to do with almost killing his son. He started to realize that whoever Eric really was, he had long planned the events that were unfolding before him, and he wasn't about to let 'Wild Bill' walk away from this alive. In order to keep Eric talking, Sam asked him another question. "What makes you think I'm here to save anything? The boys already run everything; I've been out of the circle for a long time."

"Don't try to play me for a fool, old man; you've been coaching them every step of the way. With you gone, those two idiots won't have a clue what to do next, and we will take over Simplicity right in front of their eyes, before they ever knew what hit them."

Sam did not know how much longer he could hold this calm, steady position, but he realized now why Mike had manipulated everything, and why it was so important that they believed their dad was not dead. It was not so much for his sake, as it was for everyone else. Knowing this renewed Sam's soul; he started to feel a new wave of confidence surging through him.

When Eric started to speak again, he jerked up the shotgun barrel as if he was going to shoot. Without any hesitation Sam pulled the trigger of his own gun, and from only seven paces away the bullet hit true, killing Eric instantly. Sam stood frozen in the same position, watching Eric fall backwards into a stack of hay. Finally, Sam looked at himself, to see if he had taken a bullet as well.

Within seconds, there were cowhands coming from every direction. Sam walked over and stood next to the body, still pointing his gun just in case Eric was still breathing. When he was sure Eric was dead, he holstered his gun. Looking up, he saw everybody heading his way. He knew he didn't have much time, so very quickly he grabbed Eric's cell phone from his jacket pocket. As he started to walk away, he could not help himself, but had to stop and give Hercules a hug, whispering in his ear, "Well, boy, we live to ride another day."

Stan stood there looking, but not believing his eyes. "What the hell is going on here?"

Sam, still rubbing Hercules' neck, turned to face him. "Better get Mike and Sam down here to explain it, 'cause

I quit trying to explain myself a long time ago." Then he told Hercules, "I'll see you later, boy." Then 'Wild Bill' just walked off toward the house to disappear as suddenly as he had arrived. He decided that now would be a good time to become Sam again, and as quickly as possible.

Stan was on the phone, calling Ronnie.

"Hello?"

"Ronnie, you need to get your tail down here right now, and call Mike and Sam."

"Okay, Stan, what's up?"

"You ain't gonna believe this, but I've just seen Wild Bill, and there has been a killin' down here; Eric is dead!"

"Say no more, I'm on my way."

"Okay, then, bye."

Trying to keep everyone out of the barn was damn near an impossible task. Stan did the best he could, and was glad to see Mike and Ronnie arrive.

Sam was in the house trying to remember which solution was for removing what . His adrenaline was pumping so hard that he thought, "If I don't slow down, my heart is going to jump right out of my chest." Removing the hair and beard, he jumped into the shower, running the water as hot as he could stand it. It was as though he were trying to steam-clean the guilt off of his body and soul, because no matter how it happened, no matter if it was self-defense or not, killing somebody is not a pleasant thing to deal with. The hot shower did seem to be working, and he finally started to calm down as his breathing slowly returned to normal. He knew Mike was probably in shock himself; Eric had been pretty much his right-hand man in the com center. Sam also knew that Mike would be asking many questions, but he wasn't going to cut him any slack on this deal.

Mike called Brother Phil and explained as best he could about what was going on, and told him to get with Ronnie so they could take care of Eric and have him prepared for a proper burial. Calling the hands together at the barn, Mike asked them to keep things under wraps until they could sort out this mess. Stan pointed to the main house. "You need to start right in there. I'm telling you he was here, and I watched him walk into the house."

"Thanks, Stan, I believe that's just what I'm going to do."

Mike headed to the main house almost in a panic, wondering if Sam was all right. Sam was dressed, and sitting at the kitchen table with the cell phone and videotape when Mike walked in.

"You okay, Sam?"

"Sure, Mike, I'm just fine. Couldn't be better."

Mike, hearing the sarcasm in his voice, said, "Dammit, Sam, I didn't know how this was going to unfold anymore than you did."

"I believe that, but you sure as hell knew what you were doing when you set all this up, 'Mr. Nice Guy.' I have to take my hat off to you; you really played it like a hit song. It was one thing to play with my life—that didn't bother me, after all I agreed to go along with the plan—but playing with my children's lives is a whole different story."

Being on edge, Mike didn't take to Sam's accusations very well. "I don't know what the hell you're talking about, Sam. I never tried to involve your kids in any of this."

Pushing the videotape across the table, Sam said, "Here, when you get a chance, watch this, and make of it what you will. I believe it was self-defense. In addition, here is his phone; it might be of use to you. I did my part—or should I say I did Dad's part—and now you can decide how to clean this up, Mr. Mastermind. When you figure it out, then let me know what I need to know, and then I hope like hell I can forget about the rest. Now I am going to the hospital to be with my wife and son."

"That's a damn good idea, and that's where you need to be. But let me tell you something, little brother, before you get all high and mighty on me. Don't you forget one damn thing: I walked every step behind that old man, never once running off or leaving his side. You want to know why? Because he never once left my side and I knew beyond any doubt he always had my backside guarded. You bet your sweet little ass I will clean this mess up, just as I cleaned up after shooting Philip in New York. Yeah, that's right brother, you're not the only one with blood on your hands, and God knows I would clean up another hundred messes if it means protecting our dad's name and everything he built here."

Sam sat back, taking in every word, until Mike had finished. He was surprised to hear Mike confess; he had thought Ronnie had shot Phillip. With a smile, he stood and hugged him, and said, "That is the best damn speech you've given yet. I hope I never forget this moment. It proves I'm not the only one around here with a temper problem; you're just better at controlling it. Now calm down, I was just yanking your chain. I know why you did it," Sam said.

After Sam had left, Ronnie joined up with Mike at the house.

"Hey, Mike, where is Sam?"

"He went to the hospital; we just had a little confrontation. He was rather upset about the turn of events."

"I bet he is, having a facedown like that—especially all by himself."

"Well, maybe so, but I have the feeling he was more upset with me. He figured out I was behind all this. Anyway, he was smart enough to get it on video, so come on, let's see what this tells us."

Sitting in the living room, Mike and Ronnie watched the video. Even though the sound was not the best in the world, they could still make out the entire conversation between Sam and Eric. When the tape ended, Mike could see why Sam could be angry with him.

"Well that says it all in a nutshell," Ronnie said.

"Not really. It says everything, except what we really need to know. Eric might have been the inside man, but there is somebody else out there pulling the strings."

Ronnie walked back to the kitchen. "Well, surely his belongings are still here on the ranch. Let's get busy, and see what we can find out; we need to know if he had help in all of this."

"You're right, let's get over to his place and see what we can find."

At the hospital, Sam found the entire family sitting together in the waiting room. Ben and Sarah came running to him saying, "Grappa, Grappa."

As he knelt down to get a hug, tears automatically started to fill his eyes. "Come here, you two, give Grappa a great big hug. How have you two been doing?"

Little Billy had finally wrestled lose from Donna, and was making his way to Grappa too.

"Well, look at this little man! Boy, are you growing up fast."

Getting his hugs, little Billy said, "Grappa crying."

"Grappa is just happy to see you little ones."

The rest of the family joined in with hugs and tears. When things settled down, Tara explained that Rick was making a good recovery, and they were moving him to a private room very soon. That way, they would all be able to go in and see him any time they wanted. Sam spent the rest of the day with his family, never saying a word about what had taken place that morning out at the ranch, and hoping that he would never have to.

Back at the ranch, Mike and Ronnie were finding everything they needed to put the story together. Mike had found Eric's laptop packed away, and now searched through it for clues.

"Look here, Ronnie."

"What you got?"

Mike was pointing almost in disbelief. "They're all here: every name, and addresses to boot. Some I even recognize from a long time back. As far back as when Dad was holding the monthly meetings here on the ranch. You got your phone with you?"

"Sure, what you need?"

"Call Connor; tell him I need him and Cyler to get over here. I have a plan."

Ronnie made the call, and stood back watching Mike type away on Eric's laptop. He could see Mike's eyes lighting up; it seemed the faster he typed, the more excited he got. Finally, he stopped and said, "Come on, Ronnie, we have a party to plan for."

They went back to the main house; Mike was talking so fast that Ronnie could hardly keep up with the conversation.

Ronnie jumped in. "Mike, you have got to slow down; I'm not sure what you're trying to say. You're going so fast I can't keep up."

"It's perfect, Ronnie! We got them right where we want them."

"What do you mean?"

"You know what Eric said, 'We will own it all, before the idiots know what hit them.'"

"Yeah, I remember, but what the hell has that got to do with anything? He's dead."

"Yeah, but we are the only ones that know that. I just emailed them, and told them 'the mission was complete.'"

When they sat down at the kitchen table Ronnie was still as lost as he could be. Mike was excited, and Ronnie had no clue about whatever the hell he was talking about. Mike picked up the cell phone and looked at it. "Good thing we made it back in time; no one has tried to call."

Ronnie walked to the refrigerator looking for something to drink. Mike grabbed a glass out of the cabinet and asked, "Is there any iced tea in there?"

"Sure," Ronnie put it on the counter and grabbed a Coke for himself. Both men took a couple of big swallows from their drinks, and then sat facing each other at the kitchen table.

"Aw, I don't remember when a glass of tea tasted so good," said Mike.

"Well, I'm happy for you, brother, even if I can't share your enthusiasm."

"You will very soon. As Sam said this morning, the 'Master Mind' is at work."

Eric's phone rang. Mike held his finger up to his mouth, telling Ronnie to be very quiet. Answering the call, he said, "Hello?"

"Eric, are you where you can talk?"

"Sure, I'm just trying to pack to get out of here."

"That's good. Hang on. Senator Fisher wants to speak with you."

"Hey there, Son, congratulations! You finally pulled it off."

Mike, trying to keep the conversation very simple, answered, "Yes, sir."

"All right, here's what I want you to do. Get the hell out of there, and make sure you leave nothing behind. I need you to have the body shipped to my place in Chattanooga. The rest of the group will want confirmation that Bill is actually dead. And one last thing: were you able to run the rest of the holdings into Simplicity?"

"Yes, sir."

"All right, boy, it sounds like you have everything under control. I guess we will see you in a couple of days, and then we can celebrate your accomplishments."

"Thank you, sir."

Mike hung up the phone and took some deep breaths.

"Well, come on, tell me. Who was it?" asked Ronnie.

"That, my dear brother, was Senator Fisher. He just filled in the gaps; we are now all set."

"Will you stop talking in riddles to me? I would like to know what's going on, and now you're going to tell me what the hell is happening here."

"Look, they think Eric has just killed our Dad, and they want Eric to ship the body to Senator Fisher's place in Chattanooga. That way everybody can be assured that he is really dead."

"Okay, what damn good is that to us?"

"Ronnie, I need you to get focused; we are about to pull the deal of the century off, but we don't have much time. When Connor and Cyler get here, I will put all of this in perspective for you."

Ronnie sat back, took a deep breath, and said, "Lord help us, I know we're gonna need it."

"Hey, are you hungry? I know I am."

"Yeah, I'm hungry too. Do you want me to call Sally and have her bring us something over?"

"If you don't think she would mind, that would be great."

Going back to work on the laptop, Mike was off into his own little world. Ronnie talked with Sally, and she said she would be there with food in a few minutes.

At the hospital, Sam was finally starting to come back to reality. The sleepless night, and all that he had been through that morning, had been more than he could take. He was just plain worn out; his mind and body started to shut down. Not wanting to make the long drive home to the ranch, he and Tara excused themselves and grabbed a motel room close to the hospital. Sam was sure sleep would somehow make things better.

When Connor and Cyler showed up at the ranch, it was late afternoon. Mike was ready to present his idea to them, after explaining in detail just how they had arrived at this point. He was ready to begin with what they were actually going to do.

"Okay, are you with me so far?"

They all nodded, and Ronnie spoke up. "All right, Mike, let's hear it."

"Maybe if I tell you first what was supposed to happen, then you will have a better understanding of what we are going to make happen. First, I was telling you about the company buyouts showing up in Simplicity's holdings. The kickers to the buyouts were that Eric was going to flood the vested membership roll with people from the organization. That way, by the end of next year, Simplicity would be in serious trouble when it came time to pay out the dividends. Then the organization would have been able to step in and take control, because they would have the majority vote and we wouldn't have enough money to bail Simplicity out.

"So now here is what we are going to do. I have already run the rest of the company's buyouts just as Eric started. The only thing is, I switched Dad's name to mine, and showed a fifty-four-million-dollar payout to our friend Senator Fisher. I figure he will have a fun time trying to explain that one. Then I took his membership roll and transferred it to future prospects, and added them to our mailing list. Now for the switch, they are expecting a delivery, and I need Senator Fisher's signature to make the transactions legal. So we are going to deliver Eric's body to him, and you're going to have him sign for it."

Cyler spoke up. "I get it! They were going to show good faith in their transaction of the companies, but at the same time they were going to try to bankrupt Simplicity when she couldn't make her dividend payout. That would leave the door wide open for a hostile takeover."

"You are exactly right, and they had to be sure Dad was out of the way. They weren't afraid of me or Sam, but they knew with Dad in the picture it would be an all-out war."

Ronnie joined in. "Okay, now it's starting to make sense. If you complete what they started, then in the end, Simplicity will own all their assets."

"I do believe you're catching on, brother. The best part is that if they want to recover any part of their losses, it will cost them another million dollars each to become vested members of Simplicity. How ironic is that?"

They worked out the final details and set a time schedule for carrying out the plan. When they parted company, Mike and Mary went to the hospital to visit with Rick.

By the time they had returned home, Mike had thought everything through and was sure if the timing was right they could pull this off and put a end to the lifelong war. He met up with Connor and Cyler, and handed them Eric's cell phone and two videotapes to put inside Eric's coffin. One tape was a copy of the shooting, the other was a tape of his father explaining the story of Simplicity, how it got started and how it worked for new members. They were all set to go; Brother Phil followed them to the funeral home to pick up Eric's body. Once they loaded the coffin in the hearse, Brother Phil wished them Godspeed and a safe return home.

Mike and Ronnie were already on their way to the airport to meet Conner and Cyler. Their timing could not have been better; Renny had flown in the night before, bringing Cyndi, Haley, and Gabe back from New York. Therefore, he was available to fly them over to Chattanooga. They would have time to set things up, check everything out, and plan their getaway.

Once they were in Chattanooga, things fell into place like clockwork. Renny even joined in on the escape plan. Connor rented a plain white delivery truck, and had some magnetic signs made up that read, "C and C Delivery Service, Chattanooga, Tenn." Mike completed everything on the laptop, making a final backup copy of all the files, and then he changed all the access codes so no one else could access Simplicity's system, which didn't matter much because in a few days, the changeover to New York would be completed and all the codes would be changing anyway. Connor and Cyler were set to go; Mike placed the laptop into the coffin, just to add insult to injury. In the end, he wanted them to know who the idiots really were that pulled off this stunt.

They drove out to the estate with Mike and Renny following about a mile behind them. Connor pulled the truck up to the speaker at the gate. As he pushed the intercom button a voice came on. "What can we do for you?"

"I have a special delivery for Senator Fisher."

There was a loud buzzing noise and the gates started to open. "Come on in. The guard at the front of the house will direct you where to go."

They pulled up in front of the house, and luck was smiling down on them for once. Senator Fisher himself came out, telling the guard, "We will take the delivery right here."

Connor and Cyler jumped out, pulled out the crated coffin and set it on the walkway. "Would you like help getting this inside?"

"No, that's all right; we can handle it from here."

Grabbing the clipboard, Cyler asked Senator Fisher for a signature. Standing at six feet, six inches, and weighing 380 pounds, Cyler could intimidate almost anybody. Senator Fisher, being a much shorter man, did not even hesitate.

"There you go, young man."

"Thank you, sir. Have a good evening."

Connor started up the truck just as Cyler was climbing in, and they drove out without any problem. About two miles down the road, they saw that Mike and Renny had pulled in behind them. They follow them to the rental place to return the truck. When this was completed, they climbed into the car with Mike and Renny, and were heading back to the airport within the hour, ready to fly back home. Once they were in the air they couldn't help but let go a little bit, with high fives, and laughter so hard it hurt. Mike sat back holding his stomach. "Come on, give me a break; I can't take no more."

"You should have seen it; old Cyler here stepped up to Senator Fisher and said, "I need a signature." I think

Senator Fisher would have said 'no' if Cyler had not been so intimidating; you could tell he wanted to say no," said Connor.

"Connor, come on. Give it up."

Mike was still laughing; the nervous energy was just too much. Finally, Cyler fixed everyone a drink. "Now you fellows settle down before I have to get rough."

When they arrived back in Little Rock, Mike insisted Renny come back to the ranch with them; he was sure Sam would enjoy seeing him. They had become very close over the years.

Meanwhile, back in Chattanooga things were coming apart at the seams for Senator Fisher. Finding Eric in the coffin blew him away. He was watching one of the videos when his guests started showing up. There on the big screen television was Wild Bill giving his spill on Simplicity. This was enough to drive him into an angry rage. He threw his drink at the fireplace and screamed, "Give me that other tape!" When the second tape started, he fell back in his seat. "My God, it can't be!" But this was just the beginning; when the other members of the organization arrived and started going through the laptop, watching Eric die at the hand of their enemy, things were really getting out of control.

One man jumped up, hollering at Senator Fisher, "You son of bitch, what the hell? Do you think that we are all stupid?"

"Look here, he was going to pull his own Wild Bill."

"Selling us all out, for fifty-four million dollars."

Senator Fisher was now in a fight for his life. "I swear I don't have a clue what you're talking about."

"It's all right here in black and white."

The problem with trying to pull off a con as big as Senator Fisher had is that it involved an excess of people and their money as well. Now these people were no more than a angry lynch mob, out of control and bloodthirsty, and only one thing was going to settle the score.

The Broken R family awoke the next morning to what seemed like an unscheduled family reunion. John from the Bar S had brought Jason down, and as Sam would have guessed, Ashley was with them. From out of the blue, Lance and Brett from Montana showed up with their wives Erin and Terrie. They had both settled down; Lance had gone into banking and Brett was in insurance. Molly and Frank slipped in from New York; they left poor Joe to look after everything. Uncle Alan and his family were there, and Rick was on his way home from the hospital. The women were busy trying to put everything back in order for Patty. Through it all she never once complained, or tried to blame anyone for what had happened. Sometimes the real troupers in life are overlooked, so the family was trying their best to show their appreciation. Sam was more or less back to his old self, never saying a word about what had happened that fatal morning. Mike and Mary never seemed happier. Haley and Gabe still had their heads up in the stars. Cyndi seemed to have other things on her mind, but she wasn't talking. For now, she was too busy planning to take care of their family and guest. Ronnie was back to just being a cowboy, and hoped the rumors of Wild Bill's return would just fade away.

As all the introductions and welcomes took place, Mike caught a breaking news bulletin on the TV, concerning Senator Fisher from Tennessee. Apparently he had died in a fatal car crash. Mike did not know whether he felt bad for the man or not, but in some way he knew something like this was bound to happen. Walking away, he thought that maybe this would finally bring an end to the nightmare, and his dad could finally rest in peace. When he stepped outside the door, he ran into Sam and Ronnie.

"Come on, you two, let's take a little walk."

As they walked out toward the corral, Mike explained to Sam what had taken place.

"Why didn't you tell me?"

"Now, Sam, you told me to clean up the mess and tell you only what you needed to know."

"Well, that's true; I did have trouble getting my head screwed back on right."

"Let's hope this is over with, and that we never have to do anything like this again."

"You got that right, but there's something that has been driving me crazy."

"What is it?"

"When I figured out that you were the one manipulating the idea that dad was still alive."

"Come on, Sam, you know why I did that."

"Sure, but that's not what's bothering me. Remember when I first came back, over at the house in Bryant?"

"Sure I remember; what about it?"

"Who the hell was that playing Dad's part that night?"

Ronnie and Mike both started laughing.

"You got to be kidding," Ronnie said.

"Now why would I be kidding?"

Starting to walk away, Mike turned and said, "Damn, brother, it was that story you told that gave me the whole idea to begin with."

Sam stood speechless as Mike walked back toward the house.

Ronnie walked over and put his arm around Sam's shoulder. "Mike's right, brother, haven't you ever wondered what would have happened if you had just walked out of the study that day and said 'THE SNOW IS TOO DEEP'?"

Sam was looking around at everyone visiting. "You know something Ronnie, we're nothing more than figments of our own imagination."

THE END

Printed in the United States
215909BV00001B/7/P